VOLUME THREE of CLIVE BARKER'S

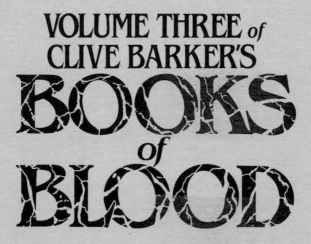

BOOKS of BLOOD

BERKLEY BOOKS, NEW YORK

This Berkley book contains the complete
text of the original edition.
It has been completely reset in a typeface
designed for easy reading and was printed
from new film.

CLIVE BARKER'S BOOKS OF BLOOD VOLUME THREE

A Berkley Book / published by arrangement with
the author

PRINTING HISTORY
First published in Great Britain by
Sphere Books Ltd. 1984
Berkley edition / October 1986

ISBN: 0-425-09347-6

A BERKLEY BOOK ® TM 757,375
Berkley Books are published by The Berkley Publishing Group,
200 Madison Avenue, New York, NY 10016.
The name "BERKLEY" and the "B" logo
are trademarks belonging to Berkley Publishing Corporation.

PRINTED IN THE UNITED STATES OF AMERICA

10   9   8   7

To Roy and Lynne

Every body is a book of blood;
Wherever we're opened, we're red.

CONTENTS

SON OF CELLULOID

ONE: TRAILER

Barberio felt fine, despite the bullet. Sure, there was a catch in his chest if he breathed too hard, and the wound in his thigh wasn't too pretty to look at, but he'd been holed before and come up smiling. At least he was free: that was the main thing. Nobody, he swore, nobody would ever lock him up again, he'd kill himself rather than be taken back into custody. If he was unlucky and they cornered him, he'd stick the gun in his mouth and blow off the top of his head. No way would they drag him back to that cell alive.

Life was too long if you were locked away and counting it in seconds. It had only taken him a couple of months to learn that lesson. Life was long, and repetitive and debilitating, and if you weren't careful you were soon thinking it would be better to die than go on existing in the shit-hole they'd put you in. Better to string yourself up by your belt in the middle of the night rather than face the tedium of another twenty-four hours, all eighty-six thousand four hundred seconds of it.

So he went for broke.

First he bought a gun on the prison black market. It cost him everything he had and a handful of IOUs he'd have to make good on the outside if he wanted to stay alive. Then he made the most obvious move in the book: he climbed the wall. And whatever god looked after the liquor-store muggers of this world was looking after him that night, because hot damn if he didn't scoot right over that wall and away without so much as a dog sniffing at his heels.

And the cops? Why they screwed it up every which way from Sunday, looking for him where he'd never gone, pulling in his brother and his sister-in-law on suspicion of harbouring him when they didn't even know he'd escaped, putting out an All-Points Bulletin with a description of his pre-prison self, twenty pounds heavier than he was now. All this he'd heard from Geraldine, a lady he'd courted in the good old days, who'd given him a dressing for his leg and the bottle of Southern Comfort that was now almost empty in his pocket. He'd taken the booze and sympathy and gone on his way, trusting to the legendary idiocy of the law and the god who'd got him so far already.

Sing-Sing he called this god. Pictured him as a fat guy with a grin that hooked from one ear to the other, a prime salami in one hand, and a cup of dark coffee in the other. In Barberio's mind Sing-Sing smelt like a full belly at Mama's house, back in the days when Mama was still well in the head, and he'd been her pride and joy.

Unfortunately Sing-Sing had been looking the other way when the one eagle-eye cop in the whole city saw Barberio draining his snake in a back alley, and recognized him from that obsolete APB. Young cop, couldn't have been more than twenty-five, out to be a hero. He was too dumb to learn the lesson of Barberio's warning shot. Instead of taking cover, and letting Barberio make a break, he'd forced the issue by coming straight down the alley at him.

Barberio had no choice. He fired.

The cop fired back. Sing-Sing must have stepped in there somewhere, spoiling the cop's aim so that the bullet that should have found Barberio's heart hit his leg, and guiding the returning shot straight into the cop's nose. Eagle-eye went down as if he'd just remembered an appointment with the ground, and Barberio was away, cursing, bleeding and scared. He'd never shot a man before, and he'd started with a cop. Quite an introduction to the craft.

Sing-Sing was still with him though. The bullet in his leg ached, but Geraldine's ministrations had stopped the blood, the liquor had done wonders for the pain, and here he was half a day later, tired but alive, having hopped half-way across a city so thick with vengeful cops it was like a psycho's parade at the Policemen's Ball. Now all he asked of his protector was a place to rest up awhile. Not for long, just enough time to catch his breath and plan his future movements. An hour or two of shut-eye wouldn't go amiss either.

Thing was, he'd got that belly-ache, the deep, gnawing pain he got more and more these days. Maybe he'd find a phone, when he'd rested for a time, and call Geraldine again, get her to sweet-talk a doctor into seeing him. He'd been planning to get out of the city before midnight, but that didn't look like a plausible option now. Dangerous as it was, he would have to stay in the locality a night and maybe the best part of the next day; make his break for the open country when he'd recouped a little energy and had the bullet taken out of his leg.

Jeez, but that belly griped. His guess was it was an ulcer, brought on by the filthy slop they called food at the penitentiary. Lots of guys had belly and shit-chute problems in there. He'd be better after a few days of pizzas and beers, he was damn sure of that.

The word *cancer* wasn't in Barberio's vocabulary. He never thought about terminal disease, especially in reference to himself. That'd be like a piece of slaughterhouse beef fretting about an ingrowing hoof as it stepped up to meet the gun. A man in his trade, surrounded by lethal tools, doesn't expect to perish from a malignancy in his belly. But that's what that ache was.

The lot at the back of the Movie Palace cinema had been a restaurant, but a fire had gutted it three years back, and the ground had never been cleared.

It wasn't a good spec for rebuilding, and no one had shown much interest in the site. The neighborhood had once been buzzing, but that was in the sixties, early seventies. For a heady decade places of entertainment—restaurants, bars, cinemas—had flourished. Then came the inevitable slump. Fewer and fewer kids came this way to spend their money: there were new spots to hit, new places to be seen in. The bars closed up, the restaurants followed. Only the Movie Palace remained as a token reminder of more innocent days in a district that was becoming tackier and more dangerous every year.

The jungle of convolvulus and rotted timbers that throttled the vacant lot suited Barberio just fine. His leg was giving him jip, he was stumbling from sheer fatigue, and the pain in his belly was worsening. A spot to lay down his clammy head was needed, and damn quick. Finish off the Southern Comfort, and think about Geraldine.

It was one thirty a.m.; the lot was a trysting ground for cats. They ran, startled, through the man-high weeds as he pushed aside some of the fencing timbers and slid into the shadows. The refuge stank of piss, human and cat, of garbage, of old fires, but it felt like a sanctuary.

Seeking the support of the back wall of the Movie Palace, Barberio leaned on his forearm and threw up a bellyful of Southern Comfort and acid. Along the wall a little way some kids had built a makeshift den of girders, fire-blackened planks and corrugated iron. Ideal, he thought, a sanctuary within a sanctuary. Sing-Sing was smiling at him, all greasy chops. Groaning a little (the belly was really bad tonight) he staggered along the wall to the lean-to den, and ducked through the door.

Somebody else had used this place to sleep in: he could feel damp sacking under his hand as he sat down, and a bottle clinked against a brick somewhere to his left. There was a smell close by he didn't want to think too much about, like the sewers were backing up. All in all, it was squalid: but it was safer than the street. He sat with his back against the wall of the Movie Palace and exhaled his fears in a long, slow breath.

No more than a block away, perhaps half a block, the babe-in-the-night wail of a cop car began, and his newly acquired sense of security sank without trace. They were closing in for the kill, he knew it. They'd just been playing him along, letting him think he was away, all the time cruising him like sharks, sleek and silent, until he was too tired to put up any resistance. Jeez: he'd killed a cop, what they wouldn't do to him once they had him alone. They'd crucify him.

O.K. Sing-Sing, what now? Take that surprised look off your face, and get me out of this.

For a moment, nothing. Then the god smiled in his mind's

eye, and quite coincidentally he felt the hinges pressing into his back.

Shit! A door. He was leaning against a door.

Grunting with pain he turned and ran his fingers around this escape hatch at his back. To judge by touch it was a small ventilation grille no more than three feet square. Maybe it let on to a crawlspace or maybe into someone's kitchen—what the hell? It was safer inside than out: that was the first lesson any newborn kid got slapped into him.

The siren song wailed on, making Barberio's skin creep. Foul sound. It quickened his heart hearing it.

His thick fingers fumbled down the side of the grille feeling for a lock of some kind, and sure as shit there was a padlock, as gritty with rust as the rest of the metalwork.

Come on Sing-Sing, he prayed, one more break is all I'm asking, let me in, and I swear I'm yours forever.

He pulled at the lock, but damn it, it wasn't about to give so easily. Either it was stronger than it felt, or he was weaker. Maybe a little of both.

The car was slinking closer with every second. The wail drowned out the sound of his own panicking breath.

He pulled the gun, the cop killer, out of his jacket pocket and pressed it into service as a snub-nosed crowbar. He couldn't get much leverage on the thing, it was too short, but a couple of cursing heaves did the trick. The lock gave, a shower of rust scales peppered his face. He only just silenced a whoop of triumph.

Now to open the grille, to get out of this wretched world into the dark.

He insinuated his fingers through the lattice and pulled. Pain, a continuum of pain that ran from his belly to his bowel to his leg, made his head spin. Open, damn you, he said to the grille, open sesame.

The door conceded.

It opened suddenly, and he fell back on to the sodden sacking. A moment and he was up again, peering into the darkness within this darkness that was the interior of the Movie Palace.

Let the cop car come, he thought buoyantly, I've got my hidey hole to keep me warm. And warm it was: almost hot in fact. The air out of the hole smelt like it had been simmering in there for a good long while.

His leg had gone into a cramp and it hurt like fuck as he dragged himself through the door and into the solid black beyond. Even as he did so the siren turned a corner nearby and the baby wail died. Wasn't that the patter of lawlike feet he could hear on the sidewalk?

He turned clumsily in the blackness, his leg a dead-weight, his foot feeling about the size of a watermelon, and pulled the grille door to after him. The satisfaction was that of pulling up a drawbridge and leaving the enemy on the other side of the moat, somehow it didn't matter that they could open the door just as easily as he had, and follow him in. Childlike, he felt sure nobody could possibly find him here. As long as he couldn't see his pursuers, his pursuers couldn't see him.

If the cops did indeed duck into the lot to look for him, he didn't hear them. Maybe he'd been mistaken, maybe they were after some other poor punk on the street, and not him. Well O.K., whatever. He had found himself a nice niche to rest up awhile, and that was fine and dandy.

Funny, the air wasn't so bad in here after all. It wasn't the stagnant air of a crawlspace or an attic, the atmosphere in the hidey hole was alive. Not fresh air, no it wasn't that, it smelt old and trapped sure enough, but it was buzzing nevertheless. It fairly sang in his ears, it made his skin tingle like a cold shower, it wormed its way up his nose and put the weirdest things in his head. It was like being high on something: he felt that good. His leg didn't hurt anymore, or if it did he was too distracted by the pictures in his head. He was filling up to overflowing with pictures: dancing girls and kissing couples, farewells at stations, old dark houses, comedians, cowboys, undersea adventures—scenes he'd never lived in a million years, but that moved him now like raw experience, true and incontestable. He wanted to cry at the farewells, except that he wanted to laugh at the comedians, except that the girls needed ogling, the cowboys needed hollering for.

What kind of place was this anyhow? He peered through the glamour of the pictures which were damn close to getting the better of his eyes. He was in a space no more than four feet wide, but tall, and lit by a flickering light that chanced through cracks in the inner wall. Barberio was too befuddled to recognize the origins of the light, and his murmuring ears couldn't make sense of the dialogue from the screen on the other side of the wall. It was "Satyricon," the second of the two Fellini movies the Palace was showing as their late-night double feature that Saturday.

Barberio had never seen the movie, never even heard of Fellini. It would have disgusted him (faggot film, Italian crap). He preferred undersea adventures, war movies. Oh, and dancing girls. Anything with dancing girls.

Funny, though he was all alone in his hidey hole, he had the weird sensation of being watched. Through the kaleidoscope of Busby Berkeley routines that was playing on the inside of his skull he felt eyes, not a few—thousands—watching him. The feeling wasn't so bad you'd want to take a drink for it, but they were always there, staring away at him like he was something worth looking at, laughing at him sometimes, crying sometimes, but mostly just gawping with hungry eyes.

Truth was, there was nothing he could do about them anyhow. His limbs had given up the ghost; he couldn't feel his hands or feet at all. He didn't know, and it was probably better that he didn't, that he'd torn open his wound getting into this place, and he was bleeding to death.

About two-fifty-five a.m., as Fellini's "Satyricon" came to its ambiguous end, Barberio died in the space between the back of the building proper and the back wall of the cinema.

The Movie Palace had once been a Mission Hall, and if he'd looked up as he died he might have glimpsed the inept fresco depicting an Angelic Host that was still to be seen through the grime, and assumed his own Assumption. But he died watching the dancing girls, and that was fine by him.

The false wall, the one that let through the light from the back of the screen, had been erected as a makeshift partition to cover the fresco of the Host. It had seemed more respectful to do that than paint the Angels out permanently, and besides the man who had ordered the alterations half-suspected that the movie house bubble would burst sooner or later. If so, he could simply demolish the wall, and he'd be back in business for the worship of God instead of Garbo.

It never happened. The bubble, though fragile, never burst,

and the movies carried on. The Doubting Thomas (his name was Harry Cleveland) died, and the space was forgotten. Nobody now living even knew it existed. If he'd searched the city from top to bottom Barberio couldn't have found a more secret place to perish.

The space however, the air itself, had lived a life of its own in that fifty years. Like a reservoir, it had received the electric stares of thousands of eyes, of tens of thousands of eyes. Half a century of movie goers had lived vicariously through the screen of the Movie Palace, pressing their sympathies and their passions on to the flickering illusion, the energy of their emotions gathering strength like a neglected cognac in that hidden passage of air. Sooner or later, it must discharge itself. All it lacked was a catalyst.

Until Barberio's cancer.

TWO: THE MAIN FEATURE

After loitering in the cramped foyer of the Movie Palace for twenty minutes or so, the young girl in the cerise and lemon print dress began to look distinctly agitated. It was almost three in the morning, and the late-night movies were well over.

Eight months had passed since Barberio had died in the back of the cinema, eight slow months in which business had been at best patchy. Still, the late-night double bill on Fridays and Saturdays always packed in the punters. Tonight it had been two Eastwood movies: spaghetti westerns. The girl in the cerise dress didn't look like much of a western fan to Birdy; it wasn't really a women's genre. Maybe she'd come for Eastwood rather than the violence, though Birdy had never seen the attraction of that eternally squinting face.

"Can I help you?" Birdy asked.

The girl looked nervously at Birdy.

"I'm waiting for my boyfriend," she said. "Dean."

"Have you lost him?"

"He went to the rest room at the end of the movie and he hasn't come out yet."

"Was he feeling . . . er . . . ill?"

"Oh no," said the girl quickly, protecting her date from this slight on his sobriety.

"I'll get someone to go and look for him," said Birdy. It was late, she was tired, and the speed was wearing off. The idea of spending any more time than she strictly needed to in this fleapit was not particularly appealing. She wanted home; bed and sleep. Just sleep. At thirty-four, she'd decided she'd grown out of sex. Bed was for sleep, especially for fat girls.

She pushed the swing door, and poked her head into the cinema. A ripe smell of cigarettes, popcorn and people enveloped her; it was a few degrees hotter in here than in the foyer.

"Ricky?"

Ricky was locking up the back exit, at the far end of the cinema.

"That smell's completely gone," he called to her.

"Good." A few months back there'd been a hell of a stench at the screen end of the cinema.

"Something dead in the lot next door," he said.

"Can you help me a minute?" she called back.

"What'd you want?"

He sauntered up the red-carpeted aisle towards her, keys jangling at his belt. His T-shirt proclaimed "Only the Young Die Good."

"Problem?" he said, blowing his nose.

"There's a girl out here. She says she lost her boyfriend in the john."

Ricky looked pained.

"In the john?"

"Right. Will you take a look? You don't mind, do you?"

And she could cut out the wisecracks for a start, he thought, giving her a sickly smile. They were hardly on speaking terms these days. Too many high times together: it always dealt a crippling blow to a friendship in the long run. Besides, Birdy'd made some very uncharitable (accurate) remarks about his associates and he'd returned the salvo with all guns blazing. They hadn't spoken for three and a half weeks after that. Now there was an uncomfortable truce, more for sanity's sake than anything. It was not meticulously observed.

He about turned, wandered back down the aisle, and took row E across the cinema to the john, pushing up seats as he went. They'd seen better days, those seats: sometime around "Now Voyager." Now they looked thoroughly shot at: in need of refurbishing, or replacing altogether. In row E alone four of the seats had been slashed beyond repair, now he counted a fifth mutilation which was new tonight. Some mindless kid bored with the movie and/or his girlfriend, and too stoned to leave. Time was he'd done that kind of thing himself: and counted it a blow for freedom against the capitalists who ran these joints. Time was he'd done a lot of damn-fool things.

Birdy watched him duck into the Men's Room. He'll get a kick out of that, she thought with a sly smile, just his sort of occupation. And to think, she'd once had the hots for him, back in the old days (six months ago) when razor-thin men with noses like Durante and an encyclopaedic knowledge of de Niro movies had really been her style. Now she saw him for what he was, flotsam from a lost ship of hope. Still a pill-freak, still a theoretical bisexual, still devoted to early Polanski movies and symbolic pacifism. What kind of dope did he have between his ears anyhow? The same as she'd had, she chided herself, thinking there was something sexy about the bum.

She waited for a few seconds, watching the door. When he failed to re-emerge she went back into the foyer for a moment, to see how the girl was going on. She was smoking a cigarette like an amateur actress who's failed to get the knack of it, leaning against the rail, her skirt hitched up as she scratched her leg.

"Tights," she explained.

"The Manager's gone to find Dean."

"Thanks," she scratched on. "They bring me out in a rash, I'm allergic to them."

There were blotches on the girl's pretty legs, which rather spoiled the effect.

"It's because I'm hot and bothered," she ventured. "Whenever I get hot and bothered, I get allergic."

"Oh."

"Dean's probably run off, you know, when I had my back turned. He'd do that. He doesn't give a f—. He doesn't care."

Birdy could see she was on her way to tears, which was a

drag. She was bad with tears. Shouting matches, even fights, O.K. Tears, no go.

"It'll be O.K." was all she could find to say to keep the tears from coming.

"No it's not," said the girl. "It won't be O.K., because he's a bastard. He treats everyone like dirt." She ground out the half-smoked cigarette with the pointed toe of her cerise shoes, taking particular care to extinguish every glowing fragment of tobacco.

"Men don't care, do they?" she said looking up at Birdy with heart-melting directness. Under the expert makeup, she was perhaps seventeen, certainly not much more. Her mascara was a little smeared, and there were arcs of tiredness under her eyes.

"No," replied Birdy, speaking from painful experience. "No they don't."

Birdy thought ruefully that she'd never looked as attractive as this tired nymphet. Her eyes were too small, and her arms were fat. (Be honest, girl, you're fat all over.) But the arms were her worst feature, she'd convinced herself of that. There were men, a lot of them, who got off on big breasts, on a sizeable ass, but no man she'd ever known liked fat arms. They always wanted to be able to encircle the wrist of their girlfriend between thumb and index finger, it was a primitive way to measure attachment. Her wrists, however, if she was brutal with herself, were practically undiscernible. Her fat hands became her fat forearms, which became, after a podgy time, her fat upper arms. Men couldn't encircle her wrists because she had no wrists, and that alienated them. Well, that was one of the reasons anyhow. She was also very bright: and that was always a drawback if you wanted men at your feet. But of the options as to why she'd never been successful in love, she plumped for the fat arms as the likeliest explanation.

Whereas this girl had arms as slender as a Balinese dancer's, her wrists looked thin as glass, and about as fragile.

Sickening, really. She was probably a lousy conversationalist to boot. God, the girl had all the advantages.

"What's your name?" she asked.

"Lindi Lee," the girl replied.

It would be.

• • •

Ricky thought he'd made a mistake. This can't be the toilet, he said to himself.

He was standing in what appeared to be the main street of a frontier town he'd seen in two hundred Westerns. A dust storm seemed to be raging, forcing him to narrow his eyes against the stinging sand. Through the swirl of the ochre-grey air he could pick out, he thought, the General Stores, the Sheriff's Office and the Saloon. They stood in lieu of the toilet cubicles. Optional tumble-weed danced by him on the hot desert wind. The ground beneath his feet was impacted sand: no sign of tiles. No sign of anything that was faintly toilet-like.

Ricky looked to his right, down the street. Where the far wall of the john should have been the street receded, in forced perspective, towards a painted distance. It was a lie, of course, the whole thing was a lie. Surely if he concentrated he'd begin to see through the mirage to find out how it had been achieved; the projections, the concealed lighting effects, the backcloths, the miniatures; all the tricks of the trade. But though he concentrated as hard as his slightly spaced-out condition would allow, he just couldn't seem to get his fingers under the edge of the illusion to strip it back.

The wind just went on blowing, the tumbleweed tumbled on. Somewhere in the storm a barndoor was slamming, opening and slamming again in the gusts. He could even smell horseshit. The effect was so damn perfect, he was breathless with admiration.

But whoever had created this extraordinary set had proved their point. He was impressed: now it was time to stop the game.

He turned back to the toilet door. It was gone. A wall of dust had erased it, and suddenly he was lost and alone.

The barndoor kept slamming. Voices called to each other in the worsening storm. Where was the Saloon and the Sheriff's office? They too had been obscured. Ricky tasted something he hadn't experienced since childhood: the panic of losing the hand of a guardian. In this case the lost parent was his sanity.

Somewhere to his left a shot sounded in the depths of the storm, and he heard something whistle in his ear, then felt a sharp pain. Gingerly he raised his hand to his earlobe and touched the place that hurt. Part of his ear had been shot away, a neat nick in his lobe. His earstud was gone, and there was blood, real blood, on his fingers. Someone had either just missed blowing off his head or was really playing silly fuckers.

"Hey, man," he appealed into the teeth of this wretched fiction, whirling around on his heel to see if he could locate the aggressor. But he could see no one. The dust had totally enclosed him: he couldn't move backwards or forwards with any safety. The gunman might be very close, waiting for him to step in his direction.

"I don't like this," he said aloud, hoping the real world would hear him somehow, and step in to salvage his tattered mind. He rummaged in his jeans pocket for a pill or two, anything to improve the situation, but he was all out of instant sunshine, not even a lowly Valium was to be found lurking in the seam of his pocket. He felt naked. What a time to be lost in the middle of Zane Grey's nightmares.

A second shot sounded, but this time there was no whistling. Ricky was certain this meant he'd been shot, but as there was neither pain nor blood it was difficult to be sure.

Then he heard the unmistakable flap of the saloon door, and the groan of another human being somewhere near. A tear opened up in the storm for a moment. Did he see the saloon through it, and a young man stumbling out, leaving behind him a painted world of tables, mirrors, and gunslingers? Before he could focus properly the tear was sewn up with sand, and he doubted the sight. Then, shockingly, the young man he'd come looking for was there, a foot away, blue-lipped with death, and falling forward into Ricky's arms. He wasn't dressed for a part in this movie anymore than Ricky was. His bomber jacket was a fair copy of a fifties style, his T-shirt bore the smiling face of Mickey Mouse.

Mickey's left eye was bloodshot, and still bleeding. The bullet had unerringly found the young man's heart.

He used his last breath to ask: "What the fuck is going on?" and died.

As last words went, it lacked style, but it was deeply felt. Ricky stared into the young man's frozen face for a moment, then the dead weight in his arms became too much, and he had no choice but to drop him. As the body hit the ground the dust seemed to turn into piss-stained tiling for an instant. Then the fiction took precedence again, and the dust swirled, and the tumbleweed tumbled, and he was standing in the middle of Main Street, Deadwood Gulch, with a body at his feet.

Ricky felt something very like cold turkey in his system. His limbs began a St. Vitus' dance, and the urge to piss came on him, very strong. Another half minute, he'd wet his pants.

Somewhere, he thought, somewhere in this wild world, there is a urinal. There is a graffiti-covered wall, with numbers for the sex-crazed to call, with "This is not a fallout shelter" scrawled on the tiles, and a cluster of obscene drawings. There are water tanks and paperless toilet roll holders and broken seats. There is the squalid smell of piss and old farts. Find it! in God's name find the real thing before the fiction does you some permanent damage.

If, for the sake of argument, the Saloon and the General Stores are the toilet cubicles, then the urinal must be behind me, he reasoned. So step back. It can't do you any more harm than staying here in the middle of the street while someone takes potshots at you.

Two steps, two cautious steps, and he found only air. But on the third—well, well, what have we here?—his hand touched a cold tile surface.

"Whoo-ee!" he said. It was the urinal: and touching it was like finding gold in a pan of trash. Wasn't that the sickly smell of disinfectant wafting up from the gutter? It was, oh boy, it was.

Still whooping, he unzipped and started to relieve the ache in his bladder, splashing his feet in his haste. What the hell: he had this illusion beat. If he turned round now he'd find the fantasy dispersed, surely. The saloon, the dead boy, the storm, all would be gone. It was some chemical throw-back, bad dope lingering in his system and playing dumb-ass games with his imagination. As he shook the last drops onto his blue suedes, he heard the hero of this movie speak.

"What you doin' pissin' in mah street, boy?"

It was John Wayne's voice, accurate to the last slurred syllable, and it was just behind him. Ricky couldn't even contemplate turning around. The guy would blow off his head for sure. It was in the voice, that threatful ease that warned: I'm ready to draw, so do your worst. The cowboy was armed, and all Ricky had in his hand was his dick, which was no match for a gun even if he'd been better hung.

Very cautiously he tucked his weapon away and zipped himself up, then raised his hands. In front of him the wavering image of the toilet wall had disappeared again. The storm howled: his ear bled down his neck.

"O.K. boy, I want you to take off that gunbelt and drop it to the ground. You hear me?" said Wayne.

"Yes."

"Take it nice and slow, and keep those hands where I can see them."

Boy, this guy was really into it.

Nice and slow, like the man said, Ricky unbuckled his belt, pulled it through the loops in his jeans and dropped it to the floor. The keys should have jangled as they hit the tiles, he hoped to God they would. No such luck. There was a clinking thud that was the sound of metal on sand.

"O.K.," said Wayne. "Now you're beginning to behave. What have you got to say for yourself?"

"I'm sorry?" said Ricky lamely.

"Sorry?"

"For pissing in the street."

"I don't reckon sorry is sufficient penitence," said Wayne.

"But really I am. It was all a mistake."

"We've had about enough of you strangers around these parts. Found that kid with his trousers round his ankles takin' a dump in the middle of the saloon. Well I call that uncouth! Where's you sons of bitches been educated anyhow? Is that what they're teaching you in them fancy schools out East?"

"I can't apologize enough."

"Damn right you can't," Wayne drawled. "You with the kid?"

"In a manner of speaking."

"What kind of fancy talk is that?" he jabbed his gun in Rick's back: it felt very real indeed. "Are you with him or not?"

"I just meant—"

"You don't mean nothing in this territory, mister, you take that from me."

He cocked the gun, audibly.

"Why don't you turn around, son and let's us see what you're made of?"

Ricky had seen this routine before. The man turns, he goes for a concealed gun, and Wayne shoots him. No debate, no time to discuss the ethics of it, a bullet would do the job better than words.

"Turn round I said."

Very slowly, Ricky turned to face the survivor of a thousand shootouts, and there was the man himself, or rather a brilliant impersonation of him. A middle period Wayne, before he'd grown fat and sick looking. A Rio Grande Wayne, dusty from the long trail and squinting from a lifetime of looking at the horizon. Ricky had never had a taste for Westerns. He hated all the forced machismo, the glorification of dirt and cheap heroism. His generation had put flowers in rifle barrels, and he'd thought that was a nice thing to do at the time; still did, in fact.

This face, so mockmanly, so uncompromising, personified a handful of lethal lies—about the glory of America's frontier origins, the morality of swift justice, the tenderness in the heart of brutes. Ricky hated the face. His hands just itched to hit it.

Fuck it, if the actor, whoever he was, was going to shoot him anyway, what was to be lost by putting his fist in the bastard's face? The thought became the act: Ricky made a fist, swung and his knuckles connected with Wayne's chin. The actor was slower than his screen image. He failed to dodge the blow, and Ricky took the opportunity to knock the gun out of Wayne's hand. He then followed through with a barrage of punches to the body, just as he'd seen in the movies. It was a spectacular display.

The bigger man reeled backwards under the blows, and tripped, his spur catching in the dead boy's hair. He lost his balance and fell in the dust, bested.

The bastard was down! Ricky felt a thrill he'd never tasted before; the exhilaration of physical triumph. My God! he'd brought down the greatest cowboy in the world. His critical faculties were overwhelmed by the victory.

The dust storm suddenly thickened. Wayne was still on the

floor, splattered with blood from a smashed nose and a broken lip. The sand was already obscuring him, a curtain drawn across the shame of his defeat.

"Get up," Ricky demanded, trying to capitalize on the situation before the opportunity was lost entirely.

Wayne seemed to grin as the storm covered him.

"Well boy," he leered, rubbing his chin, "we'll make a man of you yet . . ."

Then his body was eroded by the driving dust, and momentarily something else was there in its place, a form Ricky could make no real sense of. A shape that was and was not Wayne, which deteriorated rapidly towards inhumanity.

The dust was already a furious bombardment, filling ears and eyes. Ricky stumbled away from the scene of the fight, choking, and miraculously he found a wall, a door, and before he could make sense of where he was the roaring storm had spat him out into the silence of the Movie Palace.

There, though he'd promised himself to butch it up since he'd grown a moustache, he gave a small cry that would not have shamed Fay Wray, and collapsed.

In the foyer Lindi Lee was telling Birdy why she didn't like films very much.

"I mean, Dean likes cowboy movies. I don't really like any of that stuff. I guess I shouldn't say that to you—"

"No, that's O.K."

"—But I mean you must really love movies, I guess. 'Cause you work here."

"I like some movies. Not everything."

"Oh." She seemed surprised. A lot of things seemed to surprise her. "I like wildlife movies, you know."

"Yes . . ."

"You know? Animals . . . and stuff."

"Yes . . ." Birdy remembered her guess about Lindi Lee, that she wasn't much of a conversationalist. Got it in one.

"I wonder what's keeping them?" said Lindi.

The lifetime Ricky had been living in the duststorm had lasted no more than two minutes in real time. But then in the movies time was elastic.

"I'll go look," Birdy ventured.

"He's probably left without me," Lindi said again.

"We'll find out."

"Thanks."

"Don't fret," said Birdy, lightly putting her hand on the girl's thin arm as she passed. "I'm sure everything's O.K."

She disappeared through the swing doors into the cinema, leaving Lindi Lee alone in the foyer. Lindi sighed. Dean wasn't the first boy who'd run out on her, just because she wouldn't produce the goods. Lindi had her own ideas about when and how she'd go all the way with a boy; this wasn't the time and Dean wasn't the boy. He was too slick, too shifty, and his hair smelt of diesel oil. If he had run out on her, she wasn't going to weep buckets over the loss. As her mother always said, there were plenty more fish in the sea.

She was staring at the poster for next week's attraction when she heard a thump behind her, and there was a piebald rabbit, a fat, dozy sweetheart of a thing, sitting in the middle of the foyer staring up at her.

"Hello," she said to the rabbit.

The rabbit licked itself adorably.

Lindi Lee loved animals; she loved True Life Adventure Movies in which creatures were filmed in their native habitat to tunes from Rossini, and scorpions did squaredances while mating, and every bear-cub was lovingly called a little scamp. She lapped up that stuff. But most of all she loved rabbits.

The rabbit took a couple of hops towards her. She knelt to stroke it. It was warm and its eyes were round and pink. It hopped past her up the stairs.

"Oh I don't think you should go up there," she said.

For one thing it was dark at the top of the stairs. For another there was a sign that read "Private. Staff only" on the wall. But the rabbit seemed determined, and the clever mite kept well ahead of her as she followed it up the stairs.

At the top it was pitch black, and the rabbit had gone.

Something else was sitting there in the rabbit's place, its eyes burning bright.

With Lindi Lee illusions could be simple. No need to seduce her into a complete fiction like the boy, this one was already dreaming. Easy meat.

"Hello," Lindi Lee said, scared a little by the presence

ahead of her. She looked into the dark, trying to sort out some outline, a hint of face. But there was none. Not even a breath.

She took one step back down the stairs but it reached for her suddenly, and caught her before she toppled, silencing her quickly, intimately.

This one might not have much passion to steal, but it sensed another use here. The tender body was still budding: the orifices unused to invasions. It took Lindi up the few remaining stairs and sealed her away for future investigation.

"Ricky? Oh God, Ricky!"

Birdy knelt beside Ricky's body and shook him. At least he was still breathing, that was something, and though at first sight there seemed to be a great deal of blood, in fact the wound was merely a nick in his ear.

She shook him again, more roughly, but there was no response. After a frantic search she found his pulse: it was strong and regular. Obviously he'd been attacked by somebody, possibly Lindi Lee's absent boyfriend. In which case, where was he? Still in the john perhaps, armed and dangerous. There was no way she was going to be damn fool enough to step in there and have a look, she'd seen that routine too many times. Woman in Peril: standard stuff. The darkened room, the stalking beast. Well, instead of walking bang into that cliché she was going to do what she silently exhorted heroines to do time and again: defy her curiosity and call the cops.

Leaving Ricky where he lay, she walked up the aisle, and back into the foyer.

It was empty. Lindi Lee had either given up on her boyfriend altogether, or found somebody else on the street outside to take her home. Whichever, she'd closed the front door behind her as she left, leaving only a hint of Johnson's Baby Powder on the air behind her. O.K., that certainly made things easier, Birdy thought, as she stepped into the Ticket Office to dial the cops. She was rather pleased to think that the girl had found the common sense to give up on her lousy date.

She picked up the receiver, and immediately somebody spoke.

"Hello there," said the voice, nasal and ingratiating, "it's a little late at night to be using the phone, isn't it?"

It wasn't the operator, she was sure. She hadn't even punched a number.

Besides, it sounded like Peter Lorre.

"Who is this?"

"Don't you recognize me?"

"I want to speak to the police."

"I'd like to oblige, really I would."

"Get off the line, will you? This is an emergency! I need the police."

"I heard you first time," the whine went on.

"Who are you?"

"You already played that line."

"There's somebody hurt in here. Will you *please*—"

"Poor Rick."

He knew his name. Poor Rick, he said, as though he was a loving friend.

She felt the sweat begin in her brow: felt it sprout out of her pores. He knew Ricky's name.

"Poor, poor Rick," the voice said again. "Still I'm sure we'll have a happy ending. Aren't you?"

"This is a matter of life and death," Birdy insisted, impressed by how controlled she felt sure she was sounding.

"I know," said Lorre. "Isn't it exciting?"

"Damn you! Get off this phone! Or so help me—"

"So help you what? What can a fat girl like you hope to do in a situation like this, except blubber?"

"You fucking creep."

"My pleasure."

"Do I know you?"

"Yes and no," the tone of the voice was wavering.

"You're a friend of Ricky's, is that it?" One of the dope fiends he used to hang out with. Kind of idiot game they'd get up to. All right, you've had your stupid little joke," she said, "now get off the line before you do some serious harm."

"You're harassed," the voice said, softening. "I understand . . ." it was changing magically, sliding up an octave, "you're trying to help the man you love . . ." Its tone was feminine now, the accent altering, the slime becoming a purr. And suddenly it was Garbo.

"Poor Richard," she said to Birdy. "He's tried so hard,

hasn't he?'' She was gentle as a lamb.

Birdy was speechless: the impersonation was as faultless as that of Lorre, as female as the first had been male.

"All right, I'm impressed," said Birdy, "now let me speak to the cops."

"Wouldn't this be a fine and lovely night to go out walking, Birdy? Just we two girls together."

"You know my name."

"Of course I know your name. I'm very close to you."

"What do you mean, close to me?"

The reply was throaty laughter, Garbo's lovely laughter.

Birdy couldn't take it any more. The trick was too clever; she could feel herself succumbing to the impersonation, as though she were speaking to the star herself.

"No," she said down the phone, "you don't convince me, you hear?" Then her temper snapped. She yelled: "You're a fake!" into the mouthpiece of the phone so loudly she felt the receiver tremble, and then slammed it down. She opened the Office and went to the outer door. Lindi Lee had not simply slammed the door behind her. It was locked and bolted from the inside.

"Shit," Birdy said quietly.

Suddenly the foyer seemed smaller than she'd previously thought, and so did her reserve of cool. She mentally slapped herself across the face, the standard response for a heroine verging on hysteria. Think this through, she instructed herself. One: the door was locked. Lindi Lee hadn't done it, Ricky couldn't have done it, she certainly hadn't done it. Which implied—

Two: There was a weirdo in here. Maybe the same he, she or it that was on the phone. Which implied—

Three: He, she or it must have access to another line, somewhere in the building. The only one she knew of was upstairs, in the storeroom. But there was no way she was going up there. For reasons see Heroine in Peril. Which implied—

Four: She had to open this door with Ricky's keys.

Right, there was the imperative: get the keys from Ricky.

She stepped back into the cinema. For some reason the houselights were jumpy, or was that just panic in her optic nerve? No, they were flickering slightly; the whole interior seemed to be fluctuating, as though it were breathing.

Ignore it: fetch the keys.

She raced down the aisle, aware, as she always was when she ran, that her breasts were doing a jig, her buttocks too. A right sight I look, she thought for anyone with the eyes to see. Ricky was moaning in his faint. Birdy looked for the keys, but his belt had disappeared.

"Ricky . . ." she said close to his face. The moans multiplied.

"Ricky, can you hear me? It's Birdy, Rick. *Birdy.*"

"Birdy?"

"We're locked in, Ricky. Where are the keys?"

". . . keys?"

"You're not wearing your belt, Ricky," she spoke slowly, as if to an idiot, "where-are-your-keys?"

The jigsaw Ricky was doing in his aching head was suddenly solved, and he sat up.

"Boy!" he said.

"What boy?"

"In the john. Dead in the john."

"Dead? Oh Christ. Dead? Are you sure?"

Ricky was in some sort of trance, it seemed. He didn't look at her, he just stared into middle-distance, seeing something she couldn't.

"Where are the keys?" she asked again. *"Ricky.* It's important. Concentrate."

"Keys?"

She wanted to slap him now, but his face was already bloody and it seemed sadistic.

"On the floor," he said after a time.

"In the john? On the floor in the john?"

Ricky nodded. The movement of his head seemed to dislodge some terrible thoughts: suddenly he looked as though he was going to cry.

"It's all going to be all right," said Birdy.

Ricky's hands had found his face, and he was feeling his features, a ritual of reassurance.

"Am I here?" he inquired quietly. Birdy didn't hear him, she was steeling herself for the john. She had to go in there, no doubt about that, body or no body. Get in, fetch the keys, get out again. Do it *now*.

She stepped through the door. It occurred to her as she did so that she'd never been in a men's toilet before, and she sincerely hoped this would be the first and only occassion.

The toilet was almost in darkness. The light was flickering in the same fitful way as the lights in the cinema, but at a lower level. She stood at the door, letting her eyes accommodate the gloom, and scanned the place.

The toilet was empty. There was no boy on the floor, dead or alive.

The keys were there though. Ricky's belt was lying in the gutter of the urinal. She fished it out, the oppressive smell of the disinfectant block making her sinuses ache. Disengaging the keys from their ring she stepped out of the toilet into the comparative freshness of the cinema. And it was all over, simple as that.

Ricky had hoisted himself on to one of the seats, and was slumped in it, looking sicker and sorrier for himself than ever. He looked up as he heard Birdy emerge.

"I've got the keys," she said.

He grunted: God, he looked ill, she thought. Some of her sympathy had evaporated however. He was obviously having hallucinations, and they probably had chemical origins. It was his own damn fault.

"There's no boy in there, Ricky."

"What?"

"There's no body in the john; nobody at all. What are you on anyhow?"

Ricky looked down at his shaking hands.

"I'm not on anything. Honestly."

"Damn stupid," she said. She half-suspected that he'd set her up for this somehow, except that practical jokes weren't his style. Ricky was quite a puritan in his way: that had been one of his attractions.

"Do you need a doctor?"

He shook his head sulkily.

"Are you sure?"

"I said no," he snapped.

"O.K., I offered." She was already marching up the rake of
the aisle, muttering something under her breath. At the foyer
door she stopped and called across to him.

"I think we've got an intruder. There was somebody on the
extension line. Do you want to stand watch by the front door
while I fetch a cop?"

"In a minute."

Ricky sat in the flickering light and examined his sanity. If
Birdy said the boy wasn't in there, then presumably she was
telling the truth. The best way to verify that was to see for
himself. Then he'd be certain he'd suffered a minor reality
crisis brought on by some bad dope, and he'd go home, lay his
head down to sleep and wake tomorrow afternoon healed. Except that he didn't want to put his head in that evil-smelling
room. Suppose she was wrong, and *she* was the one having the
crisis? Weren't there such things as hallucinations of nor-
mality?

Shakily, he hauled himself up, crossed the aisle and pushed
open the door. It was murky inside, but he could see enough to
know that there were no sandstorms, or dead boys, no gun-
toting cowboys, nor even a solitary tumbleweed. It's quite a
thing, he thought, this mind of mine. To have created an alter-
native world so eerily well. It was a wonderful trick. Pity it
couldn't be turned to better use than scaring him shitless. You
win some, you lose some.

And then he saw the blood. On the tiles. A smear of blood
that hadn't come from his nicked ear, there was too much of
it. Ha! He didn't imagine it at all. There was blood, heel
marks, every sign that what he thought he'd seen, he'd seen.
But Jesus in Heaven, which was worse? To see, or not to see?
Wouldn't it have been better to be wrong, and just a little
spaced-out tonight, than right, and in the hands of a power
that could literally change the world?

Ricky stared at the trail of blood, and followed it across the
floor of the toilet to the cubicle on the left of his vision. Its
door was closed: it had been open before. The murderer, whoever he was, had put the boy in there, Ricky knew it without
looking.

"O.K.," he said, "now I've got you."

He pushed on the door. It swung open and there was the boy, propped up on the toilet seat, legs spread, arms hanging.

His eyes had been scooped out of his head. Not neatly: no surgeon's job. They'd been wrenched out, leaving a trail of mechanics down his cheek.

Ricky put his hand over his mouth and told himself he wasn't going to throw up. His stomach churned, but obeyed, and he ran to the toilet door as though any moment the body was going to get up and demand its ticket-money back.

"Birdy . . . Birdy . . ."

The fat bitch had been wrong, all wrong. There was death here, and worse.

Ricky flung himself out of the john into the body of the cinema.

The wall lights were fairly dancing behind their Deco shades, guttering like candles on the verge of extinction. Darkness would be too much; he'd lose his mind.

There was, it occurred to him, something familiar about the way the lights flickered, something he couldn't quite put his finger on. He stood in the aisle for a moment, hopelessly lost.

Then the voice came; and though he guessed it was death this time, he looked up.

"Hello Ricky," she was saying as she came along Row E towards him. Not Birdy. No, Birdy never wore a white gossamer dress, never had bruisefull lips, or hair so fine, or eyes so sweetly promising. It was Monroe who was walking towards him, the blasted rose of America.

"Aren't you going to say hello?" she gently chided.

". . . er . . ."

"Ricky. Ricky. Ricky. After all this time."

All this time? What did she mean: all this time?

"Who are you?"

She smiled radiantly at him.

"As if you didn't know."

"You're not Marilyn. Marilyn's dead."

"Nobody dies in the movies, Ricky. You know that as well as I do. You can always thread the celluloid up again—"

—that was what the flickering reminded him of, the flicker

of celluloid through the gate of a projector, one image hot on the next, the illusion of life created from a perfect sequence of little deaths.

"—and we're there again, all talking, all singing." She laughed: ice-in-a-glass laughter, "We never fluff our lines, never age, never lose our timing—"

"You're not real," said Ricky.

She looked faintly bored by the observation, as if he was being pedantic.

By now she'd come to the end of the row and was standing no more than three feet away from him. At this distance the illusion was as ravishing and as complete as ever. He suddenly wanted to take her, there, in the aisle. What the hell if she was just a fiction: fictions are fuckable if you don't want marriage.

"I want you," he said, surprised by his own bluntness.

"I want *you*," she replied, which surprised him even more. "In fact I need you. I'm very weak."

"Weak?"

"It's not easy, being the center of attraction, you know. You find you need it, more and more. Need people to look at you. All the night, all the day."

"I'm looking."

"Am I beautiful?"

"You're a goddess: whoever you are."

"I'm yours: that's who I am."

It was a perfect answer. She was defining herself through him. I am a function of you; made for you out of you. The perfect fantasy.

"Keep looking at me; looking *forever*, Ricky. I need your loving looks. I can't live without them."

The more he stared at her the stronger her image seemed to become. The flickering had almost stopped; a calm had settled over the place.

"Do you want to touch me?"

He thought she'd never ask.

"Yes," he said.

"Good." She smiled coaxingly at him, and he reached to make contact. She elegantly avoided his fingertips at the last possible moment, and ran, laughing, down the aisle towards the screen. He followed, eager. She wanted a game: that was fine by him.

She'd run into a cul-de-sac. There was no way out from this end of the cinema, and judging by the come-ons she was giving him, she knew it. She turned and flattened herself against the wall, feet spread a little.

He was within a couple of yards of her when a breeze out of nowhere billowed her skirt up around her waist. She laughed, half closing her eyes, as the surf of silk rose and exposed her. She was naked underneath.

Ricky reached for her again and this time she didn't avoid his touch. The dress billowed up a little higher and he stared, fixated, at the part of Marilyn he had never seen, the fur divide that had been the dream of millions.

There was blood there. Not much, a few fingermarks on her inner thighs. The faultless gloss of her flesh was spoiled slightly. Still he stared; and the lips parted a little as she moved her hips, and he realized the glint of wetness in her interior was not the juice of her body, but something else altogether. As her muscles moved the bloody eyes she'd buried in her body shifted, and came to rest on him.

She knew by the look on his face that she hadn't hidden them deep enough, but where was a girl with barely a veil of cloth covering her nakedness to hide the fruits of her labor?

"You killed him," said Ricky, still looking at the lips, and the eyes that peeked out between. The image was so engrossing, so pristine, it all but cancelled out the horror in his belly. Perversely, his disgust fed his lust instead of killing it. So what if she *was* a murderer: she was legend.

"Love me," she said. "Love me forever."

He came to her, knowing now full well that it was death to do so. But death was a relative matter, wasn't it? Marilyn was dead in the flesh, but alive here, either in his brain, or in the buzzing matrix of the air or both; and he could be with her.

He embraced her, and she him. They kissed. It was easy. Her lips were softer than he'd imagined, and he felt something close to pain at his crotch he wanted to be in her so much.

The willow-thin arms slipped around his waist, and he was in the lap of luxury.

"You make me strong," she said. "Looking at me that way. I need to be looked at, or I die. It's the natural state of illusions."

Her embrace was tightening; the arms at his back no longer seemed quite so willowlike. He struggled a little against the discomfort.

"No use," she cooed in his ear. "You're mine."

He wrenched his head around to look at her grip and to his amazement the arms weren't arms any longer, just a loop of something round his back, without hands or fingers or wrists.

"Jesus Christ!" he said.

"Look at me, boy," she said. The words had lost their delicacy. It wasn't Marilyn that had him in its arms any more: nothing like her. The embrace tightened again, and the breath was forced from Ricky's body, breath the tightness of the hold prevented him from recapturing. His spine creaked under the pressure, and pain shot through his body like flares, exploding in his eyes, all colors.

"You should have got out of town," said Marilyn, as Wayne's face blossomed under the sweep of her perfect cheekbones. His look was contemptuous, but Ricky had only a moment to register it before that image cracked too, and something else came into focus behind this façade of famous faces. For the last time in his life, Ricky asked the question:

"Who are you?"

His captor didn't answer. It was feeding on his fascination; even as he stared twin organs erupted out of its body like the horns of a slug, antennae perhaps, forming themselves into probes and crossing the space between its head and Ricky's.

"I need you," it said, its voice now neither Wayne nor Monroe, but a crude, uncultivated voice, a thug's voice. "I'm so fucking weak; it uses me up, being in the world."

It was mainlining on him, feeding itself, whatever it was, on his stares, once adoring—now horrified. He could feel it draining out his life through his eyes, luxuriating in the soul looks he was giving it as he perished.

He knew he must be nearly dead, because he hadn't taken a breath in a long while. It seemed like minutes, but he couldn't be sure.

Just as he was listening for the sound of his heart, the horns divided around his head and pressed themselves into his ears. Even in this reverie, the sensation was disgusting, and he wanted to cry out for it to stop. But the fingers were working their way into his head, bursting his eardrums, and passing on like inquisitive tapeworms through brain and skull. He was alive, even now, still staring at his tormentor, and he knew that the fingers were finding his eyeballs, and pressing on them now from behind.

His eyes bulged suddenly and broke from their housing, splashing from his sockets. Momentarily he saw the world from a different angle as his sense of sight cascaded down his cheek. There was his lip, his chin—

It was an appalling experience, and mercifully short. Then the feature Ricky'd lived for thirty-seven years snapped in mid-reel, and he slumped in the arms of fiction.

Ricky's seduction and death had occupied less than three minutes. In that time Birdy had tried every key on Ricky's ring, and could get none of the damn things to open the door. Had she not persisted she might have gone back into the cinema and asked for some help. But things mechanical, even locks and keys, were a challenge to her womanhood. She despised the way men felt some instinctive superiority over her sex when it came to engines, systems and logical processes, and she was damned if she was going to go whining back to Ricky to tell him she couldn't open the damn door.

By the time she'd given up the job, so had Ricky. He was dead and gone. She swore, colorfully, at the keys, and admitted defeat. Ricky clearly had a knack with these wretched things that she'd never quite grasp. Good luck to him. All she wanted now was out of this place. It was getting claustrophobic. She didn't like being locked in, not knowing who was lurking around upstairs.

And now to cap it all, the lights in the foyer were on the blink, dying away flicker by flicker.

What the hell was going on in this place anyhow?

Without warning the lights went out altogether, and beyond the doors into the cinema she was sure she heard movement. A light spilled through from the other side, stronger than torchlight, twitching, colorful.

"Ricky?" she chanced into the dark. It seemed to swallow her words. Either that or she didn't believe it was Ricky at all, and something was telling her to make her appeal, if she had to, in a whisper.

"Ricky . . .?"

The lips of the swing doors smacked together gently as something pressed on them from the other side.

". . . is that you?"

The air was electric: static was crackling off her shoes as she walked towards the door, the hairs on her arms were rigid. The light on the other side was growing brighter with every step.

She stopped advancing, thinking better of her enquiries. It wasn't Ricky, she knew that. Maybe it was the man or woman on the phone, some pebble-eyed lunatic who got off on stalking fat women.

She stook two steps back towards the Ticket Office, her feet sparking, and reached under the counter for the Mother-fucker, an iron bar which she'd kept there since she'd been trapped in the Office by three would-be thieves with shaved heads and electric drills. She'd screamed blue murder and they'd fled, but next time she swore she'd beat one (or all of them) senseless rather than be terrorized. And the Mother-fucker, all three feet of it, was her chosen weapon.

Armed now, she faced the doors.

They blew open suddenly, and a roar of white noise filled her head, and a voice through the roar said:

"Here's looking at you, kid."

An eye, a single vast eye, was filling the doorway. The noise deafened her; the eye blinked, huge and wet and lazy, scanning the doll in front of it with the insolence of the One True God, the maker of celluloid Earth and celluloid Heaven.

Birdy was terrified, no other word for it. This wasn't a look-behind-you thrill, there was no delicious anticipation, no pleasurable fright. It was real fear, bowel fear, unadorned and ugly as shit.

She could hear herself whimpering under the relentless gaze of the eye, her legs were weakening. Soon she'd fall on the carpet in front of the door, and that would be the end of her, surely.

Then she remembered Motherfucker. Dear Motherfucker, bless his phallic heart. She raised the bar in a two-handed grip and ran at the eye, swinging.

Before she made contact the eye closed, the light went out, and she was in darkness again, her retina burning from the sight.

In the darkness, somebody said: "Ricky's dead."

Just that. It was worse than the eye, worse than all the dead voices of Hollywood, because she knew somehow it was true. The cinema had become a slaughterhouse. Lindi Lee's Dean had died as Ricky had said he had, and now Ricky was dead as well. The doors were all locked, the game was down to two. Her and it.

She made a dash for the stairs, not sure of her plan of action, but certain that remaining in the foyer was suicidal. As her foot touched the bottom stair the swing doors sighed open again behind her and something came after her, fast and flickering. It was a step or two behind her as she breathlessly mounted the stairs, cursing her bulk. Spasms of brilliant light shot by her from its body like the first igniting flashes of a Roman Candle. It was preparing another trick, she was certain of it.

She reached the top of the stairs with her admirer still on her heels. Ahead, the corridor, lit by a single greasy bulb, promised very little comfort. It ran the full length of the cinema, and there were a few storerooms off it, piled with crap: posters, 3-D spectacles, mildewed stills. In one of the storerooms there was a fire door, she was sure. But which? She'd only been up here once, and that two years ago.

"Shit. Shit. Shit," she said. She ran to the first storeroom. The door was locked. She beat on it, protesting. It stayed locked. The next the same. The third the same. Even if she could remember which storeroom contained the escape route the doors were too heavy to break down. Given ten minutes and Motherfucker's help she might do it. But the Eye was at her back: she didn't have ten seconds, never mind ten minutes.

There was nothing for it but confrontation. She spun on her heel, a prayer on her lips, to face the staircase and her pursuer. The landing was empty.

She stared at the forlorn arrangement of dead bulbs and

peeling paint as if to discover the invisible, but the thing wasn't in front of her at all, it was behind. The brightness flared again at her back, and this time the Roman Candle caught, fire became light, light became image, and glories she'd almost forgotten were spilling down the corridor towards her. Unleased scenes from a thousand movies: each with its unique association. She began, for the first time, to understand the origins of this remarkable species. It was a ghost in the machine of the cinema: a son of celluloid.

"Give your soul to me," a thousand stars said.

"I don't believe in souls," she replied truthfully.

"Then give me what you give to the screen, what everybody gives. *Give me some love.*"

That's why all those scenes were playing, and replaying, and playing again, in front of her. They were all moments when an audience was magically united with the screen, bleeding through its eyes, looking and looking and looking. She'd done it herself, often. Seen a film and felt it move her so deeply it was almost a physical pain when the end credits rolled and the illusion was broken, because she felt she'd left something of herself behind, a part of her inner being lost up there amongst her heroes and her heroines. Maybe she had. Maybe the air carried the cargo of her desires and deposited them somewhere, intermingled with the cargo of other hearts, all gathering together in some niche, until—

Until this. This child of their collective passions: this technicolor seducer; trite, crass and utterly betwitching.

Very well, she thought, it's one thing to understand your executioner: another thing altogether to talk it out of its professional obligations.

Even as she sorted the enigma out she was lapping up the pictures in the thing: she couldn't help herself. Teasing glimpses of lives she'd lived, faces she'd loved. Mickey Mouse, dancing with a broom, Gish in "Broken Blossoms," Garland (with Toto at her side) watching the twister louring over Kansas, Astaire in "Top Hat," Welles in "Kane," Brando and Crawford, Tracy and Hepburn—people so engraved on our hearts they need no Christian names. And so much better to be teased by these moments, to be shown only the pre-kiss melt, not the kiss itself; the slap, not the reconciliation; the shadow, not the monster; the wound, not death.

It had her in thrall, no doubt of it. She was held by her eyes as surely as if it had them out on their stalks, and chained.

"Am I beautiful?" it said.

Yes it was beautiful.

"Why don't you give yourself to me?"

She wasn't thinking any more, her powers of analysis had drained from her, until something appeared in the muddle of images that slapped her back into herself. "Dumbo." The fat elephant. *Her* fat elephant: no more than that, the fat elephant she'd thought *was* her.

The spell broke. She looked away from the creature. For a moment, out of the corner of her eye, she saw something sickly and fly-blown beneath the glamour. They'd called her Dumbo as a child, all the kids on her block. She'd lived with that ridiculous grey horror for twenty years, never able to shake it off. Its fat body reminded her of her fat, its lost look of her isolation. She thought of it cradled in the trunk of its mother, condemned as a Mad Elephant, and she wanted to beat the sentimental thing senseless.

"It's a fucking lie!" she spat at it.

"I don't know what you mean," it protested.

"What's under all the pizzazz then? Something very nasty I think."

The light began to flicker, the parade of trailers faltering. She could see another shape, small and dark, lurking behind the curtains of light. Doubt was in it. Doubt and fear of dying. She was sure she could smell the fear off it, at ten paces.

"What are you, under there?"

She took a step towards it.

"What are you hiding? Eh?"

It found a voice. A frightened, human voice. "You've no business with me."

"You tried to kill me."

"I want to live."

"So do I."

It was getting dark this end of the corridor, and there was an old, bad smell here, of rot. She knew rot, and this was something animal. Only last spring, when the snow had melted, she'd found something very dead in the yard behind her apart-

ment. Small dog, large cat, it was difficult to be sure.
Something domestic that had died of cold in the sudden snows
the December before. Now it was besieged with maggots:
yellowish, greyish, pinkish: a pastel fly machine with a
thousand moving parts.

It had around it the same stink that lingered here. Maybe
that was somehow the flesh behind the fantasy.

Taking courage, her eyes still stinging with "Dumbo," she
advanced on the wavering mirage, Motherfucker raised in case
the thing tried any funny business.

The boards beneath her feet were creaking, but she was too
interested in her quarry to listen to their warnings. It was time
she got a hold of this killer, shook it and made it spit its secret.

They'd almost gone the length of the corridor now, her advancing, it retreating. There was nowhere left for the thing to
go.

Suddenly the floorboards folded up into dusty fragments
under her weight and she was falling through the floor in a
cloud of dust. She dropped Motherfucker as she threw out her
hands to catch hold of something, but it was all worm-ridden,
and crumbled in her grasp.

She fell awkwardly and landed hard on something soft.
Here the smell of rot was incalculably stronger, it coaxed the
stomach into the throat. She reached out her hand to right
herself in the darkness, and on every side there was slime and
cold. She felt as though she'd been dumped in a case of par-
tially-gutted fish. Above her, the anxious light shone through
the boards as it fell on her bed. She looked, though God
knows she didn't want to, and she was lying in the remains of
a man, his body spread by his devourers over quite an area.
She wanted to howl. Her instinct was to tear off her skirt and
blouse, both of which were gluey with matter; but she couldn't
go naked, not in front of the son of celluloid.

It still looked down at her.

"Now you know," it said, lost.

"This is you—"

"This is the body I once occupied, yes. His name was
Barberio. A criminal; nothing spectacular. He never aspired to
greatness."

"And you?"

"His cancer. I'm the piece of him which did aspire, that did long to be more than a humble cell. I am a dreaming disease. No wonder I love the movies."

The son of celluloid was weeping over the edge of the broken floor, its true body exposed now it had no reason to fabricate a glory.

It was a filthy thing, a tumor grown fat on wasted passion. A parasite with the shape of a slug, and the texture of raw liver. For a moment a toothless mouth, badly molded, formed at its head end and said: "I'm going to have to find a new way to eat your soul."

It flopped down into the crawlspace beside Birdy. Without its shimmering coat of many technicolors it was the size of a small child. She backed away as it stretched a sensor to touch her, but avoidance was a limited option. The crawlspace was narrow, and further along it was blocked with what looked to be broken chairs and discarded prayer books. There was no way out but the way she'd come, and that was fifteen feet above her head.

Tentatively, the cancer touched her foot, and she was sick. She couldn't help it, even though she was ashamed to be giving in to such primitive responses. It revolted her as nothing ever had before; it brought to mind something aborted, a bucket case.

"Go to hell," she said to it, kicking at its head, but it kept coming, its diarrheal mass trapping her legs. She could feel the churning motion of its innards as it rose up to her.

Its bulk on her belly and groin was almost sexual, and revolted as she was by her own train of thought she wondered dimly if such a thing aspired to sex. Something about the insistence of its forming and reforming feelers against her skin, probing tenderly beneath her blouse, stretching to touch her lips, only made sense as desire. Let it come then, she thought, let it come if it has to.

She let it crawl up her until it was entirely perched on her body, fighting every moment the urge to throw it off—and then she sprang her trap.

She rolled over.

She'd weighed 225 pounds at the last count, and she was probably more now. The thing was beneath her before it could work out how or why this had happened, and its pores were oozing the sick sap of tumors.

It fought, but it couldn't get out from under, however much it squirmed. Birdy dug her nails into it and began to tear at its sides, taking cobs of it, spongy cobs that set more fluids gushing. Its howls of anger turned into howls of pain. After a short while, the dreaming disease stopped fighting.

Birdy lay still for a moment. Underneath her, nothing moved.

At last, she got up. It was impossible to know if the tumor was dead. It hadn't, by any standards that she understood, lived. Besides, she wasn't touching it again. She'd wrestle the Devil himself rather than embrace Barberio's cancer a second time.

She looked up at the corridor above her and despaired. Was she now to die in here, like Barberio before her? Then, as she glanced down at her adversary, she noticed the grille. It hadn't been visible while it was still night outside. Now dawn was breaking, and columns of dishwater light were creeping through the lattice.

She bent to the grille, pushed it hard, and suddenly the day was in the crawlspace with her, all around her. It was a squeeze to get through the small door, and she kept thinking every moment that she felt the thing crawling across her legs, but she hauled herself into the world with only bruised breasts to complain of.

The abandoned lot hadn't changed substantially since Barberio's visit there. It was merely more nettle-thronged. She stood for a while breathing in drafts of fresh air, then made for the fence and the street beyond it.

The fat woman with the haggard look and the stinking clothes was given a wide berth by newsboys and dogs alike as she made her way home.

THREE: CENSORED SCENES

It wasn't the end.

The police went to the Movie Palace just after nine-thirty.

Birdy went with them. The search revealed the mutilated bodies of Dean and Ricky, as well as the remains of "Sonny" Barberio. Upstairs, in the corner of the corridor, they found a cerise shoe.

Birdy said nothing, but she knew. Lindi Lee had never left.

She was put on trial for a double murder nobody really thought she'd committed, and acquitted for lack of evidence. It was the order of the court that she be put under psychiatric observation for a period of not less than two years. The woman might not have committed murder, but it was clear she was a raving lunatic. Tales of walking cancers do nobody's reputation much good.

In the early summer of the following year Birdy gave up eating for a week. Most of the weight loss in that time was water, but it was sufficient to encourage her friends that she was at last going to tackle the Big Problem.

That weekend, she went missing for twenty-fours hours.

Birdy found Lindi Lee in a deserted house in Seattle. She hadn't been so difficult to trace: it was hard for poor Lindi to keep control of herself these days, never mind avoid would-be pursuers. As it happened her parents had given up on her several months previous. Only Birdy had continued to look, paying for an investigator to trace the girl, and finally her patience was rewarded with the sight of the frail beauty, frailer than ever but still beautiful sitting in this bare room. Flies roamed the air. A turd, perhaps human, sat in the middle of the floor.

Birdy had a gun out before she opened the door. Lindi Lee looked up from her thoughts, or maybe *its* thoughts, and smiled at her. The greeting lasted a moment only before the parasite in Lindi Lee recognized Birdy's face, saw the gun in her hand and knew exactly what she'd come to do.

"Well," it said, getting up to meet its visitor.

Lindi Lee's eyes burst, her mouth burst, her cunt and ass, her ears and nose all burst, and the tumor poured out of her in shocking pink rivers. It came worming out of her milkless breasts, out of a cut in her thumb, from an abrasion on her thigh. Wherever Lindi Lee was open, it came.

Birdy raised the gun and fired three times. The cancer stretched once towards her, fell back, staggered and collapsed. Once it was still, Birdy calmly took the acid bottle out of her pocket, unscrewed the top and emptied the scalding contents on human limb and tumor alike. It made no shout as it dissolved, and she left it there, in a patch of sun, a pungent smoke rising from the confusion.

She stepped out into the street, her duty done, and went her way, confidently planning to live long after the credits for this particular comedy had rolled.

RAWHEAD REX

Of all the conquering armies that had tramped the streets of Zeal down the centuries, it was finally the mild tread of the Sunday tripper that brought the village to its knees. It had suffered Roman legions, and the Norman conquest, it had survived the agonies of Civil War, all without losing its identity to the occupying forces. But after centuries of boot and blade it was to be the tourists—the new barbarians—that bested Zeal, their weapons courtesy and hard cash.

It was ideally suited for the invasion. Forty miles south east of London, amongst the orchards and hopfields of the Kentish Weald, it was far enough from the city to make the trip an adventure, yet close enough to beat a quick retreat if the weather turned foul. Every weekend between May and October Zeal was a watering hole for parched Londoners. They would swarm through the village on each Saturday that promised sun, bringing their dogs, their plastic balls, their litters of children, and their children's litter, disgorging them in bawling hordes onto the village green, then returning to "The Tall Man" to compare traffic stories over glasses of warm beer.

For their part the Zealots weren't unduly distressed by the Sunday trippers; at least they didn't spill blood. But their very lack of aggression made the invasion all the more insidious.

Gradually these city-weary people began to work a gentle but permanent change on the village. Many of them set their hearts on a home in the country; they were charmed by stone cottages set amongst churning oaks, they were enchanted by doves in the churchyard yews. Even the air, they'd say as they inhaled deeply, even the air smells fresher here. It smells of England.

At first a few, then many, began to make bids for the empty barns and deserted houses that littered Zeal and its outskirts. They could be seen every fine weekend, standing in the nettles and rubble, planning how to have a kitchen extension built, and where to install the jacuzzi. And although many of them, once back in the comfort of Kilburn or St. John's Wood, chose to stay there, every year one or two of them would strike a reasonable bargain with one of the villagers, and buy themselves an acre of the good life.

So, as the years passed and the natives of Zeal were picked off by old age, the civil savages took over in their stead. The occupation was subtle, but the change was plain to the knowing eye. It was there in the newspapers the Post Office began to stock—what native of Zeal had ever purchased a copy of "Harpers and Queen" magazine, or leafed through "The Times Literary Supplement"? It was there, that change, in the bright new cars that clogged the one narrow street, laughingly called the High Road, that was Zeal's backbone. It was there too in the buzz of gossip at "The Tall Man," a sure sign that the affairs of the foreigners had become fit subject for debate and mockery.

Indeed, as time went by the invaders found a yet more permanent place in the heart of Zeal, as the perennial demons of their hectic lives, Cancer and Heart Disease, took their toll, following their victims even into his newfound land. Like the Romans before them, like the Normans, like all invaders, the commuters made their profoundest mark upon this usurped turf not by building on it, but by being buried under it.

It was clammy the middle of that September; Zeal's last September.

Thomas Garrow, the only son of the late Thomas Garrow, was sweating up a healthy thirst as he dug in the corner of the Three Acre Field. There'd been a violent rainstorm the previous day, Thursday, and the earth was sodden. Clearing

the ground for sowing next year hadn't been the easy job
Thomas thought it'd be, but he'd sworn blind he'd have the
field finished by the end of the week. It was heavy labor, clearing stones, and sorting out the detritus of out-of-date
machinery his father, lazy bastard, had left to rust where it
lay. Must have been some good years, Thomas thought, some
pretty fine damn years, that his father could afford to let good
machinery waste away. Come to think of it, that he could have
afforded to leave the best part of three acres unploughed;
good healthy soil too. This was the Garden of England after
all: land was money. Leaving three acres fallow was a luxury
nobody could afford in these straitened times. But Jesus, it
was hard work: the kind of work his father had put him to in
his youth, and he'd hated with a vengeance ever since.

Still, it had to be done.

And the day had begun well. The tractor was healthier after
its overhaul, and the morning sky was rife with gulls, across
from the coast for a meal of freshly turned worms. They'd
kept him raucous company as he worked, their insolence and
their short tempers always entertaining. But then, when he
came back to the field after a liquid lunch in "The Tall Man,"
things began to go wrong. The engine started to cut out for
one, the same problem that he'd just spent £200 having seen
to; and then, when he'd only been back at work a few minutes,
he'd found the stone.

It was an unspectacular lump of stuff: poking out of the soil
perhaps a foot, its visible diameter a few inches short of a
yard, its surface smooth and bare. No lichen even; just a few
grooves in its face that might have once been words. A love
letter perhaps, a "Kilroy was here" more likely, a date and a
name likeliest of all. Whatever it had once been, monument or
milestone, it was in the way now. He'd have to dig it up, or
next year he'd lose a good three yards of ploughable land.
There was no way a plough could skirt around a boulder that
size.

Thomas was surprised that the damn thing had been left in
the field for so long without anyone bothering to remove it.
But then it was a long spell since the Three Acre Field had been
planted: certainly not in his thirty-six years. And maybe, now
he came to think of it, not in his father's lifetime either. For

some reason (if he'd ever known the reason he'd forgotten it)
this stretch of Garrow land had been left fallow for a good
many seasons, maybe even for generations. In fact there was a
suspicion tickling the back of his skull that someone, probably
his father, had said no crop would ever grow in that particular
spot. But that was plain nonsense. If anything plant life, albeit
nettles and convolvulus, grew thicker and ranker in this forsaken three acres than in any other plot in the district. So there
was no reason on earth why hops shouldn't flourish here.
Maybe even an orchard: though that took more patience and
love than Thomas suspected he possessed. Whatever he chose
to plant, it would surely spring up from such rich ground with
a rare enthusiasm, and he'd have reclaimed three acres of
good land to bolster his shaky finances.

If he could just dig out that bloody stone.

He'd half thought of hiring in one of the earth movers from
the building site at the North End of the village, just to haul
itself across here and get its mechanical jaws working on the
problem. Have the stone out and away in two seconds flat.
But his pride resisted the idea of running for help at the first
sign of a blister. The job was too small anyhow. He'd dig it
out himself, the way his father would have done. That's what
he'd decided. Now, two and a half hours later, he was regretting his haste.

The ripening warmth of the afternoon had soured in that
time, without much of a breeze to stir it around, had become
stifling. Over from the Downs came a stuttering roll of
thunder, and Thomas could feel the static crawling at the nape
of his neck, making the short hairs there stand up. The sky
above the field was empty now: the gulls, too fickle to hang
around once the fun was over, had taken some salt-smelling
thermal.

Even the earth, that had given up a sweet-sharp flavor as the
blades turned it that morning, now smelt joyless; and as he
dug the black soil out from around the stone his mind returned
helplessly to the putrefaction that made it so very rich. His
thoughts circled vacuously on the countless little deaths on
every spadeful of soil he dug. This wasn't the way he was used
to thinking, and the morbidity of it distressed him. He stopped
for a moment, leaning on his spade, and regretting the fourth

pint of Guinness he'd downed at lunch. That was normally a harmless enough ration, but today it swilled around in his belly, he could hear it, as dark as the soil on his spade, working up a scum of stomach acid and half-digested food.

Think of something else, he told himself, or you'll get to puking. To take his mind off his belly, he looked at the field. It was nothing out of the ordinary; just a rough square of land bounded by an untrimmed hawthorn hedge. One or two dead animals lying in the shadow of the hawthorn: a starling; something else, too far gone to be recognizable. There was a sense of absence, but that wasn't so unusual. It would soon be autumn, and the summer had been too long, too hot for comfort.

Looking up higher than the hedge he watched the mongol-headed cloud discharge a flicker of lightning to the hills. What had been the brightness of the afternoon was now pressed into a thin line of blue at the horizon. Rain soon, he thought, and the thought was welcome. Cool rain; perhaps a downpour like the previous day. Maybe this time it would clear the air good and proper.

Thomas stared back down at the unyielding stone, and struck it with his spade. A tiny arc of white flame flew off.

He cursed, loudly and inventively: the stone, himself, the field. The stone just sat there in the moat he'd dug around it, defying him. He'd almost run out of options: the earth around the thing had been dug out two feet down; he'd hammered stakes under it, chained it and then got the tractor going to haul it out. No joy. Obviously he'd have to dig the moat deeper, drive the stakes further down. He wasn't going to let the damn thing beat him.

Grunting his determination he set to digging again. A fleck of rain hit the back of his hand, but he scarcely noticed it. He knew by experience that labor like this took singularity of purpose: head down, ignore all distractions. He made his mind blank. There was just the earth, the spade, the stone and his body.

Push down, scoop up. Push down, scoop up, a hypnotic rhythm of effort. The trance was so total he wasn't sure how long he worked before the stone began to shift.

The movement woke him. He stood upright, his vertebrae

clicking, not quite certain that the shift was anything more than a twitch in his eye. Putting his heel against the stone, he pushed. Yes, it rocked in its grave. He was too drained to smile, but he felt victory close. He had the bugger.

The rain was starting to come on heavier now, and it felt fine on his face. He drove a couple more stakes in around the stone to unseat it a little further: he was going to get the better of the thing. You'll see, he said, you'll see. The third stake went deeper than the first two, and it seemed to puncture a bubble of gas beneath the stone, a yellowish cloud smelling so foul he stepped away from the hole to snatch a breath of purer air. There was none to be had. All he could do was hawk up a wad of phlegm to clear his throat and lungs. Whatever was under the stone, and there was something animal in the stench, it was very rotten.

He forced himself back down to the work, taking gasps of the air into his mouth, not through his nostrils. His head felt tight, as though his brain was swelling and straining against the dome of his skull, pushing to be let out.

"Fuck you," he said and beat another stake under the stone. His back felt as though it was about to break. On his right hand a blister had bust. A cleg sat on his arm and feasted itself, unswatted.

"Do it. Do it. Do it." He beat the last stake in without knowing he was doing it.

And then, the stone began to roll.

He wasn't even touching it. The stone was being pushed out of its seating from beneath. He reached for his spade, which was still wedged beneath the stone. He suddenly felt possessive of it; it was his, a part of him, and he didn't want it near the hole. Not now; not with the stone rocking like it had a geyser under it about to blow. Not with the air yellow, and his brain swelling up like a marrow in August.

He pulled hard on his spade: it wouldn't come.

He cursed it, and took two hands to the job, keeping at arm's length from the hole as he hauled, the increasing motion of the stone slinging up showers of soil, lice, and pebbles.

He heaved at the spade again, but it wouldn't give. He didn't stop to analyze the situation. The work had sickened him, all he wanted was to get his spade, *his* spade, out of the hole and get the hell out of there.

The stone bucked, but still he wouldn't let go of the spade, it had become fixed in his head that he had to have it before he could leave. Only when it was back in his hands, safe and sound, would he obey his bowels, and run.

Beneath his feet the ground began to erupt. The stone rolled away from the tomb as if feather light, a second cloud of gas, more obnoxious than the first, seemed to blow it on its way. At the same time the spade came out of the hole, and Thomas saw what had hold of it.

Suddenly there was no sense in heaven or earth.

There was a hand, a living hand, clutching the spade, a hand so wide it could grasp the blade with ease.

Thomas knew the moment well. The splitting earth: the hand: the stench. He knew it from some nightmare he'd heard at his father's knee.

Now he wanted to let go of the spade, but he no longer had the will. All he could do was obey some imperative from underground, to haul until his ligaments tore and his sinews bled.

Beneath the thin crust of earth, Rawhead smelt the sky. It was pure ether to his dulled senses, making him sick with pleasure. Kingdoms for the taking, just a few inches away. After so many years, after the endless suffocation, there was light on his eyes again, and the taste of human terror on his tongue.

His head was breaking surface now, his black hair wreathed with worms, his scalp seething with tiny red spiders. They'd irritated him a hundred years, those spiders burrowing into his marrow, and he longed to crush them out. Pull, pull, he willed the human, and Thomas Garrow pulled until his pitiful body had no strength left, and inch by inch Rawhead was hoisted out of his grave in a shroud of prayers.

The stone that had pressed on him for so long had been removed, and he was dragging himself up easily now, sloughing off the grave earth like a snake its skin. His torso was free. Shoulders twice as broad as a man's; lean, scarred arms stronger than any human. His limbs were pumping with blood like a butterfly's wings, juicing with resurrection. His long, lethal fingers rhythmically clawed the ground as they gained strength.

Thomas Garrow just stood and watched. There was nothing in him but awe. Fear was for those who still had a chance of life: he had none.

Rawhead was out of his grave completely. He began to stand upright for the first in centuries. Clods of damp soil fell from his torso as he stretched to his full height, a yard above Garrow's six feet.

Thomas Garrow stood in Rawhead's shadow with his eyes still fixed on the gaping hole the King had risen from. In his right hand he still clutched his spade. Rawhead picked him up by the hair. His scalp tore under the weight of his body, so Rawhead seized Garrow round the neck, his vast hand easily enclosing it.

Blood ran down Garrow's face from his scalp, and the sensation stirred him. Death was imminent, and he knew it. He looked down at his legs, thrashing uselessly below him, then he looked up and stared directly into Rawhead's pitiless face.

It was huge, like the harvest moon, huge and amber. But this moon had eyes that burned in its pallid, pitted face. They were for all the world like wounds, those eyes, as though somebody had gouged them in the flesh of Rawhead's face then set two candles to flicker in the holes.

Garrow was entranced by the vastness of this moon. He looked from eye to eye, and then to the wet slits that were its nose, and finally, in a childish terror, down to the mouth. God, that mouth. It was so wide, so cavernous it seemed to split the head in two as it opened. That was Thomas Garrow's last thought. That the moon was splitting in two, and falling out of the sky on top of him.

Then the King inverted the body, as had always been his way with his dead enemies, and drove Thomas head first into the hole, winding him down into the very grave his forefathers had intended to bury Rawhead in forever.

By the time the thunderstorm proper broke over Zeal, the King was a mile away from the Three Acre Field, sheltering in the Nicholson barn. In the village everyone went about their business, rain or no rain. Ignorance was bliss. There was no Cassandra amongst them, nor had "Your Future in the Stars" in that week's "Gazette" even hinted at the sudden deaths to come to a Gemini, three Leos, a Sagittarian and a minor star system of others in the next few days.

The rain had come with the thunder, fat cool spots of it, which rapidly turned into a downpour of monsoonal ferocity. Only when the gutters became torrents did people begin to take shelter.

On the building site the earth mover that had been roughly landscaping Ronnie Milton's back garden sat idling in the rain, receiving a second washdown in two days. The driver had taken the downpour as a signal to retire into the hut to talk race horses and women.

In the doorway of the Post Office three of the villagers watched the drains backing up, and tutted that this always happened when it rained, and in half an hour there'd be a pool of water in the dip at the bottom of the High Street so deep you could sail a boat on it.

And down in the dip itself, in the vestry of St. Peter's, Declan Ewan, the Verger, watched the rain pelting down the hill in eager rivulets, and gathering into a little sea outside the vestry gate. Soon be deep enough to drown in, he thought, and then, puzzled by why he imagined drowning, he turned away from the window and went back to the business of folding vestments. A strange excitement was in him today: and he couldn't, wouldn't, didn't want to suppress it. It was nothing to do with the thunderstorm, though he'd always loved them since he was a child. No: there was something else stirring him up, and he was damned if he knew what. It was like being a child again. As if it was Christmas, and any minute Santa, the first Lord he'd ever believed in, would be at the door. The very idea made him want to laugh out loud, but the vestry was too sober a place for laughter, and he stopped himself, letting the smile curl inside him, a secret hope.

While everyone else took refuge from the rain, Gwen Nicholson was getting thoroughly drenched. She was still in the yard behind the house, coaxing Amelia's pony towards the barn. The thunder had made the stupid beast jittery, and it didn't want to budge. Now Gwen was soaked and angry.

"Will you come on, you brute?" she yelled at it over the
noise of the storm. The rain lashed the yard, and pummelled
the top of her head. Her hair was flattened. *"Come on! Come
on!"*

The pony refused to budge. Its eyes showed crescents of
white in its fear. And the more the thunder rolled and crackled
around the yard the less it wanted to move. Angrily, Gwen
slapped it across the backside, harder than she strictly needed
to. It took a couple of steps in response to the blow, dropping
steaming turds as it went, and Gwen took the advantage. Once
she had it moving she could drag it the rest of the way.

"Warm barn," she promised it; "Come on, it's wet out
here, you don't want to stay out here."

The barn door was slightly ajar. Surely it must look like an
inviting prospect, she thought, even to a pea-brained pony.
She dragged it to within spitting distance of the barn, and one
more slap got it through the door.

As she'd promised the damn thing, the interior of the barn
was sweet and dry, though the air smelt metallic with the
storm. Gwen tied the pony to the crossbar in its stall and
roughly threw a blanket over its glistening hide. She was
damned if she was going to swab the creature down, that was
Amelia's job. That was the bargain she'd made with her
daughter whan they'd agreed to buy the pony: that all the
grooming and clearing out would be Amelia's responsibility,
and to be fair to her, she'd done what she promised, more or
less.

The pony was still panicking. It stamped and rolled its eyes
like a bad tragedian. There were flecks of foam on its lips. A
little apologetically Gwen patted its flank. She'd lost her
temper. Time of the month. Now she regretted it. She only
hoped Amelia hadn't been at her bedroom window watching.

A gust of wind caught the barn door and it swung closed.
The sound of rain on the yard outside was abruptly muted. It
was suddenly dark.

The pony stopped stamping. Gwen stopped stroking its
side. Everything stopped: her heart too, it seemed.

Behind her a figure that was almost twice her size rose from
beyond the bales of hay. Gwen didn't see the giant, but her in-

nards churned. Damn periods, she thought, rubbing her lower belly in a slow circle. She was normally as regular as clockwork, but this month she'd come on a day early. She should go back to the house, get changed, get clean.

Rawhead stood and looked at the nape of Gwen Nicholson's neck, where a single nip would easily kill. But there was no way he could bring himself to touch this woman; not today. She had the blood cycle on her, he could taste its tang, and it sickened him. It was taboo, that blood, and he had never taken a woman poisoned by its presence.

Feeling the damp between her legs, Gwen hurried out of the barn without looking behind her, and ran through the downpour back to the house, leaving the fretting pony in the darkness of the barn.

Rawhead heard the woman's feet recede, heard the housedoor slam.

He waited, to be sure she wouldn't come back, then he padded across to the animal, reached down and took hold of it. The pony kicked and complained, but Rawhead had in his time taken animals far bigger and far better armed than this.

He opened his mouth. The gums were suffused with blood as the teeth emerged from them, like claws unsheathed from a cat's paw. There were two rows on each jaw, two dozen needle-sharp points. They gleamed as they closed around the meat of the pony's neck. Thick, fresh blood poured down Rawhead's throat; he gulped it greedily. The hot taste of the world. It made him feel strong and wise. This was only the first of many meals he would take, he'd gorge on anything that took his fancy and nobody would stop him, not this time. And when he was ready he'd throw those pretenders off his throne, he'd cremate them in their houses, he'd slaughter their children and wear their infants' bowels as necklaces. *This place was his*. Just because they'd tamed the wilderness for a while didn't mean they owned the earth. It was his, and nobody would take it from him, not even the holiness. He was wise to that too. They'd never subdue him again.

He sat cross-legged on the floor of the barn, the grey-pink intestines of the pony coiled around him, planning his tactics as best he could. He'd never been a great thinker. Too much appetite: it overwhelmed his reason. He lived in the eternal present of his hunger and his strength, feeling only the crude territorial instinct that would sooner or later blossom into carnage.

The rain didn't let up for over an hour.

Ron Milton was becoming impatient: a flaw in his nature that had given him an ulcer and a top flight job in Design Consultancy. What Milton could get done for you, couldn't be done quicker. He was the best: and he hated sloth in other people as much as in himself. Take this damn house, for instance. They'd promised it would be finished by mid-July, garden landscaped, driveway laid, everything, and here he was, two months after that date, looking at a house that was still far from habitable. Half the windows without glass, the front door missing, the garden an assault course, the driveway a mire.

This was to be his castle: his retreat from a world that made him dyspeptic and rich. A haven away from the hassles of the city, where Maggie could grow roses, and the children could breathe clean air. Except that it wasn't ready. Damn it, at this rate he wouldn't be in until next spring. Another winter in London: the thought made his heart sink.

Maggie joined him, sheltering him under her red umbrella.

"Where are the kids?" he asked.

She grimaced. "Back at the hotel, driving Mrs. Blatter crazy."

Enid Blatter had borne their cavortings for half a dozen weekends through the summer. She'd had kids of her own, and she handled Debbie and Ian with aplomb. But there was a limit, even to her fund of mirth and merriment.

"We'd better get back to town."

"No. Please let's stay another day or two. We can go back on Sunday evening. I want us all to go to the Harvest Festival Service on Sunday."

Now it was Ron's turn to grimace.

"Oh hell."

"It's all part of village life, Ronnie. If we're going to live here, we have to become part of the community."

He whined like a little boy when he was in this kind of

mood. She knew him so well she could hear his next words before he said them.

"I don't want to."

"Well we've no choice."

"We can go back tonight."

"Ronnie—"

"There's nothing we can do here. The kids are bored, you're miserable . . ."

Maggie had set her features in concrete; she wasn't going to budge an inch. He knew that face as well as she knew his whining.

He studied the puddles that were forming in what might one day be their front garden, unable to imagine grass there, roses there. It all suddenly seemed impossible.

"You go back to town if you like, Ronnie. Take the kids. I'll stay here. Train it home on Sunday night."

Clever, he thought, to give him a get out that's more unattractive than staying put. Two days in town looking after the kids alone? No thank you.

"O.K. You win. We'll go to the Harvest-bloody-Festival."

"Martyr."

"As long as I don't have to pray."

Amelia Nicholson ran into the kitchen, her round face white, and collapsed in front of her mother. There was greasy vomit on her green plastic mackintosh, and blood on her green plastic wellingtons.

Gwen yelled for Denny. Their little girl was shivering in her faint, her mouth chewing at a word, or words, that wouldn't come.

"What is it?"

Denny was thundering down the stairs.

"For Christ's sake—"

Amelia was vomiting again. Her face was practically blue.

"What's wrong with her?"

"She just came in. You'd better ring for an ambulance."

Denny put his hand on her cheek.

"She's in shock."

"Ambulance, Denny . . ." Gwen was taking off the green

mackintosh, and loosening the child's blouse. Slowly, Denny stood up. Through the rain-laced window he could see into the yard: the barn door flapped open and closed in the wind. Somebody was inside; he glimpsed movement.

"For Christ's sake—ambulance!" Gwen said again.

Denny wasn't listening. There was somebody in his barn, on his property, and he had a strict ritual for trespassers.

The barn door opened again, teasing. Yes! Retreating into the dark. Interloper.

He picked up the rifle beside the door, keeping his eyes on the yard as much as he could. Behind him, Gwen had left Amelia on the kitchen floor and was dialing for help. The girl was moaning now: she was going to be O.K. Just some filthy trespasser scaring her, that's all. On his land.

He opened the door and stepped into the yard. He was in his shirtsleeves and the wind was bitingly cold, but the rain had stopped. Underfoot the ground glistened, and drips fell from every eave and portico, a fidgety percussion that accompanied him across the yard.

The barn door swung listlessly ajar again, and this time stayed open. He could see nothing inside. Half wondered if a trick of the light had—

But no. He'd seen someone moving in here. The barn wasn't empty. Something (not the pony) was watching him even now. They'd see the rifle in his hands, and they'd sweat. Let them. Come into his place like that. Let them think he was going to blow their balls off.

He covered the distance in a half a dozen confident strides and stepped into the barn.

The pony's stomach was beneath his shoe, one of its legs to his right, the upper shank gnawed to the bone. Pools of thickening blood reflected the holes in the roof. The mutilation made him want to heave.

"All right," he challenged the shadows. "Come out." He raised his rifle. "You hear me you bastard? Out I said, or I'll blow you to Kingdom Come."

He meant it too.

At the far end of the barn something stirred amongst the bales.

Now I've got the son of a bitch, thought Denny. The trespasser got up, all nine feet of him, and stared at Denny.

"Jee-sus."

And without warning it was coming at him, coming like a locomotive smooth and efficient. He fired into it, and the bullet struck its upper chest, but the wound hardly slowed it.

Nicholson turned and ran. The stones of the yard were slippery beneath his shoes, and he had no turn of speed to outrun it. It was at his back in two beats, and on him in another.

Gwen dropped the phone when she heard the shot. She raced to the window in time to see her sweet Denny eclipsed by a gargantuan form. It howled as it took him, and threw him up into the air like a sack of feathers. She watched helplessly as his body twisted at the apex of its journey before plummeting back down to earth again. It hit the yard with a thud she felt in her every bone, and the giant was at his body like a shot, treading his loving face to muck.

She screamed; trying to silence herself with her hand. Too late. The sound was out and the giant was looking at her, straight at her, its malice piercing the window. Oh God, it had seen her, and now it was coming for her, loping across the yard, a naked engine, and grinning a promise at her as it came.

Gwen snatched Amelia off the floor and hugged her close, pressing the girl's face against her neck. Maybe she wouldn't see: she mustn't see. The sound of its feet slapping on the wet yard got louder. Its shadow filled the kitchen.

"Jesus help me."

It was pressing at the window, its body so wide that it cancelled out the light, its lewd, revolting face smeared on the watery pane. Then it was smashing through, ignoring the glass that bit into its flesh. It smelled child meat. It wanted child meat. It would *have* child meat.

Its teeth were spilling into view, widening that smile into an obscene laugh. Ropes of saliva hung from its jaw as it clawed the air, like a cat after a mouse in a cage, pressing further and further in, each swipe closer to the morsel.

Gwen flung open the door into the hall as the thing lost patience with snatching and began to demolish the window-frame and clamber through. She locked the door after her while crockery smashed and wood splintered on the other side, then she began to load all the hall furniture against it. Tables, chairs, coatstand, knowing even as she did it, that it would be matchwood in two seconds flat. Amelia was kneeling on the hall floor where Gwen had set her down. Her face was a thankful blank.

All right, that was all she could do. Now, upstairs. She picked up her daughter, who was suddenly air light, and took the stairs two at a time. Halfway up, the noise in the kitchen below stopped utterly.

She suddenly had a reality crisis. On the landing where she stood all was peace and calm. Dust gathered minutely on the windowsills, flowers wilted; all the infinitesimal domestic procedures went on as though nothing had happened.

"Dreaming it," she said. God, yes: dreaming it.

She sat down on the bed Denny and she had slept in together for eight years, and tried to think straight.

Some vile menstrual nightmare, that's what it was, some rape fantasy out of all control. She lay Amelia on the pink eiderdown (Denny hated pink but suffered it for her sake) and stroked the girl's clammy forehead.

"Dreaming it."

Then the room darkened, and she looked up knowing what she'd see.

It was there, the nightmare, all over the upper windows, its spidery arms spanning the width of the glass, clinging like an acrobat to the frame, its repellent teeth sheathing and unsheathing as it gawped at her terror.

In one swooping movement she snatched Amelia up from the bed and dived towards the door. Behind her, glass shattered, and a gust of cold air swept into the bedroom. It was coming.

She ran across the landing to the top of the stairs but it was after her in a heart's beat, ducking through the bedroom door, its mouth a tunnel. It whooped as it reached to steal the mute parcel in her arms, huge in the confined space of the landing.

She couldn't outrun it, she couldn't outfight it. Its hands fixed on Amelia with insolent ease, and tugged.

The child screamed as it took her, her fingernails raking four furrows across her mother's face as she left her arms.

Gwen stumbled back, dizzied by the unthinkable sight in front of her, and lost balance at the top of the stairs. As she fell backwards she saw Amelia's tear-stained face, dollstiff, being fed between those rows of teeth. Then her head hit the bannister, and her neck broke. She bounced down the last six steps a corpse.

The rainwater had drained away a little by early evening, but the artificial lake at the bottom of the dip still flooded the road to a depth of several inches. Serenely, it reflected the sky. Pretty, but inconvenient. Reverend Coot quietly reminded Declan Ewan to report the blocked drains to the County Council. It was the third time of asking, and Declan blushed at the request.

"Sorry, I'll . . ."

"All right. No problem, Declan. But we really must get them cleared."

A vacant look. A beat. A thought.

"Autumn fall always clogs them again, of course."

Coot made a roughly cyclical gesture, intending a sort of observation about how it really wouldn't make that much difference when or if the Council cleared the drains, then the thought disappeared. There were more pressing issues. For one, the Sunday Sermon. For a second, the reason why he couldn't make much sense of sermon writing this evening. There was an unease in the air today, that made every reassuring word he committed to paper curdle as he wrote it. Coot went to the window, back to Declan, and scratched his palms. They itched: maybe an attack of eczema again. If he could only speak; find some words to shape his distress. Never, in his forty-five years, had he felt so incapable of communication; and never in those years had it been so vital that he talk.

"Shall I go now?" Declan asked.

Coot shook his head.

"A moment longer. If you would."

He turned to the Verger. Declan Ewan was twenty-nine, though he had the face of a much older man. Bland, pale features: his hair receding prematurely.

What will this eggface make of my revelation? thought Coot. He'll probably laugh. That's why I can't find the words, because I don't want to. I'm afraid of looking stupid. Here I am, a man of the cloth, dedicated to the Christian Mysteries.

For the first time in forty odd years I've had a real glimpse of something, a vision maybe, and I'm scared of being laughed at. Stupid man, Coot, stupid, stupid man.

He took off his glasses. Declan's empty features became a blur. Now at least he didn't have to look at the smirking.

"Declan, this morning I had what I can only describe as a . . . as a . . . visitation."

Declan said nothing, nor did the blur move.

"I don't quite know how to say this . . . our vocabulary's impoverished when it comes to these sorts of things . . . but frankly I've never had such a direct, such an unequivocal, manifestation of—"

Coot stopped. Did he mean God?

"God," he said, not sure that he did.

DeClan said nothing for a moment. Coot risked returning his glasses to their place. The egg hadn't cracked.

"Can you say what it was like?" Declan asked, his equilibrium absolutely unspoiled.

Coot shook his head; he'd been trying to find the words all day, but the phrases all seemed so predictable.

"What was it like?" Declan insisted.

Why didn't he understand that there were no words? I must try, thought Coot, I *must*.

"I was at the Altar after Morning Prayer . . ." he began, "and I felt something going through me. Like electricity almost. It made my hair stand on end. Literally on end."

Coot's hand was running through his short-cropped hair as he remembered the sensation. The hair standing bolt upright, like a field of grey-ginger corn. And that buzzing at the temples, in his lungs, at his groin. It had actually given him a hardon; not that he was going to be able to tell Declan that. But he'd stood there at the Altar with an erection so powerful it was like discovering the joy of lust all over again.

"I won't claim . . . I *can't* claim it was our Lord God—"

(Though he wanted to believe that; that his God was the Lord of the Hardon.) "—I can't even claim it was Christian. But something happened today. I felt it."

Declan's face was still impenetrable. Coot watched it for several seconds, impatient for its disdain.

"Well?" he demanded.

"Well what?"

"Nothing to say?"

The egg frowned for a moment, a furrow in its shell. Then it said:

"God help us," almost in a whisper.

"What?"

"I felt it too. Not quite as you describe: not quite an electric shock. But something."

"Why God help us, Declan? Are you afraid of something?"

He made no reply.

"If you know something about these experiences that I don't . . . please tell me. I want to know, to understand. God, I *have* to understand."

Declan pursed his lips. "Well . . ." his eyes became more indecipherable than ever; and for the first time Coot caught a glimpse of a ghost behind Declan's eyes. Was it despair, perhaps?

"There's a lot of history to this place you know," he said, "a history of things . . . on this site."

Coot knew Declan had been delving into Zeal's history. Harmless enough pastime: the past was the past.

"There's been a settlement here for centuries, stretches back well before Roman occupation. No one knows how long. There's probably always been a temple on this site."

"Nothing odd about that." Coot offered up a smile, inviting Declan to reassure him. A part of him wanted to be told everything was well with his world: even if it was a lie.

Declan's face darkened. He had no reassurance to give. "And there was a forest here. Huge. The Wild Woods." Was it still despair behind the eyes? Or was it nostalgia? "Not some tame little orchard. A forest you could lose a city in; full of beasts . . ."

"Wolves you mean? Bears?'

Declan shook his head.

"There were things that owned this land. Before Christ. Before civilization. Most of them didn't survive the destruction of their natural habitat: too primitive I suppose. But strong. Not like us; not human. Something else altogether."

"So what?"

"One of them survived as late as the fourteen hundreds.

There's a carving of it being buried. It's on the Altar.''

"On the Altar?''

"Underneath the cloth. I found it a while ago; never thought much of it. Till today. Today I . . . tried to touch it.''

He produced his fist, and unclenched it. The flesh of his palm was blistered. Pus ran from the broken skin.

"It doesn't hurt,'' he said. ''In fact it's quite numb. Serves me right, really. I should have known.''

Coot's first thought was that the man was lying. His second was that there was some logical explanation. His third was his father's dictum: ''Logic is the last refuge of a coward.''

Declan was speaking again. This time he was seeping excitement.

"They called it Rawhead.''

"What?''

"The beast they buried. It's in the history books. Rawhead it was called, because its head was huge, and the color of the moon, and raw, like meat.''

Declan couldn't stop himself now. He was beginning to smile.

"It ate children,'' he said, and beamed like a baby about to receive its mother's tit.

It wasn't until early on the Saturday morning that the atrocity at the Nicholson Farm was discovered. Mick Glossop had been driving up to London, and he'd taken the road that ran beside the farm, ("Don't know why. Don't usually. Funny really.'') and Nicholson's Friesian herd was kicking up a row at the gate, their udders distended. They'd clearly not been milked in twenty-four hours. Glossop had stopped his jeep on the road and gone into the yard.

The body of Denny Nicholson was already crawling with flies, though the sun had barely been up an hour. Inside the house the only remains of Amelia Nicholson were shreds of a dress and a casually discarded foot. Gwen Nicholson's unmutilated body lay at the bottom of the stairs. There was no sign of a wound or any sexual interference with the corpse.

By nine-thirty Zeal was swarming with police, and the shock of the incident registered on every face in the street. Though there were conflicting reports as to the state of the bodies there was no doubt of the brutality of the murders. Especially the child, dismembered presumably. Her body taken away by her killer for God knows what purpose.

The Murder Squad set up a Unit at "The Tall Man," while house to house interviews were conducted throughout the village. Nothing came immediately to light. No strangers seen in the locality; no more suspicious behavior from anyone than was normal for a poacher or a bent building merchant. It was Enid Blatter, she of the ample bust and the motherly manner, who mentioned that she hadn't seen Thorn Garrow for over twenty-four hours.

They found him where his killer had left him, the worse for a few hours of picking. Worms at his head and gulls at his legs. The flesh of his shins, where his trousers had slid out of his boots, was pecked to the bone. When he was dug up families of refugee lice scurried from his ears.

The atmosphere in the hotel that night was subdued. In the bar Detective Sergeant Gissing, down from London to head the investigation, had found a willing ear in Ron Milton. He was glad to be conversing with a fellow Londoner, and Milton kept them both in Scotch and water for the best part of three hours.

"Twenty years in the force," Gissing kept repeating, "and I've never seen anything like it."

Which wasn't strictly true. There'd been that whore (or selected highlights thereof) he'd found in a suitcase at Euston's left luggage department, a good decade ago. And the addict who'd taken it upon himself to hypnotize a polar bear at London Zoo: he'd been a sight for sore eyes when they dredged him out of the pool. He'd seen a good deal, had Stanley Gissing—

"But this . . . never seen anything like it," he insisted. "Fair made me want to puke."

Ron wasn't quite sure why he listened to Gissing; it was just something to while the night away. Ron, who'd been a radical in his younger days, had never liked policemen much, and there was some quirky satisfaction to be had from getting this self-satisfied prat pissed out of his tiny skull.

"He's a fucking lunatic," Gissing said, "you can take my word for it. We'll have him easy. A man like that isn't in con-

trol, you see. Doesn't bother to cover his tracks, doesn't even
care if he lives or dies. God knows, any man who can tear a
seven-year-old girl to shreds like that, he's on the verge of
going bang. Seen 'em.''

"Yes?"

"Oh yes. Seen 'em weep like children, blood all over 'em
like they was just out of the abattoir, and tears on their faces.
Pathetic.''

"So, you'll have him."

"Like that," said Gissing, and snapped his fingers. He got
to his feet, a little unsteadily, "Sure as God made little apples,
we'll have him." He glanced at his watch and then at the
empty glass.

Ron made no further offers of refills.

"Well," said Gissing, "I must be getting back to town. Put
in my report."

He swayed to the door and left Milton to the bill.

Rawhead watched Gissing's car crawl out of the village and
along the north road, the headlights making very little impres-
sion on the night. The noise of the engine made Rawhead
nervous though, as it over-revved up the hill past the Nicholson Farm. It roared and coughed like no beast he had en-
countered before, and somehow the homo sapiens had control
of it. If the Kingdom was to be taken back from the usurpers,
sooner or later he would have to best one of these beasts.
Rawhead swallowed his fear and prepared for the confrontation.

The moon grew teeth.

In the back of the car Stanley was near as damnit asleep,
dreaming of little girls. In his dreams these charming nym-
phettes were climbing a ladder on their way to bed, and he was
on duty beside the ladder watching them climb, catching
glimpses of their slightly soiled knickers as they disappeared
into the sky. It was a familiar dream, one that he would never
have admitted to, not even drunk. Not that he was ashamed
exactly; he knew for a fact many of his colleagues entertained
peccadilloes every bit as offbeat as, and some a good deal less
savory than, his. But he was possessive of it: it was his particular dream, and he wasn't about to share it with anyone.

In the driving seat the young officer who had been chauffeur-

ing Gissing around for the best part of six months was waiting
for the old man to fall well and truly asleep. Then and only
then could he risk turning the radio on to catch up with the
cricket scores. Australia were well down in the Test: a late
rally seemed unlikely. Ah, now there was a career, he thought
as he drove. Beats this routine into a cocked hat.

Both lost in their reveries, driver and passenger, neither
caught sight of Rawhead. He was stalking the car now, his
giant's stride easily keeping pace with it as it navigated the
winding, unlit road.

All at once his anger flared, and roaring, he left the field for
the tarmac.

The driver swerved to avoid the immense form that skipped
into the burning headlights, its mouth issuing a howl like a
pack of rabid dogs.

The car skidded on the wet ground, its left wing grazing the
bushes that ran along the side of the road, a tangle of branches
lashing the windscreen as it careered on its way. On the back
seat Gissing fell off the ladder he was climbing, just as the car
came to the end of its hedgerow tour and met an iron gate.
Gissing was flung against the front seat, winded but unin-
jured. The impact took the driver over the wheel and through
the window in two short seconds. His feet, now in Gissing's
face, twitched.

From the road Rawhead watched the death of the metal
box. Its tortured voice, the howl of its wrenched flank, the
shattering of its face, frightened him. But it was dead.

He waited a few cautious moments before advancing up the
road to sniff the crumpled body. There was an aromatic smell
in the air, which pricked his sinuses, and the cause of it, the
blood of the box, was dribbling out of its broken torso, and
running away down the road. Certain now that it must be finished, he approached.

There was someone alive in the box. None of the sweet
childflesh he savored so much, just tough malemeat. It was a
comical face that peered at him. Round, wild eyes. Its silly
mouth opened and closed like a fish's. He kicked the box to
make it open, and when that didn't work he wrenched off the
doors. Then he reached and drew the whimpering male out of
his refuge. Was this one of the species that had subdued him?

This fearful mite, with its jellylips? He laughed at its pleas, then turned Gissing on his head, and held him upside down by one foot. He waited until the cries died down, then reached between the twitching legs and found the mite's manhood. Not large. Quite shrunk, in fact, by fear. Gissing was blathering all kinds of stuff: none of it made any sense. The only sound Rawhead understood from the mouth of the man was this sound he was hearing now, this high-pitched shriek that always attended a gelding. Once finished, he dropped Gissing beside the car.

A fire had begun in the smashed engine, he could smell it. He was not so much a beast that he feared fire. Respected it yes: but not feared. Fire was a tool, he'd used it many times: to burn out enemies, to cremate them in their beds.

Now he stepped back from the car as the flame found the petrol and fire erupted into the air. Heat balled towards him, and he smelt the hair on the front of his body crisp, but he was too entranced by the spectacle not to look. The fire followed the blood of the beast, consuming Gissing, and licking along the rivers of petrol like an eager dog after a trail of piss. Rawhead watched, and learned a new and lethal lesson.

In the chaos of his study Coot was unsuccessfully fighting off sleep. He'd spent a good deal of the evening at the Altar, some of it with Declan. Tonight there'd be no praying, just sketching. Now he had a copy of the Altar carving on his desk in front of him, and he'd spent an hour just staring at it. The exercise had been fruitless. Either the carving was too ambiguous, or his imagination lacked breadth. Whichever, he could make very little sense of the image. It pictured a burial certainly, but that was about all he was able to work out. Maybe the body was a little bigger than that of the mourners, but nothing exceptional. He thought of Zeal's pub, "The Tall Man," and smiled. It might well have pleased some Medieval wit to picture the burial of a brewer under the Altar cloth.

In the hall, the sick clock struck twelve-fifteen, which meant it was almost one. Coot got up from his desk, stretched, and switched off the lamp. He was surprised by the brilliance of the moonlight streaming through the crack in the curtain. It

was a full, harvest moon, and the light, though cold, was luxuriant.

He put the guard in front of the fire, and stepped into the
darkened hallway, closing the door behind him. The clock
ticked loudly. Somewhere over towards Goudhurst, he heard
the sound of an ambulance siren.

What's happening? he wondered, and opened the front
door to see what he could see. There were car headlights on the
hill, and the distant throb of blue police lights, more rhythmical than the ticking at his back. Accident on the north road.
Early for ice, and surely not cold enough. He watched the
lights, set on the hill like jewels on the back of a whale, winking away. It was quite chilly, come to think of it. No weather
to be standing in the—

He frowned; something caught his eye, a movement in the
far corner of the churchyard, underneath the trees. The moonlight etched the scene in monochrome. Black yews, grey
stones, a white chrysanthemum strewing its petals on a grave.
And black in the shadow of the yews, but outlined clearly
against the slab of a marble tomb beyond, a giant.

Coot stepped out of the house in slippered feet.

The giant was not alone. Somebody was kneeling in front of
it, a smaller, more human shape, its face raised and clear in
the light. It was Declan. Even from a distance it was clear that
he was smiling up at his master.

Coot wanted to get closer; a better look at the nightmare.
As he took his third step his foot crunched on a piece of
gravel.

The giant seemed to shift in the shadows. Was it turning to
look at him? Coot chewed on his heart. No, let it be deaf;
please God, let it not see me, make me invisible.

The prayer was apparently answered. The giant made no
sign of having seen his approach. Taking courage Coot advanced across the pavement of gravestones, dodging from
tomb to tomb for cover, barely daring to breathe. He was
within a few feet of the tableau now and he could see the way
the creature's head was bowed towards Declan; he could hear
the sound like sandpaper on stone it was making at the back of
its throat. But there was more to the scene.

Declan's vestments were torn and dirtied, his thin chest
bare. Moonlight caught his sternum, his ribs. His state, and
his position, were unequivocal. This was adoration—pure
and simple. The Coot heard the splashing; he stepped closer
and saw that the giant was directing a glistening rope of its
urine onto Declan's upturned face. It spashed into his slackly
opened mouth, it ran over his torso. The gleam of joy didn't
leave Declan's eyes for a moment as he received this baptism,
indeed he turned his head from side to side in his eagerness to
be totally defiled.

The smell of the creature's discharge wafted across to Coot.
It was acidic, vile. How could Declan bear to have a drop of it
on him, much less bathe in it? Coot wanted to cry out, stop
the depravity, but even in the shadow of the yew the shape of
the beast was terrifying. It was too tall and too broad to be
human.

This was surely the Beast of the Wild Woods Declan had
been trying to describe; this was the childdevourer. Had
Declan guessed, when he eulogized about the monster, what
power it would have over his imagination? Had he known all
along that if the beast were to come sniffing for him he'd kneel
in front of it, call it Lord (before Christ, before Civilization,
he'd said), let it discharge its bladder on to him, and smile?

Yes. Oh yes.

And so let him have his moment. Don't risk your neck for
him, Coot thought, he's where he wants to be. Very slowly he
backed off towards the Vestry, his eyes still fixed on the
degradation in front of him. The baptism dribbled to a halt,
but Declan's hands, cupped in front of him, still held a quan-
tity of fluid. He put the heels of his hands to his mouth, and
drank.

Coot gagged, unable to prevent himself. For an instant he
closed his eyes to shut out the sight, and opened them again to
see that the shadowy head had turned towards him and was
looking at him with eyes that burned in the blackness.

"Christ Almighty."

It saw him. For certain this time, it saw him. It roared, and
its head changed shape in the shadow, its mouth opened so
horribly wide.

"Sweet Jesus."

Already it was charging towards him, antelope-lithe, leaving its acolyte slumped beneath the tree. Coot turned and ran, ran as he hadn't in many a long year, hurdling the graves as he fled. It was just a few yards: the door, some kind of safety. Not for long maybe, but time to think, to find a weapon. Run, you old bastard. Christ the race, Christ the prize. Four yards.

Run.

The door was open.

Almost there; a yard to go—

He crossed the threshold and swung round to slam the door on his pursuer. But no! Rawhead had shot his hand through the door, a hand three times the size of a human hand. It was snatching at the empty air, trying to find Coot, the roars relentless.

Coot threw his full weight against the oak door. The door stile, edged with iron, bit into Rawhead's forearm. The roar became a howl: venom and agony mingled in a din that was heard from one end of Zeal to the other.

It stained the night up as far as the north road, where the remains of Gissing and his driver were being scraped up and parcelled in plastic. It echoed round the icy walls of the Chapel of Rest where Denny and Gwen Nicholson were already beginning to degenerate. It was heard too in the bedrooms of Zeal, where living couples lay side by side, maybe an arm numbed under the other's body; where the old lay awake working out the geography of the ceiling; where children dreamt of the womb, and babies mourned it. It was heard again and again as Rawhead raged at the door.

The howl made Coot's head swim. His mouth babbled prayers, but the much needed support from on high showed no sign of coming. He felt his strength ebbing away. The giant was steadily gaining access, pressing the door open inch by inch. Coot's feet slid on the too-well polished floor, his muscles were fluttering as they faltered. This was a contest he had no chance of winning, not if he tried to match his strength to that of the beast, sinew for sinew. If he was to see tomorrow morning, he needed some strategy.

Coot pressed harder against the wood, his eyes darting around the hallway looking for a weapon. It mustn't get in: it mustn't have mastery over him. A bitter smell was in his nostrils. For a moment he saw himself naked and kneeling in front of the giant, with its piss beating on his skull. Hard on the heels of that picture, came another flurry of depravities. It was all he could do not to let in, let the obscenities get a permanent hold. Its mind was working its way into his, a thick wedge of filth pressing its way through his memories, encouraging buried thoughts to the surface. Wouldn't it ask for worship, just like any God? And wouldn't its demands be plain, and real? Not ambiguous, like those of the Lord he'd served up 'til now. That was a fine thought: to give himself up to this certainty that beat on the other side of of the door, and lie open in front of it, and let it ravage him.

Rawhead. Its name was a pulse in his ear—Raw. Head.

In desperation, knowing his fragile mental defenses were within an ace of collapsing, his eyes alighted on the clothes stand to the left of the door.

Raw. Head. Raw. Head. The name was an imperative. Raw. Head. Raw. Head. It evoked a skinned head, its defenses peeled back, a thing close to bursting, no telling if it was pain or pleasure. But easy to find out—

It almost had possession of him, he knew it: it was now or never. He took one arm from the door and stretched towards the rack for a walking stick. There was one amongst them he wanted in particular. He called it his cross country stick, a yard and a half of stripped ash, well used and resilient. His fingers coaxed it towards him.

Rawhead had taken advantage of the lack of force behind the door; its leathery arm was working its way in, indifferent to the way the door jamb scored the skin. The hand, its fingers strong as steel, had caught the folds of Coot's jacket.

Coot raised the ash stick and brought it down on Rawhead's elbow, where the bone was vulnerably close to the surface. The weapon splintered on impact, but it did its job. On the other side of the door the howl began again, and Rawhead's arm was rapidly withdrawn. As the fingers slid out Coot slammed the door and bolted it. There was a short hiatus, seconds only, before the attack began again, this time a two-fisted beating on the door. The hinges began to buckle; the wood groaned. It would be a short time, a very short time, before it gained access. It was strong; and now it was furious too.

Coot crossed the hall and picked up the phone. Police, he said, and began to dial. How long before it put two and two together, gave up on the door, and moved to the windows? They were leaded, but that wouldn't keep it out for long. He had minutes at the most, probably seconds, depending on its brain power.

His mind, loosed from Rawhead's grasp, was a chorus of fragmented prayers and demands. If I die, he found himself thinking, will I be rewarded in Heaven for dying more brutally than any country vicar might reasonably expect? Is there compensation in paradise for being disembowelled in the front hall of your own Vestry?

There was only one officer left on duty at the Police Station: the rest were up on the north road, clearing up after Gissing's party. The poor man could make very little sense of Reverend Coot's pleas, but there was no mistaking the sound of splintering wood that accompanied the babbles, nor the howling in the background.

The officer put the phone down and radioed for help. The patrol on the north road took twenty, maybe twenty-five seconds to answer. In that time Rawhead had smashed the central panel of the Vestry door, and was now demolishing the rest. Not that the patrol knew that. After the sights they'd faced up there, the chauffeur's charred body, Gissing's missing manhood, they had become insolent with experience, like hour-old war veterans. It took the officer at the Station a good minute to convince them of the urgency in Coot's voice. In that time Rawhead had gained access.

In the hotel Ron Milton watched the parade of lights blinking on the hill, heard the sirens, and Rawhead's howls, and was besieged by doubts. Was this really the country village he had intended to settle himself and his family in? He looked down at Maggie, who had been woken by the noise but was now asleep again, her bottle of sleeping tablets almost empty on the bedside cabinet. He felt, though she would have laughed at him for it, protective towards her: he wanted to be her hero.

She was the one who took the self-defense night classes however, while he grew overweight on expense account lunches. It made him inexplicably sad to watch her sleep, knowing he had so little power over life and death.

Rawhead stood in the hall of the Vestry in a confetti of shattered wood. His torso was pinpricked with splinters, and dozens of tiny wounds bled down his heaving bulk. His sour sweat permeated the hall like incense.

He sniffed the air for the man, but he was nowhere near. Rawhead bared his teeth in frustration, expelling a thin whistle of air from the back of his throat, and loped down the hall towards the study. There was warmth there, his nerves could feel it at twenty yards, and there was comfort too. He overturned the desk and shattered two of the chairs, partly to make more room for himself, mostly out of sheer destructiveness, then threw away the fire guard and sat down. Warmth surrounded him: healing, living warmth. He luxuriated in the sensation as it embraced his face, his lean belly, his limbs. He felt it heat his blood too, and so stir memories of other fires, fires he'd set in fields of burgeoning wheat.

And he recalled another fire, the memory of which his mind tried to dodge and duck, but he couldn't avoid thinking about it: the humiliation of that night would be with him forever. They'd picked their season so carefully: high summer, and no rain in two months. The undergrowth of the Wild Woods was tinder dry, even the living tree caught the flame easily. He had been flushed out of his fortress with streaming eyes, confused and fearful, to be met with spikes and nets on every side, and that . . . *thing* they had, that sight that could subdue him.

Of course they weren't courageous enough to kill him; they were too superstitious for that. Besides, didn't they recognize his authority, even as they wounded him, their terror a homage to it? So they buried him alive: and that was worse than death. Wasn't that the very worst: Because he could live an age, ages, and never die, not even locked in the earth. Just left to wait a hundred years, and suffer, and another hundred and another, while the generations walked the ground above his head and lived and died and forgot him. Perhaps the women didn't forget him: he could smell them even through the earth, when they came close to his grave, and though they might not have known it they felt anxious, they persuaded their men to abandon the place altogether, so he was left absolutely alone, with not even a gleaner for company. Loneliness was their revenge on him, he thought, for the times he and his brothers had taken women into the woods, spread them out, spiked and loosed them again, bleeding but fertile. They would die having the children of those rapes; no woman's anatomy could survive the thrashing of a hybrid, its teeth, its anguish. That was the only revenge he and his brothers ever had on the big-bellied sex.

Rawhead stroked himself and looked up at the gilded reproduction of "The Light of the World" that hung above Coot's mantelpiece. The image woke no tremors of fear or remorse in him: it was a picture of a sexless martyr, doe-eyed and woebegone. No challenge there. The true power, the only power that could defeat him, was apparently gone: lost beyond recall, its place usurped by a virgin shepherd. He ejaculated, silently, his thin semen hissing on the hearth. The world was his to rule unchallenged. He would have warmth, and food in abundance. Babies even. Yes, babymeat, that was the best. Just dropped mites, still blind from the womb.

He stretched, sighing in anticipation of that delicacy, his brain awash with atrocities.

From his refuge in the crypt Coot heard the police cars squealing to a halt outside the Vestry, then the sound of feet on the gravel path. He judged there to be at least half a dozen. It would be enough, surely.

Cautiously he moved through the darkness towards the stairs.

Something touched him: he almost yelled, biting his tongue a moment before the cry escaped.

"Don't go now," a voice said from behind him. It was Declan, and he was speaking altogether too loudly for comfort. The thing was above them, somewhere, it would hear them if he wasn't careful. Oh God, it mustn't hear.

"It's up above us," said Coot in a whisper.

"I know."

The voice seemed to come from his bowels not from his throat; it was bubbled through filth.

"Let's have him come down here shall we? He wants you, you know. He wants me to—"

"What's happened to you?"

Declan's face was just visible in the dark. It grinned; lunatic.

"I think he might want to baptize you too. How'd you like that? Like that would you? He pissed on me: you see him? And that wasn't all. Oh no, he wants more than that. He wants everything. Hear me? Everything."

Declan grabbed hold of Coot, a bear hug that stank of the creature's urine.

"Come with me?" he leered in Coot's face.

"I put my trust in God."

Declan laughed. Not a hollow laugh; there was genuine compassion in it for this lost soul.

"He *is* God," he said. "He was here before this fucking shithouse was built, you know that."

"So were dogs."

"Uh?"

"Doesn't mean I'd let them cock their legs on me."

"Clever old fucker aren't you?" said Declan, the smile inverted. "He'll show you. You'll change."

"No, Declan. Let go of me—"

The embrace was too strong.

"Come on up the stairs, fuckface. Mustn't keep God waiting."

He pulled Coot up the stairs, arms still locked round him. Words, all logical argument, eluded Coot: was there nothing he could say to make the man see his degradation? They made an ungainly entrance into the Church, and Coot automatically looked towards the altar, hoping for some reassurance, but he got none. The altar had been desecrated. The cloths had been torn and smeared with excrement, the cross and candlesticks were in the middle of a fire of prayerbooks that burned healthily on the altar steps. Smuts floated around the Church, the air was grimy with smoke.

"You did this?"

Declan grunted.

"He wants me to destroy it all. Take it apart stone by stone if I have to."

"He wouldn't dare."

"Oh he'd dare. He's not scared of Jesus, he's not scared of . . ."

The certainty lapsed for a telling instant, and Coot leapt on the hesitation.

"There's something here he *is* scared of, though, isn't there, or he'd have come in here himself, done it all himself . . ."

Declan wasn't looking at Coot. His eyes had glazed.

"What is it, Declan? What is it he doesn't like? You can tell me—"

Declan spat in Coot's face, a wad of thick phlegm that hung on his cheek like a slug.

"None of your business."

"In the name of Christ, Declan, look at what he's done to you."

"I know my master when I see him—"

Declan was shaking

"—and so will you."

He turned Coot round to face the south door. It was open, and the creature was there on the threshold, stooping gracefully to duck under the porch. For the first time Coot saw Rawhead in a good light, and the terrors began in earnest. He had avoided thinking too much of its size, its stare, its origins. Now, as it came towards him with slow, even stately steps, his heart conceded its mastery. It was no mere beast, despite its mane, and its awesome array of teeth; its eyes lanced him through and through, gleaming with a depth of contempt no animal could ever muster. Its mouth opened wider and wider, the teeth gliding from the gums, two, three inches long, and still the mouth was gaping wider. When there was nowhere to run, Declan let Coot go. Not that Coot could have moved anyway: the stare was too insistent. Rawhead reached out and picked Coot up. The world turned on its head—

There were seven officers, not six as Coot had guessed. Three of them were armed, their weapons brought down from London on the order of Detective Sergeant Gissing. The late, soon to be decorated posthumously, Detective Sergeant Gissing. They were led, these seven good men and true, by Sergeant Ivanhoe Baker. Ivanhoe was not an heroic man, either by inclination or education. His voice, which he had prayed would give the appropriate orders when the time came without betraying him, came out as a strangled yelp as Rawhead appeared from the interior of the Church.

"I can see it!" he said. Everybody could: it was nine feet tall, covered in blood, and it looked like Hell on legs. Nobody needed it pointed out. The guns were raised without Ivanhoe's instruction: and the unarmed men, suddenly feeling naked, kissed their truncheons and prayed. One of them ran.

"Hold your ground!" Ivanhoe shrieked; if those sons of bitches turned tail he'd be left on his own. They hadn't issued him with a gun, just authority, and that was not much comfort.

Rawhead was still holding Coot up, at arm's length, by the neck. The Reverend's legs dangled a foot above the ground, his head lolled back, his eyes were closed. The monster displayed the body for his enemies, proof of power.

"Shall we . . . please . . . can we . . . shoot the bastard?" One of the gunmen inquired.

Ivanhoe swallowed before answering. "We'll hit the vicar."

"He's dead already." said the gunman.

"We don't know that."

"He must be dead. Look at him—"

Rawhead was shaking Coot like an eiderdown, and his stuffing was falling out, much to Ivanhoe's intense disgust. Then, almost lazily, Rawhead flung Coot at the police. The body hit the gravel a little way from the gate and lay still. Ivanhoe found his voice—

"Shoot!"

The gunmen needed no encouragement; their fingers were depressing the triggers before the syllable was out of his mouth.

Rawhead was hit by three, four, five bullets in quick succession, most of them in the chest. They stung him and he put up an arm to protect his face, covering his balls with the other hand. This was a pain he hadn't anticipated. The wound he'd received from Nicholson's rifle had been forgotten in the bliss of the bloodletting that came soon after, but these barbs hurt him, and they kept coming. He felt a twinge of fear. His instinct was to fly in the face of these popping, flashing rods, but the pain was too much. Instead, he turned and made his retreat, leaping over the tombs as he fled towards the safety of hills. There were copses he knew, burrows and caves, where he could hide and find time to think this new problem through. But first he had to elude them.

They were after him quickly, flushed with the ease of their victory, leaving Ivanhoe to find a vase on one of the graves, empty it of chrysanthemums, and be sick.

Out of the dip there were no lights along the road, and Rawhead began to feel safer. He could melt into the darkness, into the earth, he'd done it a thousand times. He cut across a field. The barley was still unharvested, and heavy with its grain. He trampled it as he ran, grinding seed and stalk. At his back his pursuers were already losing the chase. The car they'd piled into had stopped in the road, he could see its lights, one blue, two white, way behind him. The enemy was shouting a confusion of orders, words Rawhead didn't understand. No matter; he knew men. They were easily frightened. They would not look far for him tonight; they'd use the dark as an excuse to call off the search, telling themselves that his wounds were probably fatal anyhow. Trusting children that they were.

He climbed to the top of the hill and looked down into the valley. Below the snake of the road, its eyes the headlights of the enemy's car, the village was a wheel of warm light, with flashing blues and reds at its hub. Beyond, in every direction, the impenetrable black of the hills, over which the stars hung in loops and clusters. By day this would seem a counterpane valley, toytown small. By night it was fathomless, more his than theirs.

His enemies were already returning to their hovels, as he'd known they would. The chase was over for the night.

He lay down on the earth and watched a meteor burn up as it fell to the southwest. It was a brief, bright streak, which edgelit a cloud, then went out. Morning was many long, healing hours in the future. He would soon be strong again: and then, then—he'd burn them all away.

Coot was not dead: but so close to death it scarcely made any difference. Eighty percent of the bones in his body were fractured or broken: his face and neck were a maze of lacerations:

one of his hands was crushed almost beyond recognition. He would certainly die. It was purely a matter of time and inclination.

In the village those who had glimpsed so much as a fragment of the events in the dip were already elaborating on their stories; and the evidence of the naked eye lent credence to the most fantastic inventions. The chaos in the churchyard, the smashed door of the Vestry: the cordoned-off car on the north road. Whatever had happened that Saturday night it was going to take a long time to forget.

There was no harvest festival service, which came as no surprise to anyone.

Maggie was insistent: "I want us all to go back to London."

"A day ago you wanted us to stay here. Get to be part of the community."

"That was on Friday, before all this . . . this . . . There's a maniac loose, Ron."

"If we go now, we won't come back."

"What are you talking about; of course we'll come back."

"If we leave once the place is threatened, we give up on it altogether."

"That's ridiculous."

"You were the one who was so keen on us being visible, being seen to join in village life. Well, we'll have to join in the deaths too. And I'm going to stay—see it through. You can go back to London. Take the kids."

"No."

He sighed, heavily.

"I want to see him caught: whoever he is. I want to know it's all been cleared up, see it with my own eyes. That's the only way we'll ever feel safe here."

Reluctantly, she nodded.

"At least let's get out of the hotel for a while. Mrs. Blatter's going loopy. Can't we go for a drive? Get some air—"

"Yes, why not?"

It was a balmy September day: the countryside, always willing to spring a surprise, was gleaming with life. Late flowers shone in the roadside hedges, birds dipped over the road as they drove. The sky was azure, the clouds a fantasia in cream. A few miles outside the village all the horrors of the previous night began to evaporate and the sheer exuberance of the day began to raise the family's spirits. With every mile they drove out of Zeal Ron's fears diminished. Soon, he was singing.

On the back seat Debbie was being difficult. One moment "I'm hot Daddy," the next: "I want an orange juice Daddy;" the next: "I have to pee."

Ron stopped the car on an empty stretch of road, and played the indulgent father. The kids had been through a lot; today they could be spoiled.

"All right, darling, you can have a pee here, then we'll go and find an ice cream for you."

"Where's the la-la?" she said. Damn stupid phrase; mother-in-law's euphemism.

Maggie chipped in. She was better with Debbie in these moods than Ron. "You can go behind the hedge," she said.

Debbie looked horrified. Ron exchanged a half-smile with Ian.

The boy had a put-upon look on his face. Grimacing, he went back to his dogeared comic.

"Hurry up, can't you?" he muttered. "Then we can go somewhere proper."

Somewhere proper, thought Ron. He means a town. He's a city kid: it's going to take a while to convince him that a hill with a view *is* somewhere proper. Debbie was still being difficult.

"I can't go here Mummy—"

"Why not?"

"Somebody might see me."

"Nobody's going to see you darling," Ron reassured her. "Now do as your Mummy says." He turned to Maggie, "Go with her, love."

Maggie wasn't budging.

"She's O.K."

"She can't climb over the gate on her own."

"Well you go, then."

Ron was determined not to argue; he forced a smile. "Come on," he said.

Debbie got out of the car and Ron helped her over the iron gate into the field beyond. It was already harvested. It smelt ... earthy.

"Don't look," she admonished him, wide-eyed, "you *mustn't* look."

She was already a manipulator, at the ripe old age of nine. She could play him better than the piano she was taking lessons on. He knew it, and so did she. He smiled at her and closed his eyes.

"All right. See? I've got my eyes closed. Now hurry up, Debbie. Please."

"Promise you won't peek."

"I won't peek." My God, he thought, she's certainly making a production number out of this. "Hurry up."

He glanced back towards the car. Ian was sitting in the back, still reading, engrossed in some cheap heroics, his face set as he stared into the adventure. The boy was so serious: the occasional half-smile was all Ron could ever win from him. It wasn't a put-on, it wasn't a fake air of mystery. He seemed content to leave all the performing to his sister.

Behind the hedge Debbie pulled down her Sunday knickers and squatted, but after all the fuss her pee wouldn't come. She concentrated but that just made it worse.

Ron looked up the field towards the horizon. There were gulls up there, squabbling over a titbit. He watched them awhile, impatience, growing.

"Come on love," he said.

He looked back at the car, and Ian was watching him now, his face slack with boredom; or something like it. Was there something else there: a deep resignation? Ron thought. The boy looked back to his comic book "Utopia" without acknowledging his father's gaze.

Then Debbie screamed: an ear-piercing shriek.

"Christ!" Ron was clambering over the gate in an instant, and Maggie wasn't far behind him.

"Debbie!"

Ron found her standing against the hedge, staring at the ground, blubbering, face red. "What's wrong, for God's sake?"

She was yabbering incoherently. Ron followed her eye.

"What's happened?" Maggie was having difficulty getting over the gate.

"It's all right . . . it's all right."

There was a dead mole almost buried in the tangle at the edge of the field, its eyes pecked out, its rotting hide crawling with flies.

"Oh God, Ron." Maggie looked at him accusingly, as though he'd put the damn thing there with malice afore-thought.

"It's all right, sweetheart," she said, elbowing past her husband and wrapping Debbie up in her arms.

Her sobs quietened a bit. City kids, thought Ron. They're going to have to get used to that sort of thing if they're going to live in the country. No roadsweepers here to brush up the runover cats every morning. Maggie was rocking her, and the worst of the tears were apparently over.

"She'll be all right," Ron said.

"Of course she will, won't you, darling?" Maggie helped her pull up her knickers. She was still snivelling, her need for privacy forgotten in her unhappiness.

In the back of the car Ian listened to his sister's caterwauling and tried to concentrate on his comic. Anything for attention, he thought. Well, she's welcome.

Suddenly, it went dark.

He looked up from the page, his heart loud. At his shoulder, six inches away from him, something stooped to peer into the car, its face like Hell. He couldn't scream, his tongue refused to move. All he could do was flood the seat and kick uselessly as the long, scarred arms reached through the window towards him. The nails of the beast gouged his ankles, tore his sock. One of his new shoes fell off in the strug-gle. Now it had his foot and he was being dragged across the wet seat towards the window. He found his voice. Not quite *his* voice, it was a pathetic, a silly-sounding voice, not the equal of the mortal terror he felt. And all too late anyway; it was dragging his legs through the window, and his bottom was almost through now. He looked through the back window as it hauled his torso into the open air and in a dream he saw Daddy at the gate, his face looking so, so ridiculous. He was climbing the gate, coming to help, coming to save him but he was far too slow. Ian knew he was beyond salvation from the beginning, because he'd died this way in his sleep on a hundred occasions and Daddy never got there in time. The mouth was wider even than he'd dreamed it, a hole which he was being delivered into, head first. It smelt like the dustbins at the back of the school canteen, times a million. He was sick down its throat, as it bit the top of his head off.

Ron had never screamed in his life. The scream had always belonged to the other sex, until that instant. Then, watching the monster stand up and close its jaws around his son's head, there was no sound appropriate but a scream.

Rawhead heard the cry, and turned, without a trace of fear on his face, to look at the source. Their eyes met. The King's glance penetrated Milton like a spike, freezing him to the road and to the marrow. It was Maggie who broke its hold, her voice a dirge.

"Oh . . . please . . . no."

Ron shook Rawhead's look from his head, and started towards the car, towards his son. But the hesitation had given Rawhead a moment's grace he scarcely needed anyway, and he was already away, his catch clamped between his jaws, spilling out to right and left. The breeze carried motes of Ian's blood back down the road towards Ron; he felt them spot his face in a gentle shower.

Declan stood in the chancel of St. Peter's and listened for the hum. It was still there. Sooner or later he'd have to go to the source of that sound and destroy it, even if it meant, as it well might, his own death. His new master would demand it. But that was par for the course; and the thought of death didn't distress him; far from it. In the last few days he'd realized ambitions that he'd nurtured (unspoken, even unthought) for years.

Looking up at the black bulk of the monster as it rained piss on him he'd found the purest joy. If that experience, which would once have disgusted him, could be so consummate, what might death be like? rarer still. And if he could contrive to die by Rawhead's hand, by that wide hand that smelt so rank, wouldn't that be the rarest of the rare?

He looked up at the altar, and at the remains of the fire the police had extinguished. They'd searched for him after Coot's death, but he had a dozen hiding places they would never find, and they'd soon given up. Bigger fish to fry. He collected a fresh armful of *Songs of Praise* and threw them down amongst the damp ashes. The candlesticks were warped, but still recognizable. The cross had disappeared, either shrivelled away or removed by some light-fingered officer of the law. He tore a few handfuls of hymns from the books, and lit a match. The old songs caught easily.

Ron Milton was tasting tears, and it was a taste he'd forgotten. It was many years since he'd wept, especially in front of other males. But he didn't care any longer: these bastard policemen weren't human anyway. They just looked at him while he poured out his story, and nodded like idiots.

"We've drafted men in from every division within fifty miles, Mr. Milton," said the bland face with the understanding eyes. "The hills are being scoured. We'll have it, whatever it is."

"It took my child, you understand me? It killed him, in front of me—"

They didn't seem to appreciate the horror of it all.

"We're doing what we can."

"It's not enough. This thing . . . it's not human."

Ivanhoe, with the understanding eyes, knew bloody well how unhuman it was.

"There's people coming from the Ministry of Defense: we can't do much more 'til they've had a look at the evidence," he said. Then added, as a sop: "It's all public money sir."

"You fucking idiot! What does it matter what it costs to kill it? It's not human. It's out of Hell."

Ivanhoe's look lost compassion.

"If it came out of Hell, sir," he said, "I don't think it would have found the Reverend Coot such easy pickings."

Coot: that was his man. Why hadn't he thought of that before? Coot.

Ron had never been much of a man of God. But he was prepared to be openminded, and now that he'd seen the opposition, or one of its troops, he was ready to reform his opinions. He'd believe anything, anything at all, if it gave him a weapon against the Devil.

He must get to Coot.

"What about your wife?" the officer called after him. Maggie was sitting in one of the side offices, dumb with sedation, Debbie asleep beside her. There was nothing he could do for them. They were as safe here as anywhere.

He must get to Coot, before he died.

He'd know, whatever Reverends know; and he'd understand the pain better than these monkeys. Dead sons were the crux of the Church after all.

As he got into the car it seemed for a moment he smelt his son: the boy who would have carried his name (Ian Ronald Milton he'd been christened), the boy who was his sperm made flesh, who he'd had circumsized like himself. The quiet child who'd looked out of the car at him with such resignation in his eyes.

This time the tears didn't begin. This time there was just an anger that was almost wonderful.

It was half past eleven at night. Rawhead Rex lay under the moon in one of the harvested fields to the southwest of the Nicholson Farm. The stubble was darkening now, and there was a tantalizing smell of rotting vegetable matter off the earth. Beside him lay his dinner, Ian Ronald Milton, face up on the field, his midriff torn open. Occasionally the beast would lean up on one elbow and paddle its fingers in the cooling soup of the boy child's body, fishing for a delicacy.

Here, under the full moon, bathing in silver, stretching his limbs and eating the flesh of human kind, he felt irresistible. His fingers drew a kidney off the plate beside him and he swallowed it whole.

Sweet.

Coot was awake, despite the sedation. He knew he was dying, and the time was too precious to doze through. He didn't know the name of the face that was interrogating him in the yellow gloom of his room, but the voice was so politely insistent he had to listen, even though it interrupted his peacemaking with God. Besides, they had questions in common: and they all circled, those questions, on the beast that had reduced him to this pulp.

"It took my son," the man said. "What do you know about the thing? Please tell me. I'll believe whatever you tell me—" Now *there* was desperation—"Just explain—"

Time and again, as he'd lain on that hot pillow, confused thoughts had raced through Coot's mind. Declan's baptism; the embrace of the beast; the altar; his hair rising and his flesh too. Maybe there was something he could tell the father at his bedside.

". . . in the church . . ."

Ron leaned closer to Coot; he smelt of earth already.

". . . the altar . . . it's afraid . . . the altar . . ."

"You mean the cross? It's afraid of the cross?"

"No . . . not—"

"Not—"

The body creaked once, and stopped. Ron watched death come over the face: the saliva dry on Coot's lips, the iris of his remaining eye contract. He watched a long while before he rang for the nurse, then quietly made his escape.

There was somebody in the Church. The door, which had been padlocked by the police, was ajar, the lock smashed. Ron pushed it open a few inches and slid inside. There were no lights on in the Church, the only illumination was a bonfire on the altar steps. It was being tended by a young man Ron had seen on and off in the village. He looked up from his fire-watching, but kept feeding the flames the guts of books.

"What can I do for you?" he asked, without interest.

"I came to—" Ron hesitated. What to tell this man: the truth? No, there was something wrong here.

"I asked you a frigging question," said the man. "What do you want?"

As he walked down the aisle towards the fire Ron began to see the questioner in more detail. There were stains, like mud, on his clothes, and his eyes had sunk in their orbits as if his brain had sucked them in.

"You've got no right to be in here—"

"I thought anyone could come into a church," said Ron,

staring at the burning pages as they blackened.

"Not tonight. You get the fuck out of here." Ron kept walking towards the altar.

"You get the fuck out, I said!"

The face in front of Ron was alive with leers and grimaces: there was lunacy in it.

"I came to see the altar; I'll go when I've seen it, and not before."

"You've been talking to Coot. That it?"

"Coot?"

"What did the old wanker tell you? It's all a lie, whatever it was; he never told the truth in his frigging life, you know that? You take it from me. He used to get up there—" he threw a prayerbook at the pulpit "—and tell fucking lies!"

"I want to see the altar for myself. We'll see if he was telling lies—"

"No you won't!"

The man threw another handful of books on to the fire and stepped down to block Ron's path. He smelt not of mud but of shit. Without warning, he pounced. His hands seized Ron's neck, and the two of them toppled over. Declan's fingers reaching to gouge at Ron's eyes: his teeth snapping at his nose.

Ron was surprised at the weakness of his own arms; why hadn't he played squash the way Maggie had suggested, why were his muscles so ineffectual? If he wasn't careful this man was going to kill him.

Suddenly a light, so bright it could have been a midnight dawn, splashed through the west window. A cloud of screams followed close on it. Firelight, dwarfing the bonfire on the altar steps, dyed the air. The stained glass danced.

Declan forgot his victim for an instant, and Ron rallied. He pushed the man's chin back, and got a knee under his torso, then he kicked hard. The enemy went reeling, and Ron was up and after him, a fistful of hair securing the target while the ball of his other hand hammered at the lunatic's face 'til it broke. It wasn't enough to see the bastard's nose bleed, or to hear the cartilage mashed; Ron kept beating and beating until his fist bled. Only then did he let Declan drop.

● ● ●

Outside, Zeal was ablaze.

Rawhead had made fires before, many fires. But petrol was a new weapon, and he was still getting the hang of it. It didn't take him long to learn. The trick was to wound the wheeled boxes, that was easy. Open their flanks and out their blood would pour, blood that made his head ache. The boxes were easy prey, lined up on the pavement like bullocks to be slaughtered. He went amongst them demented with death, splashing their blood down the High Street and igniting it. Streams of liquid fire poured into gardens, over thresholds. Thatches caught; wood-beamed cottages went up. In minutes Zeal was burning from end to end.

In St. Peter's, Ron dragged the filthied cloth off the altar, trying to block out all thoughts of Debbie and Margaret. The police would move them to a place of safety, for certain. The issue at hand must take precedence.

Beneath the cloth was a large box, its front panel roughly carved. He took no notice of the design; there were more urgent matters to attend to. Outside, the beast was loose. He could hear its triumphant roars, and he felt eager, yes eager, to go to it. To kill it or be killed. But first, the box. It contained power, no doubt about that; a power that was even now raising the hairs on his head, that was working at his cock, giving him an aching hardon. His flesh seemed to seethe with it, it elated him like love. Hungry, he put his hands on the box, and a shock that seemed to cook his joints ran up both his arms. He fell back, and for a moment he wondered if he was going to remain conscious, the pain was so bad, but it subsided, in moments. He cast around for a tool, something to get him into the box without laying flesh to it.

In desperation he wrapped his hand with a piece of the altar cloth and snatched one of the brass candleholders from the edge of the fire. The cloth began to smolder as the heat worked its way through to his hand. He stepped back to the altar and beat at the wood like a madman until it began to splinter. His hands were numb now; if the heated candlesticks were burning his palms he couldn't feel it. What did it matter anyhow? There was a weapon here: a few inches away from him, if only he could get to it, to wield it. His erection throbbed, his balls tingled.

"Come to me," he found himself saying, "come on, come on. Come to me. Come to me." Like he was willing it into his embrace, this treasure, like it was a girl he wanted, his hardon wanted, and he was hypnotizing her into his bed.

"Come to me, come to me—"

The wood façade was breaking. Panting now, he used the corners of the candlestick base to lever larger chunks of timber away. The altar was hollow, as he'd known it would be. And empty.

Empty.

Except for a ball of stone, the size of a small football. Was this his prize? He couldn't believe how insignificant it looked: and yet the air was still electric around him; his blood still danced. He reached through the hole he'd made in the altar and picked the relic up.

Outside, Rawhead was jubilating.

Images flashed before Ron's eyes as he weighed the stone in his deadened hand. A corpse with its feet burning. A flaming cot. A dog, running along the street, a living ball of fire. It was all outside, waiting to unfold.

Against the perpetrator, he had this stone.

He'd trusted God, just for half a day, and he got shat on. It was just a stone: just a fucking *stone*. He turned the football over and over in his hand, trying to make some sense of its furrows and its mounds. Was it meant to *be* something, perhaps; was he missing its deeper significance?

There was a knot of noise at the other end of the church; a crash, a cry, from beyond the door a whoosh of flame.

Two people staggered in, followed by smoke and pleas.

"He's burning the village," said a voice Ron knew. It was that benign policeman who hadn't believed in Hell; he was trying to keep his act together, perhaps for the benefit of his companion, Mrs. Blatter from the hotel. The nightdress she'd run into the street wearing was torn. Her breasts were exposed; they shook with her sobs; she didn't seem to know she was naked, didn't even know where she was.

"Christ in Heaven help us," said Ivanhoe.

"There's no fucking Christ in here," came Declan's voice.

He was standing up, and reeling towards the intruders. Ron couldn't see his face from where he stood, but he knew it must be near as damn it unrecognizable. Mrs. Blatter avoided him as he staggered towards the door, and she ran towards the altar. She'd been married here: on the very spot he'd built the fire.

Ron stared at her body entranced.

She was considerably overweight, her breasts sagging, her belly overshadowing her cunt so he doubted if she could even see it. But it was for this his cockhead throbbed, for this his head reeled—

Her image was in his hand. God yes, she was there in his hand, she was the living equivalent of what he held. A woman. The stone was the statue of a woman, a Venus grosser than Mrs. Blatter, her belly swelling with children, tits like mountains, cunt a valley that began at her navel and gaped to the world. All this time, under the cloth and the cross, they'd bowed their heads to a goddess.

Ron stepped off the altar and began to run down the aisle, pushing Mrs. Blatter, the policeman and the lunatic aside.

"Don't go out," said Ivanhoe, "It's right outside."

Ron held the Venus tight, feeling her weight in his hands and taking security from her. Behind him, the Verger was screeching a warning to his Lord. Yes, it was a warning for sure.

Ron kicked open the door. On every side, fire. A flaming cot, a corpse (it was the postmaster) with its feet burning, a dog skinned by fire, hurtling past. And Rawhead, of course, silhouetted against a panorama of flames. It looked around, perhaps because it heard the warnings the Verger was yelling, but more likely, he thought, because it knew, knew without being told, that the woman had been found.

"Here!" Ron yelled, "I'm here! I'm here!"

It was coming for him now, with the steady gait of a victor closing in to claim its final and absolute victory. Doubt surged up in Ron. Why did it come so surely to meet him, not seeming to care about the weapon he carried in his hands?

Hadn't it seen, hadn't it heard the warning?

Unless—

Oh God in Heaven.

—Unless Coot had been wrong. Unless it*was* only a stone he
held in his hand, a useless, meaningless lump of stone.

Then a pair of hands grabbed him around the neck.

The lunatic.

A low voice spat the word "Fucker" in his ear.

Ron watched Rawhead approaching, heard the lunatic
screeching now: "Here he is. Fetch him. Kill him. Here he is."

Without warning the grip slackened, and Ron half-turned to
see Ivanhoe dragging the lunatic back against the Church wall.
The mouth in the Verger's broken face continued to screech.

"He's here! Here!"

Ron looked back at Rawhead: the beast was almost on him,
and he was too slow to raise the stone in self-defense. But
Rawhead had no intention of taking him. It was Declan he was
smelling and hearing. Ivanhoe released Declan as Rawhead's
huge hands veered past Ron and fumbled for the lunatic.
What followed was unwatchable. Ron couldn't bear to see the
hands take Declan apart: but he heard the gabble of pleas
become whoops of disbelieving grief. When he next looked
round there was nothing recognizably human on ground or
wall—

—And Rawhead was coming for him now, coming to do the
same or worse. The huge head craned round to fix on Ron, its
maw gaping, and Ron saw how the fire had wounded
Rawhead. The beast had been careless in the enthusiasm for
destruction: fire had caught its face and upper torso. Its body
hair was crisped, its mane was stubble, and the flesh on the left
hand side of its face was black and blistered. The flames had
roasted its eyeballs, they were swimming in a gum of mucus
and tears. That was why it had followed Declan's voice and
bypassed Ron; it could scarcely see.

But it must see now. It must.

"Here . . . here . . ." said Ron, "Here I am!" Rawhead
heard. He looked without seeing, his eyes trying to focus.

"Here! I'm here!"

Rawhead growled in his chest. His burned face pained him;
he wanted to be away from here, away in the cool of a birch
thicket, moonwashed.

His dimmed eyes found the stone; the homo sapien was
nursing it like a baby. It was difficult for Rawhead to see

clearly, but he knew. It ached in his mind, that image. It pricked him it teased him.

It was just a symbol of course, a sign of the power, not the power itself, but his mind made no such distinction. To him the stone was the thing he feared most: the bleeding woman, her gaping hole eating seed and spitting children. It was life, that hole, that woman, it was endless fecundity. It terrified him.

Rawhead stepped back, his own shit running freely down his leg. The fear on his face gave Ron strength. He pressed home his advantage, closing in after the retreating beast, dimly aware that Ivanhoe was rallying allied around him, armed figures waiting at the corners of his vision, eager to bring the fireraiser down.

His own strength was failing him. The stone, lifted high above his head so Rawhead could see it plainly, seemed heavier by the moment.

"Go on," he said quietly to the gathering Zealots. "Go on, take him. Take him . . ."

They began to close in, even before he finished speaking.

Rawhead smelt them more than saw them: his hurting eyes were fixed on the woman.

His teeth slid from their sheaths in preparation for the attack. The stench of humanity closed in around him from every direction.

Panic overcame his superstitions for one moment and he snatched down towards Ron, steeling himself against the stone. The attack took Ron by surprise. The claws sank in his scalp, blood poured down over his face.

Then the crowd closed in. Human hands, weak, white human hands were laid on Rawhead's body. Fists beat on his spine, nails raked his skin.

He let Ron go as somebody took a knife to the backs of his legs and hamstrung him. The agony made him howl the sky down, or so it seemed. In Rawhead's roasted eyes the stars reeled as he fell backwards on the road, his back cracking under him. They took the advantage immediately, overpowering him by sheer weight of numbers. He snapped off a finger here, a face there, but they would not be stopped now. Their hatred was old; in their bones, did they but know it.

He thrashed under their assault for as long as he could, but knew death was certain. There would be no resurrection this time, no waiting in the earth for an age until their descendants forgot him. He'd be snuffed out absolutely, and there would be nothingness.

He became quieter at the thought, and looked up as best he could to where the little father was standing. Their eyes met, as they had on the road when he'd taken the boy. But now Rawhead's look had lost its power to transfix. His face was empty and sterile as the moon, defeated long before Ron slammed the stone down between his eyes. The skull was soft: it buckled inwards and a slop of brain splattered the road.

The King went out. It was suddenly over, without ceremony or celebration. Out, once and for all. There was no cry.

Ron left the stone where it lay, half buried in the face of the beast. He stood up groggily, and felt his head. His scalp was loose, his fingertips touched his skull, blood came and came. But there were arms to support him, and nothing to fear if he slept.

It went unnoticed, but in death Rawhead's bladder was emptying. A stream of urine pulsed from the corpse and ran down the road. The rivulet steamed in the chilling air, its scummy nose sniffing left and right as it looked for a place to drain, After a few feet it found the gutter and ran along it awhile to a crack in the tarmac; there it drained off into the welcoming earth.

CONFESSIONS OF A (PORNOGRAPHER'S) SHROUD

He had been flesh once. Flesh, and bone, and ambition. But that was an age ago, or so it seemed, and the memory of that blessed state was fading fast.

Some traces of his former life remained; time and exhaustion couldn't take everything from him. He could picture clearly and painfully the faces of those he'd loved and hated. They stared through at him from the past, clear and luminous. He could still see the sweet, goodnight expressions in his children's eyes. And the same look, less sweet but no less goodnight, in the eyes of the brutes he had murdered.

Some of those memories made him want to cry, except that there were no tears to be wrung out of his starched eyes. Besides, it was far too late for regret. Regret was a luxury reserved for the living, who still had the time, the breath and the energy to act.

He was beyond all that. He, his mother's little Ronnie (oh, if she could see him now), he was almost three weeks dead. Too late for regrets by a long chalk.

He'd done all he could do to correct the errors he'd made. He'd spun out his span to its limits and beyond, stealing himself precious time to sew up the loose ends of his frayed existence. Mother's little Ronnie had always been tidy: a paragon of neatness. That was one of the reasons he'd enjoyed accountancy. The pursuit of a few misplaced pence through

hundreds of figures was a game he relished; and how satisfying, at the end of the day, to balance the books. Unfortunately
life was not so perfectable, as now, too late in the day, he
realized. Still, he'd done his best, and that, as Mother used to
say, was all anybody could hope to do. There was nothing left
but to confess, and having confessed, go to his Judgement
empty-handed and contrite. As he sat, draped over the use-
shined seat in the Confessional Box of St. Mary Magdalene's,
he fretted that the shape of his usurped body would not hold
out long enough for him to unburden himself of all the sins
that languished in his linen heart. He concentrated, trying to
keep body and soul together for these last, vital few minutes.

Soon Father Rooney would come. He would sit behind the
lattice divide of the Confessional and offer words of consola-
tion, of understanding, of forgiveness; then, in the remaining
minutes of his stolen existence, Ronnie Glass would tell his
story.

He would begin by denying that most terrible stain on his
character: the accusation of pornographer.

Pornographer.

The thought was absurd. There wasn't a pornographer's
bone in his body. Anyone who had known him in his thirty-
two years would have testified to that. My Christ, he didn't
even like sex very much. That was the irony. Of all the people
to be accused of peddling filth, he was about the most unlikely. When it had seemed everyone about him was parading
their adulteries like third legs, he had lived a blameless existence. The forbidden life of the body happened, like car accidents, to other people; not to him. Sex was simply a
roller coaster ride that one might indulge in once every year or
so. Twice might be tolerable; three times nauseating. Was it
any surprise then, that in nine years of marriage to a good
Catholic girl this good Catholic boy only fathered two
children?

But he'd been a loving man in his lustless way, and his wife
Bernadette had shared his indifference to sex, so his unen-
thusiastic member had never been a bone of contention between them. And the children were a joy. Samantha was
already growing into a model of politeness and tidiness, and
Imogen (though scarcely two) had her mother's smile.

Life had been fine, all in all. He had almost owned a featureless semi-detached house in the leafier suburbs of South London. He had possessed a small garden, Sunday-tended: a soul the same. It had been, as far as he could judge, a model life, unassuming and dirt-free.

And it would have remained so, had it not been for that worm of greed in his nature. Greed had undone him, no doubt.

If he hadn't been greedy, he wouldn't have looked twice at the job that Maguire had offered him. He would have trusted his instinct, taken one look around the pokey smoke-filled office above the Hungarian pastry shop in Soho, and turned tail. But his itch for wealth diverted him from the plain truth—that he was using all his skills as an accountant to give a gloss of credibility to an operation that stank of corruption. He'd known that in his heart, of course. Known that despite Maguire's ceaseless talk of Moral Rearmament, his fondness for his children, his obsession with the gentlemanly art of Bonsai, the man was a louse. The lowest of the low. But he'd successfully shut out that knowledge, and contented himself with the job in hand: balancing the books. Maguire was generous: and that made the blindness easier to induce. He even began to like the man and his associates. He'd got used to seeing the shambling bulk that was Dennis "Dork" Luzzati, a fresh cream pastry perpetually hovering at his fat lips; got used, too, to little three-fingered Henry B. Henry, with his card tricks and his patter, a new routine every day. They weren't the most sophisticated of conversationalists, and they certainly wouldn't have been welcome at the Tennis Club, but they seemed harmless enough.

It was a shock then, a terrible shock, when he eventually drew back the veil and saw Dork, Henry and Maguire for the beasts they really were.

The revelation had occurred by accident.

One night, finishing some tax work late, Ronnie had caught a cab down to the warehouse, planning to deliver his report to Maguire by hand. He'd never actually visited the warehouse, though he'd heard it mentioned between them often enough. Maguire had been stock piling his supplies of books there for some months. Mostly cookery books, from Europe, or so

Ronnie had been told. That night, that last night of clean-
liness, he walked into the truth, in all its full-color glory.

Maguire was there, in one of the plain brick rooms, sitting
on a chair surrounded by packages and boxes. An unshaded
bulb threw a halo on to his thinning scalp; it glistened, pinkly.
Dork was there too, engrossed in a cake. Henry B. was playing
Patience. Piled high on every side of the trio there were
magazines, thousand upon thousand of them, their covers
shining, virginal, and somehow fleshy.

Maguire looked up from his calculations.

"Glassy," he said. He always used that nickname.

Ronnie stared into the room, guessing, even from a
distance, what these heaped treasures were.

"Come on in," said Henry B. "Good for a game?"

"Don't look so serious," soothed Maguire, "this is just
merchandise."

"A kind of numb horror drew Ronnie to approach one of
the stacks of magazines, and open the top copy.

Climax Erotica, the cover read, *Full Color Pornography for
the Discriminating Adult. Text in English, German and
French.* Unable to prevent himself he began to look through
the magazine, his face stinging with embarrassment, only half-
hearing the barrage of jokes and threats that Maguire was
shooting off.

Swarms of obscene images flew out of the pages, horribly
abundant. He'd never seen anything like it in his life. Every
sexual act possible between consenting adults (and a few only
doped acrobats would consent to) were chronicled in glorious
detail. The performers of these unspeakable acts smiled,
glassy-eyed, at Ronnie as they swarmed up out of a grease of
sex, neither shame nor apology on their lust-filled faces. Every
slit, every slot, every pucker and pimple of their bodies was exposed, naked beyond nakedness. The pouting, panting excess
of it turned Ronnie's stomach to ash.

He closed the magazine and glanced at another pile beside
it. Different faces, same furious coupling. Every depravity
was catered for somewhere. The titles alone testified to the
delights to be found inside. *Bizarre Women in Chains*, one
read. *Enslaved by Rubber*, another promised. *Labrador*

Lover, a third portrayed, in perfect focus down to the last wet whisker.

Slowly Michael Maguire's cigarette-worn voice filtered through into Ronnie's reeling brain. It cajoled, or tried to; and worse it mocked him, in its subtle way, for his naiveté.

"You had to find out sooner or later," he said. "I suppose it may as well be sooner, eh? No harm in it. All a bit of fun."

Ronnie shook his head violently, trying to dislodge the images that had taken root behind his eyes. They were multiplying already, invading a territory that had been so innocent of such possibilities. In his imagination, labradors scampered around in leather, drinking from the bodies of bound whores. It was frightening the way these pictures flowed out into his eyes, each page a new abomination. He felt he'd choke on them unless he acted.

"Horrible," was all he could say. "Horrible. Horrible. Horrible."

He kicked a pile of *Bizarre Women in Chains*, and they toppled over, the repeated images of the cover sprawling across the dirty floor.

"Don't do that," said Maguire, very quietly.

"Horrible," said Ronnie. "They're all horrible."

"There's a big market for them."

"Not me!" he said, as though Maguire was suggesting he had some personal interest in them.

"All right, so you don't like them. He doesn't like them, Dork."

Dork was wiping cream off his short fingers with a dainty handkerchief.

"Why not?"

"Too dirty for him."

"Horrible," said Ronnie again.

"Well you're in this up to your neck, my son," said Maguire. His voice was the Devil's voice, wasn't it? Surely the Devil's voice, "You may as well grin and bear it."

Dork guffawed, "Grin and bare it; I like it Mick, I like it."

Ronnie looked up at Maguire. The man was forty-five, maybe fifty; but his face had a fretted, cracked look, old before its years. The charm was gone; it was scarcely human, the face he locked eyes with. Its sweat, its bristles, its puckered mouth made it resemble, in Ronnie's mind, the proffered backside of one of the red-raw sluts in the magazines.

"We're all known villains here," the organ was saying, "and we've got nothing to lose if we're caught again."

"Nothing," said Dork.

"Whereas you, my son, you're a spit-clean professional. Way I see it, if you want to go gabbing about this dirty business, you're going to lose your reputation as a nice, honest accountant. In fact I'd venture to suggest you'll never work again. Do you take my meaning?"

Ronnie wanted to hit Maguire, so he did; hard too. There was a satisfying snap as Maguire's teeth met at speed, and blood came quickly from between his lips. It was the first time Ronnie had fought since his schooldays, and he was slow to avoid the inevitable retaliation. The blow that Maguire returned sent him sprawling, bloodied, amongst the Bizarre Women. Before he could clamber to his feet Dork had slammed his heel into Ronnie's face, grinding the gristle in his nose. While Ronnie blinked back the blood Dork hoisted him to his feet, and held him up as a captive target for Maguire. The ringed hand became a fist, and for the next five minutes Maguire used Ronnie as a punchbag, starting below the belt and working up.

Ronnie found the pain curiously reassuring; it seemed to heal his guilty psyche better than a string of Hail Marys. When the beating was over, and Dork had let him out, defaced, into the dark, there wasn't any anger left in him, only a need to finish the cleansing Maguire had begun.

He went home to Bernadette that night and told her a lie about being mugged in the street. She was so consoling, it made him sick to be deceiving her, but he had no choice. That night, and the night after, were sleepless. He lay in his own bed, just a few feet from that of his trusting spouse, and tried to make sense of his feelings. He knew in his bones the truth would sooner or later become public knowledge. Better surely to go to the police, come clean. But that took courage, and his heart had never felt weaker. So he prevaricated through the Thursday night and the Friday, letting the bruises yellow and the confusion settle.

Then on Sunday, the shit hit the fan.

The lowest of the Sunday filth sheets had his face on the front cover: complete with the banner headline: "The Sex Empire of Ronald Glass." Inside, were photographs, snatched from innocent circumstance and construed as guilt. Glass appearing to look pursued. Glass appearing to look devious. His natural hirsuteness made him seem ill-shaven; his neat hair cut suggested the prison aesthetic favored by some of the criminal fraternity. Being short sighted he squinted; photographed squinting he looked like a lustful rat.

He stood in the newsagents, staring at his own face, and knew his personal Armageddon was on the horizon. Shaking, he read the terrible lies inside.

Somebody, he never exactly worked out who, had told the whole story. The pornography, the brothels, the sex shops, the cinemas. The secret world of smut that Maguire had masterminded was here detailed in every sordid particular. Except that Maguire's name did not appear. Neither did Dork's, nor Henry's. It was Glass, Glass all the way: his guilt was transparent. He had been framed, neat as anything. A corrupter of children, the leader called him, Little Boy Blue grown fat and horny.

It was too late to deny anything. By the time he got back to the house Bernadette had gone, with the children in tow. Somebody had got to her with the news, probably salivating down the phone, delighting in the sheer dirt of it.

He stood in the kitchen, where the table was laid for a breakfast the family hadn't yet eaten, and would now never eat, and he cried. Not a great deal: his supply of tears was strictly limited, but enough to feel the duty done. Then, having finished with his gesture of remorse, he sat down, like any decent man who has been deeply wronged, and planned murder.

In many ways getting the gun was more difficult than anything that followed. It required some careful thought, some soft words, and a good deal of hard cash. It took him a day and a half to locate the weapon he wanted, and to learn how to use it.

Then, in his own good time, he went about his business.

Henry B. died first. Ronnie shot him in his own stripped pinewood kitchen in up-and-coming Islington. He had a cup of freshly brewed coffee in his three-fingered hand and a look of almost pitiable terror on his face. The first shot struck him in the side, denting his shirt, and causing a little blood to come. Far less than Ronnie had been steeling himself for however. More confident, he fired again. The second shot hit his intended in the neck: and that seemed to be the killer. Henry B. pitched forward like a comedian in a silent movie, not relinquishing the coffee cup until the moment before he hit the floor. The cup spun in the mingled dregs of coffee and life, and rattled, at last, to a halt.

Ronnie stepped over to the body and fired a third shot straight through the back of Henry B.'s neck. This last bullet was almost casual; swift and accurate. Then he escaped easily out of the back gate, almost elated by the ease of the act. He felt as though he'd cornered and killed a rat in his cellar; an unpleasant duty that needed to be done.

The frisson lasted five minutes. Then he was profoundly sick.

Anyway, that was Henry. All out of tricks.

Dork's death was rather more sensational. He ran out of time at the Dog Track; indeed, he was showing Ronnie his winning ticket when he felt the long-bladed knife insinuate itself between his fourth and fifth ribs. He could scarcely believe he was being murdered, the expression on his pastry-fattened face was one of complete amazement. He kept looking from side to side at the punters milling around as though at any moment one of them would point, and laugh, and tell him that this was all a joke, a premature birthday game.

Then Ronnie twisted the blade in the wound (he'd read that this was surely lethal) and Dork realized that, winning ticket or not, this wasn't his lucky day.

His heavy body was carried along in the crush of the crowd for a good ten yards until it became wedged in the teeth of the turnstile. Only then did someone feel the hot gush from Dork, and scream.

By then Ronnie was well away.

Content, feeling cleaner by the hour, he went back to the house. Bernadette had been in, collecting clothes and favorite ornaments. He wanted to say to her: take everything, it means nothing to me, but she'd slipped in and gone again, like a ghost of a housewife. In the kitchen the table was still set for that final Sunday breakfast. There was dust on the cornflakes in the children's bowls; the rancid butter was beginning to grease the air. Ronnie sat through the late afternoon, through the dusk, through until the early hours of the following morning, and tasted his new found power over life and death. Then he went to bed in his clothes, no longer caring to be tidy, and slept the sleep of the almost good.

It wasn't so hard for Maguire to guess who'd wasted Dork and Henry B. Henry, though the idea of that particular worm turning was hard to swallow. Many of the criminal community had known Ronald Glass, had laughed with Maguire over the little deception that was being played upon the innocent. But no one had believed him capable of such extreme sanctions against his enemies. In some seedier quarters he was now being saluted for his sheer bloody mindedness; others, Maguire included, felt he had gone too far to be welcomed into the fold like a strayed sheep. The general opinion was that he be dispatched, before he did any more damage to the fragile balance of power.

So Ronnie's days became numbered. They could have been counted on the three fingers of Henry B.'s hand.

They came for him on the Saturday afternoon and took him quickly, without him having time to wield a weapon in his defense. They escorted him to a Salami and Cooked Meats warehouse, and in the icy white safety of the cold storage room they hung him from a hook and tortured him. Anyone with any claim to Dork's or Henry B.'s affections was given an opportunity to work out their grief on him. With knives, with hammers, with oxyacetylene torches. They shattered his knees and his elbows. They put out his eardrums, burned the flesh off the soles of his feet.

Finally, about eleven or so, they began to lose interest. The clubs were just getting into their rhythm, the gaming tables were beginning to simmer, it was time to be done with justice and get out on the town.

That was when Micky Maguire arrived, dressed to kill in his best bib and tucker. Ronnie knew he was there somewhere in

the haze, but his senses were all but out, and he only half saw
the gun levelled at his head, half felt the noise of the blast
bounce around the white-tiled room.

A single bullet, immaculately placed, entered his brain
through the middle of his forehead. As neat as even he could
have wished, like a third eye.

His body twitched on its hook a moment, and died.

Maguire took his applause like a man, kissed the ladies,
thanked his dear friends who had seen this deed done with
him, and went to play. The body was dumped in a black
plastic bag on the edge of Epping Forest, early on Sunday
morning, just as the dawn chorus was tuning up in the ash
trees and the sycamores. And that, to all intents and purposes,
was the end of that. Except that it was the beginning.

Ronnie's body was found by a jogger, out before seven on the
following Monday. In the day between his being dumped and
being found his corpse had already begun to deteriorate.

But the pathologist had seen far, far worse. He watched
dispassionately while the two mortuary technicians stripped
the body, folded the clothes and placed them in tagged plastic
bags. He waited patiently and attentively while the wife of the
deceased was ushered into his echoing domain, her face ashen,
her eyes swelled to bursting with too many tears. She looked
down at her husband without love, staring at the wounds and
at the marks of torture quite unflinchingly. The pathologist
had a whole story written behind this last confrontation between Sex-King and untroubled wife. Their loveless marriage,
their arguments over his despicable way of life, her despair,
his brutality, and now, her relief that the torment was finally
over and she was released to start a new life without him. The
pathologist made a mental note to look up the pretty widow's
address. She was delicious in her indifference to mutilation; it
made his mouth wet to think of her.

Ronnie knew Bernadette had come and gone; he could sense
too the other faces that popped into the mortuary just to peer
down at the Sex-King. He was an object of fascination, even in
death, and it was a horror he hadn't predicted, buzzing
around in the cool coils of his brain, like a tenant who refuses

to be ousted by the bailiffs, still seeing the world hovering around him, and not being able to act upon it.

In the days since his death there had been no hint of escape from this condition. He had sat here, in his own dead skull, unable to find a way out into the living world, and unwilling, somehow, to relinquish life entirely and leave himself to Heaven. There was still a will to revenge in him. A part of his mind, unforgiving of trespasses, was prepared to postpone Paradise in order to finish the job he had shared. The books needed balancing; and until Michael Maguire was dead Ronnie could not go to his atonement.

In his round bone prison he watched the curious come and go, and knotted up his will.

The pathologist did his work on Ronnie's corpse with all the respect of an efficient fish gutter, carelessly digging the bullet out of his cranium, and nosing around in the stews of smashed bone and cartilage that had formerly been his knees and elbows. Ronnie didn't like the man. He'd leered at Bernadette in a highly unprofessional way; and now, when he was playing the professional, his callousness was positively shameful. Oh for a voice; for a fist, for a body to use for a time. Then he'd show this meat merchant how bodies should be treated. The will was not enough though: it needed a focus, and a means of escape.

The pathologist finished his report and his rough sewing, flung his juice-shiny gloves and his stained instruments on to the trolley beside the swabs and the alcohol, and left the body to the assistants.

Ronnie heard the swing doors close behind him as the man departed. Water was running somewhere, splashing into the sink; the sound irritated him.

Standing beside the table on which he lay, the two technicians discussed their shoes. Of all things, shoes. The banality of it, thought Ronnie, the life-decaying banality of it.

"You know them new heels, Lenny? The ones I got to put on my brown suedes? Useless. No bleeding good at all."

"I'm not surprised."

"And the price I paid for them. Look at that; just look at that. Worn through in a month."

"Paper thin."

"They are, Lenny, they're paper thin. I'm going to take them back."

"I would."

"I am."

"I would."

This mindless conversation, after those hours of torture, of sudden death, of the post mortem that he'd so recently endured, was almost beyond endurance. Ronnie's spirit began to buzz round and round in his brain like an angry bee trapped in an upturned jam-jar, determined to get out and start stinging—

Round and round; like the conversation.

"Paper bloody thin."

"I'm not surprised."

"Bloody foreign. These soles. Made in fucking Korea."

"Korea?"

"That's why they're paper thin."

It was unforgivable: the trudging stupidity of these people. That they should live and act and *be:* while he buzzed on and on, boiling with frustration. Was that fair?

"Neat shot, eh Lenny?"

"What?"

"The stiff. Old what's his name the Sex King. Bang in the middle of the forehead. See that? Pop goes the weasel."

Lenny's companion, it seemed, was still preoccupied with his paper thin sole. He didn't reply. Lenny inquisitively inched back the shroud from Ronnie's forehead. The lines of sawn and scalped flesh were inelegantly sewn, but the bullet hole itself was neat.

"Look at it."

The other glanced round at the dead face. The head wound had been cleaned after the probing pincers had worked at it. The edges were white and puckered.

"I thought they usually went for the heart," said the sole searcher.

"This wasn't any street fight. It was an execution; formal like," said Lenny, poking his little finger into the wound. "It's a perfect shot. Bang in the middle of the forehead. Like he had three eyes."

"Yeah . . ."

The shroud was tossed back over Ronnie's face. The bee buzzed on; round and round.

"You hear about third eyes, don't you?"

"Do you?"

"Stella read me something about it being the center of the body."

"That's your navel. How can your forehead be the center of your body?"

"Well . . ."

"That's your navel."

"No, it's more your spiritual center."

The other didn't deign to respond.

"Just about where this bullet hole is," said Lenny, still lost in admiration for Ronnie's killer.

The bee listened. The bullet hole was just one of many holes in his life. Holes where his wife and children should have been. Holes winking up at him like sightless eyes from the pages of the magazines, pink and brown and hairlipped. Holes to the right of him, holes to the left—

Could it be, at last, that he had found here a hole that he could profit by? Why not leave by the wound?

His spirit braced itself, and made for his brow, creeping through his cortex with a mixture of trepidation and excitement. Ahead, he could sense the exit door like the light at the end of a long tunnel. Beyond the hole, the warp and weft of his shroud glittered like a promised land. His sense of direction was good; the light grew as he crept, the voices became louder. Without fanfare Ronnie's spirit spat itself into the outside world: a tiny seepage of soul. The motes of fluid that carried his will and his consciousness were soaked up by his shroud like tears by tissues.

His flesh and blood body was utterly deserted now; an icy bulk fit for nothing but the flames.

Ronnie Glass existed in a new world: a white linen world like no state he had lived or dreamed before.

Ronnie Glass was his shroud.

Had Ronnie's pathologist not been forgetful he wouldn't have come back into the mortuary at that moment, trying to locate the diary he'd written the Widow Glass' number in;

and, had he not come in, he would have lived. As it was—

"Haven't you started on this one yet?" he snapped at the technicians.

They murmured some apology or other. He was always testy at this time of night; they were used to his tantrums.

"Get on with it," he said, stripping the shroud off the body and flinging it to the floor in irritation, "before the fucker walks out of here in disgust. Don't want to get our little hotel a bad reputation, do we?"

"Yes, sir. I mean, no sir."

"Well don't stand there: parcel it up. There's a widow wants him dispatched as soon as possible. I've seen all I need to see of him."

Ronnie lay on the floor in a crumpled heap, slowly spreading his influence through this new found land. It felt good to have a body, even if it was sterile and rectangular. Bringing a power of will to bear he hadn't known he possessed, Ronnie took full control of the shroud.

At first it refused life. It had always been passive: that was its condition. It wasn't use to occupation by spirits. But Ronnie wasn't to be beaten now. His will was an imperative. Against all rules of natural behavior it stretched and knotted the sullen linen into a semblance of life.

The shroud rose.

The pathologist had located his little black book, and was in the act of pocketing it when this white curtain spread itself in his path, stretching like a man who has just woken from a deep sleep.

Ronnie tried to speak; but the only voice he could find was a whisper of the cloth on the air, too light, too insubstantial to be heard over the complaints of frightened men. And frightened they were. Despite the pathologist's call for assistance, none was forthcoming. Lenny and his companion were sliding away towards the swing doors, gaping mouths babbling entreaties to any local god who would listen.

The pathologist backed off against the post mortem table, quite out of gods.

"Get out of my sight," he said.

Ronnie embraced him, tightly.

"Help," said the pathologist, almost to himself. But help

was gone. It was running down the corridors, still babbling, keeping its back to the miracle that was taking place in the mortuary. The pathologist was alone, wrapped up in this starched embrace, murmuring, at the last, some apologies he had found beneath his pride.

"I'm sorry, whoever you are. Whatever you are. I'm sorry."

But there was an anger in Ronnie that would not have any truck with late converts; no pardons or reprieves were available. This fish-eyed bastard, this son of the scalpel had cut and examined his old body as though it was a side of beef. It made Ronnie livid to think of this creep's oh-so-cool appraisal of life, death and Bernadette. The bastard would die, here, amongst his remains, and let that be an end to his callous profession.

The corners of the shroud were forming into crude arms now, as Ronnie's memory shaped them. It seemed natural to recreate his old appearance in this new medium. He made hands first: then digits: even a rudimentary thumb. He was like a morbid Adam raised out of linen.

Even as they formed, the hands had the pathologist about the neck. As yet they had no sense of touch in them, and it was difficult to judge how hard to press on the throbbing skin, so he simply used all the strength he could muster. The man's face blackened, and his tongue, the color of a plum, stuck out from his mouth like a spear head, sharp and hard. In his enthusiasm, Ronnie broke his neck. It snapped suddenly, and the head fell backwards at a horrid angle. The vain apologies had long since stopped.

Ronnie dropped him to the polished floor, and stared down at the hands he had made, with eyes that were still two pin pricks in a sheet of stained cloth.

He felt certain of himself in this body, and God, he was strong; he'd broken the bastard's neck without exerting himself at all. Occupying this strange, bloodless physique he had a new freedom from the constraints of humanity. He was alive suddenly to the life of the air, feeling it now fill and billow him. Surely he could fly, like a sheet in the wind, or if it suited him knot himself into a fist and beat the world into submission. The prospects seemed endless.

And yet . . . he sensed that this possession was at best temporary. Sooner or later the shroud would want to resume its former life as an idle piece of cloth, and its true, passive nature would be restored. This body had not been given to him, merely loaned; it was up to him to use it to the best of his vengeful abilities. He knew the priorities. First and foremost to find Michael Maguire and dispatch him. Then, if he still had the time left, he would see the children. But it wasn't wise to go visiting as a flying shroud. Better by far to work at this illusion of humanity, and see if he could sophisticate the effect.

He'd seen what freak creases could do, making faces appear in a crumpled pillow, or in the folds of a jacket hanging on the back of the door. More extraordinary still, there was the Shroud of Turin, in which the face and body of Jesus Christ had been miraculously imprinted. Bernadette had been sent a postcard of the Shroud, with every wound of lance and nail in place. Why couldn't he make the same miracle, by force of will? Wasn't he resurrected too?

He went to the sink in the morgue and turned off the running tap, then stared into the mirror to watch his will take shape. The surface of the shroud was already twitching and scurrying as he demanded new forms of it. At first there was only the primitive outline of his head, roughly shaped, like that of a snowman. Two pits for eyes: a lumpen nose. But he concentrated, willing the linen to stretch itself to the limits of its elasticity. And behold! it worked, it really worked! The threads complained, but acquiesced to his demands, forming in exquisite reproduction the nostrils, and then the eyelids; the upper lip: now the lower. He traced from memory the contours of his lost face like an adoring lover, and remade them in every detail. Now he began to make a column for the neck, filled with air, but looking deceptively solid. Below that the shroud swelled into a manly torso. The arms were already formed; the legs followed quickly on. And it was done.

He was remade, in his own image.

The illusion was not perfect. For one thing, he was pure white, except for the stains, and his flesh had the texture of cloth. The creases of his face were perhaps too severe, almost cubist in appearance, and it was impossible to coax the cloth to make a semblance of either hair or nails. But he was as ready for the world as any living shroud could hope to be.

It was time to go out and meet his public.

"Your game, Micky."

Maguire seldom lost at poker. He was too clever, and that used face too unreadable; his tired, bloodshot eyes never let anything out. Yet, despite his formidable reputation as a winner, he never cheated. That was his bond with himself. There was no lift in winning if there was a cheat involved. It was just stealing then; and that was for the criminal classes. He was a businessman, pure and simple.

Tonight, in the space of two and a half hours, he'd pocketed a tidy sum. Life was good. Since the deaths of Dork, Henry B. Henry and Glass, the police had been too concerned with Murder to take much notice of the lower orders of Vice. Besides, their palms were well crossed with silver; they had nothing to complain about. Inspector Wall, a drinking companion of many years' standing, had even offered Maguire protection from the lunatic killer who was apparently on the loose. The irony of the idea pleased Maguire mightily.

It was almost three a.m. Time for bad girls and boys to be in their beds, dreaming of crimes for the morrow. Maguire rose from the table, signifying the end of the night's gambling. He buttoned up his waistcoat and carefully reknotted his lemon water-ice silk tie.

"Another game next week?" he suggested.

The defeated players agreed. They were used to losing money to their boss, but there were no hard feelings amongst the quarter. There was a tinge of sadness perhaps: they missed Henry B. and Dork. Saturday nights had been such joyous affairs. Now there was a muted tone over the proceedings.

Perlgut was the first to leave, stubbing out his cheroot in the brimming ashtray.

"Night, Mick."

"Night, Frank. Give the kids a kiss from their Uncle Mick, eh?"

"Will do."

Perlgut shuffled off, with his stuttering brother in tow.

"G-g-g-goodnight."

"Night, Ernest."

The brothers clattered down the stairs.

Norton was the last to go, as always.

"Shipment tomorrow?" he asked.

"Tomorrow's Sunday," said Maguire. He never worked on Sundays; it was a day for the family.

"Not, today's Sunday," said Norton, not trying to be pedantic, just letting it come naturally. "Tomorrow's Monday."

"Yes."

"Shipment Monday?"

"I hope so."

"You going to the warehouse?"

"Probably."

"I'll pick you up then: we can run down together."

"Fine."

Norton was a good man. Humorless, but reliable.

"Night then."

"Night."

His three-inch heels were steel-tipped; they sounded like a woman's stilettos on the stairs. The door slammed below.

Maguire counted his profits, drained his glass of Cointreau, and switched out the light in the gaming room. The smoke was already staling. Tomorrow he'd have to get somebody to come up and open the window, let some fresh Soho smells in there. Salami and coffee beans, commerce and sleaze. He loved it, loved it with a passion, like a babe loves a tit.

As he descended the stairs into the darkened sex shop he heard the exchange of farewells in the street outside, followed by the slamming of car doors and the purring departure of expensive cars. A good night with good friends, what more could any man reasonably ask?

At the bottom of the stairs he stopped for a moment. The blinking streetsign lights opposite illuminated the shop sufficiently for him to make out the rows of magazines. Their plastic-bound faces glinted; siliconed breasts and spanked buttocks swelled from the covers like overripe fruit. Faces dripping mascara pouted at him, offering every lonely satisfaction paper could promise. But he was unmoved; the time had long since passed when he found any of that stuff of interest. It was simply currency to him; he was neither disgusted nor aroused by it. He was a happily married man after after all, with a wife whose imagination barely stretched beyond page two of the *Kama Sutra*, and whose children were slapped soundly if they spoke one questionable word.

In the corner of the shop, where the Bondage and Domination material was displayed, something rose from the floor. Maguire found it hard to focus in the intermittent light. Red, blue. Red, blue. But it wasn't Norton, nor one of the Perlguts.

It was a face he knew however, smiling at him against the background of "Roped and Raped" magazines. Now he saw: it was Glass, clear as day, and, despite the colored lights, white as a sheet.

He didn't try to reason how a dead man could be staring at him, he just dropped his coat and his jaw, and ran.

The door was locked, and the key was one of two dozen on his ring. Oh Jesus, why did he have so many keys? Keys to the warehouse, keys to the greenhouse, keys to the whorehouse. And only that twitching light to see them by. Red, blue. Red, blue.

He rummaged amongst the keys and by some magical chance the first he tried slotted easily in the lock and turned like a finger in hot grease. The door was open, the street ahead.

But Glass glided up behind him soundlessly, and before he could step over the threshold he had thrown something around Maguire's face, a cloth of some kind. It smelt of hospitals, of ether or disinfectant or both. Maguire tried to cry out but a fist of cloth was being thrust down his throat. He gagged on it, the vomit reflex making his system revolt. In response the assassin just tightened his grip.

In the street opposite a girl Maguire knew only as Natalie (Model: seeks interesting position with strict disciplinarian) was watching the struggle in the doorway of the shop with a doped look on her vapid face. She'd seen murder once or twice; she'd seen rape aplenty, and she wasn't about to get involved. Besides, it was late, and the insides of her thighs ached. Casually she turned away down the pink lit corridor, leaving the violence to take its course. Maguire made a mental note to have the girl's face carved up one of these days. If he survived; which seemed less likely by the moment. The red, blue, red, blue was unfixable now, as his airless brain went colorblind, and though he seemed to snatch a grip on his would-be assassin, the hold seemed to evaporate, leaving cloth, empty cloth, running through his sweating hands like silk.

Then someone spoke. Not behind him, not the voice of his assassin, but in front. In the street, Norton. It was Norton. He'd returned for some reason, God love him, and he was getting out of his car ten yards down the street, shouting Maguire's name.

The assassin's chokehold faltered and gravity claimed Maguire. He fell heavily, the world spinning, to the pavement, his face purple in the lurid light.

Norton ran towards his boss, fumbling for his gun amongst the bric-à-brac in his pocket. The white-suited assassin was already backing off down the street, unprepared to take on another man. He looked, thought Norton, for all the world like a failed member of the Klu Klux Klan; a hood, a robe, a cloak. Norton dropped to one knee, took a double-handed aim at the man and fired. The result was startling. The figure seemed to balloon up, his body losing its shape, becoming a flapping mass of white cloth, with a face loosely imprinted on it. There was a noise like the snapping of Monday-washed sheets on a line, a sound that was out of place in this grimy backstreet. Norton's confusion left him responseless for a moment, and the mansheet seemed to rise in the air, illusory.

At Norton's feet, Maguire was coming round, groaning. He was trying to speak but having difficulty making himself understood through his bruised larynx and throat. Norton bent closer to him. He smelt of vomit and fear.

"Glass," he seemed to be saying.

It was enough. Norton nodded, said hush. That was the face, of course, on the sheet. Glass, the imprudent accountant. He'd watched the man's feet fried, watched the whole vicious ritual; not to his taste at all.

Well, well: Ronnie Glass had some friends apparently, friends not above revenge.

Norton looked up, but the wind had lifted the ghost above the rooftops and away.

• • •

That had been a bad experience; the first taste of failure. Ronnie remembered it still, the desolation of that night. He'd lain, heaped in a rat-run corner of a derelict factory south of the river, and calmed the panic in his fibers. What good was this trick he'd mastered if he lost control of it the instant he was threatened? He must plan more carefully, and wind his will up until it would brook no resistance. Already he sensed that his energy was ebbing: and there was a hint of difficulty in restructuring his body this second time round. He had no time to waste with fumbled failures. He must corner the man where he could not possibly escape.

Police investigations at the mortuary had led round in circles for half a day; and now into the night. Inspector Wall of the Yard had tried every technique he knew. Soft words, hard words, promises, threats, seductions, surprises, even blows. Still Lenny told the same story; a ridiculous story he swore would be corroborated when his fellow technician came out of the catatonic state he'd now taken refuge in. But there was no way the Inspector could take the story seriously. A shroud that walked? How could he put that in his report? No, he wanted something concrete, even if it was a lie.

"Can I have a cigarette?" asked Lenny for the umpteenth time. Wall shook his head.

"Hey, Fresco—" Wall addressed his righthand man, Al Kincaid. "I think it's time you searched the lad again."

Lenny knew what another search implied; it was a euphemism for a beating. Up against the wall, legs spread, hands on head: wham! His stomach jumped at the thought.

"Listen . . ." he implored.

"What, Lenny?"

"I didn't do it."

"Of course you did it," said Wall, picking his nose. "We just want to know why. Didn't you like the old fucker? Make dirty remarks about your ladyfriends, did he? He had a bit of a reputation for that, I understand."

Al Fresco smirked.

"Was that why you nobbled him?"

"For God's sake," said Lenny, "you think I'd tell you a

fucking story like that if I didn't see it with my own fucking eyes.''

"Language," chided Fresco.

"Shrouds don't fly," said Wall, with understandable conviction.

"Then where is the shroud, eh?" reasoned Lenny.

"You incinerated it, you ate, it, how the fuck should I know?"

"Language," said Lenny quietly.

The phone rang before Fresco could hit him. He picked it up, spoke and handed it to Wall. Then he hit Lenny, a friendly slap that drew a little blood.

"Listen," said Fresco, breathing with lethal proximity to Lenny as if to suck the air out of his mouth, "We know you did it, see? You were the only one in the morgue *alive* to do it, see? We just want to know why. That's all. Just why."

"Fresco." Wall had covered the receiver as he spoke to the muscleman.

"Yes, sir."

"It's Mr. Maguire."

"Mr. Maguire?"

"Micky Maguire."

Fresco nodded.

"He's very upset."

"Oh yeah? Why's that?"

"He thinks he's been attacked, by the man in the morgue. The pornographer."

"Glass," said Lenny, "Ronnie Glass."

"Ronald Glass, like the man says," said Wall, grinning at Lenny.

"That's ridiculous," said Fresco.

"Well I think we ought to do our duty to an upstanding member of the community, don't you? Duck in to the morgue will you, make sure—"

"Make sure?"

"That the bastard's still down there—"

"Oh."

Fresco exited, confused but obedient.

Lenny didn't understand any of this: but he was past caring. What the hell was it to him anyway? He started to play with his balls through a hole in his lefthand pocket. Wall watched him with disdain.

"Don't do that," he said. "You can play with yourself as much as you like once we've got you tucked up in a nice, warm cell."

Lenny shook his head slowly, and removed his hand from his pocket. Just wasn't his day.

Fresco was already back from down the hall, a little breathless.

"He's there," he said, visibly brightened by the simplicity of the task.

"Of course he is," said Wall.

"Dead as a Dodo," said Fresco.

"What's a Dodo?" asked Lenny.

Fresco looked blank.

"Turn of phrase," he said testily.

Wall of the Yard was back on the line, talking to Maguire. The man at the other end sounded well spooked; and his reassurances seemed to do little good.

"He's all present and correct, Micky. You must have been mistaken."

Maguire's fear ran back through the phone line like a mild electric charge.

"I saw him, damn you."

"Well, he's lying down there with a hole in the middle of his head, Micky. So tell me how *can* you have seen him?"

"I don't know," said Maguire.

"Well then."

"Listen . . . if you get the chance, drop by will you? Same arrangement as usual. I could put some nice work your way."

Wall didn't like talking business on the phone, it made him uneasy.

"Later, Micky."

"O.K. Call by?"

"I will."

"Promise?"

"Yes."

Wall put down the receiver and stared at the suspect. Lenny was back to pocket billiards again. Crass little animal; another search was clearly called for.

"Fresco," said Wall in dovelike tones, "will you please teach Lenny not to play with himself in front of police officers?"

In his fortress in Richmond, Maguire cried like a baby.

He'd seen Glass, no doubt of it. Whatever Wall believed about the body being at the mortuary, he knew otherwise. Glass was out, on the street, footloose and fancyfree, despite the fact that he'd blown a hole in the bastard's head.

Maguire was a God-fearing man, and he believed in life after death, though until now he'd never questioned how it would come about. This was the answer, this blank-faced son of a whore stinking of ether: this was the way the afterlife would be. It made him weep, fearing to live, and fearing to die.

It was well past dawn now; a peaceful Sunday morning. Nothing would happen to him in the safety of the "Ponderosa," and in full daylight. This was his castle, built with his hardwon thievings. Norton was here, armed to the teeth. There were dogs at every gate. No one, living or dead, would dare challenge his supremacy in this territory. Here, amongst the portraits of his heroes: Louis B. Mayer, Dillinger, Churchill; amongst his family; amidst his good taste, his money, his *objets d'art*, here he was his own man. If the mad accountant came for him he'd be blasted in his tracks, ghost or no ghost. *Finis.*

After all, wasn't he Michael Roscoe Maguire, an empire builder? Born with nothing, he'd risen by virtue of his stockbroker's face and his maverick's heart. Once in a while, maybe, and only under very controlled conditions, he might let his darker appetites show; as at the execution of Glass. He'd taken genuine pleasure in that little scenario; *his* the *coup de grâce, his* the infinite compassion of the killing stroke. But his life of violence was all but behind him now. Now he was a bourgeois, secure in his fortress.

Raquel woke at eight, and busied herself with preparing breakfast.

"You want anything to eat?" she asked Maguire.

He shook his head. His throat hurt too much.

"Coffee?"

"Yes."

"You want it in here?"

He nodded. He liked sitting in front of the window that overlooked the lawn and the greenhouse. The day was brightening; fat, fleecy clouds bucked the wind, their shadows, passing over the perfect green. Maybe he'd take up painting, he thought, like Winston. Commit his favorite landscapes to canvas; maybe a view of the garden, even a nude of Raquel, immortalized in oils before her tits sagged beyond all hope of support.

She was back purring at his side, with the coffee.

"You, O.K.?" she asked.

Dumb bitch. Of course he wasn't O.K.

"Sure," he said.

"You've got a visitor."

"What?" He sat up straight in the leather chair. "Who?"

She was smiling at him.

"Tracy," she said. "She wants to come in and cuddle."

He expelled a hiss of air from the sides of his mouth. Dumb, dumb bitch.

"You want to see Tracy?"

"Sure."

The little accident, as he was fond of calling her, was at the door, still in her dressing gown.

"Hi, Daddy."

"Hello, sweetheart."

She sashayed across the room towards him, her mother's walk in embryo.

"Mummy says you're ill."

"I'm getting better."

"I'm glad."

"So am I."

"Shall we go out today?"

"Maybe."

"See the fair?"

"Maybe."

She pouted fetchingly, perfectly in control of the effect. Raquel's trick all over again. He just hoped to God she wasn't going to grow up as dumb as her mother.

"We'll see," he said, hoping to imply yes, but knowing he meant no.

She hoisted herself on to his knee and he indulged her tales of a five year old's mischiefs for a while, then sent her packing. Talking made his throat hurt, and he didn't feel too much like the loving father today.

Alone again, he watched the shadows waltz on the lawn.

The dogs began to bark after eleven. Then, after a short while, they fell silent. He got up to find Norton, who was in the kitchen doing a jigsaw with Tracy. "The Hay-Wain" in two thousand pieces. One of Raquel's favorites.

"You check the dogs, Norton?"

"No, boss."

"Well fucking do it."

He didn't often swear in front of the child; but he felt ready to go bang. Norton snapped to it. As he opened the back door Maguire could smell the day. It was tempting to step outside the house. But the dogs barked in a way that set his head thumping and his palms prickling. Tracy had her head down to the business of the jigsaw, her body tense with anticipation of her father's anger. He said nothing, but went straight back into the lounge.

From his chair he could see Norton striding across the lawn. The dogs weren't making a sound now. Norton disappeared from sight behind the greenhouse. A long wait. Maguire was just beginning to get agitated, when Norton appeared again, and looked up at the house, shrugging at Maguire, and speaking. Maguire unlocked the sliding door, opened it and stepped on to the patio. The day met him: balmy.

"What are you saying?" he called to Norton.

"The dogs are fine," Norton returned.

Maguire felt his body relax. Of course the dogs were O.K.; why shouldn't they bark a bit, what else were they for? He was damn near making a fool of himself, pissing his pants just because the dogs barked. He nodded to Norton and stepped off the patio on to the lawn. Beautiful day, he thought. Quickening his pace he crossed the lawn to the greenhouse, where his carefully nurtured Bonsai trees bloomed. At the door of the greenhouse Norton was waiting dutifully, going through his pockets, looking for mints.

"You want me here, sir?"

"No."

"Sure?"

"Sure," he said magnanimously, "you go back up and play with the kid."

Norton nodded.

"Dogs are fine," he said again.

"Yeah."

"Must have been the wind stirred them up."

There was a wind. Warm, but strong. It stirred the line of copper beeches that bounded the garden. They shimmered, and showed the paler undersides of their leaves to the sky, their movement reassuring in its ease and gentility.

Maguire unlocked the greenhouse and stepped into his haven. Here in this artificial Eden were his true loves, nurtured on coos and cuttlefish manure. His Sargent's Juniper, that had survived the rigors of Mount Ishizuchi; his flowering quince, his Yeddo Spruce (Picea Jesoensis), his favorite dwarf, that he'd trained, after several failed attempts, to cling to a stone. All beauties: all minor miracles of winding trunk and cascading needles, worthy of his fondest attention.

Content, mindless for a while of the outside world, he pottered amongst his flora.

The dogs had fought over possession of Ronnie as though he were a plaything. They'd caught him breaching the wall and surround him before he could make his escape, grinning as they seized him, tore him and spat him out. He escaped only because Norton had approached, and distracted them from their fury for a moment.

His body was torn in several places after their attack. Confused, concentrating to try and keep his shape coherent, he had narrowly avoided being spotted by Norton.

Now he crept out of hiding. The fight had sapped him of energy, and the shroud gaped, so that the illusion of substance was spoiled. His belly was torn open; his left leg all but severed. The stains had multiplied; mucus and dog shit joining the blood.

But the will, the will was all. He had come so close; this was not the time to relinquish his grip and let nature take its course. He existed in mutiny against nature, that was his state; and for the first time in his life (and death) he felt an elation. To be unnatural: to be in defiance of system and sanity, was that so bad? He was shitty, bloody, dead and resurrected in a piece of stained cloth; he was a nonsense. *Yet he was.* No one could deny him being, as long as he had the will to be. The thought was delicious: like finding a new sense in a blind, deaf world.

He saw Maguire in the greenhouse and watched him awhile. The enemy was totally absorbed in his hobby; he was even whistling the National Anthem as he tended his flowering charges. Ronnie moved closer to the glass, and closer, his voice an oh-so-gentle moan in the failing weave.

Maguire didn't hear the sigh of cloth on the window, until Ronnie's face pressed flat to the glass, the features smeared and misshapen. He dropped the Yeddo Spruce. It shattered on the floor, its branches broken.

Maguire tried to yell, but all he could squeeze from his vocal cords was a strangled yelp. He broke for the door, as the face, huge with greed for revenge, broke the glass. Maguire didn't quite comprehend what happened next. The way the head and the body seemed to flow through the broken pane, defying physics, and reassembled in his sanctum, taking on the shape of a human being.

No, it wasn't quite human. It had the look of a stroke victim, its white mask and its white body sagged down the right side, and it dragged its torn leg after it as it lunged at him.

He opened the door and retreated into the garden. The thing followed, speaking now, arms extended towards him.

"Maguire . . ."

It said his name in a voice so soft he might have imagined it. But no, it spoke again.

"Recognize me, Maguire?" it said.

And of course he did, even with its stroke-stricken, billowing features it was clearly Ronnie Glass.

"Glass," he said.

"Yes," said the ghost.

"I don't want—" Maguire began, then faltered. What

didn't he want? To speak with this horror, certainly. To know that it existed; that too. To die, most of all.

"I don't want to die."

"You will," said the ghost.

Maguire felt the gust of the sheet as it flew in his face, or perhaps it was the wind that caught this insubstantial monster and threw it around him.

Whichever, the embrace stank of ether, and disinfectant, and death. Arms of linen tightened around him, the gaping face was pressed on to his, as though the thing wanted to kiss him.

Instinctively Maguire reached round his attacker, and his hands found the rent the dogs had made in the shroud. His fingers gripped the open edge of the cloth, and he pulled. He was satisfied to hear the linen tearing along its weave, and the bearhug fell away from him. The shroud bucked in his hand, the liquefied mouth wide in a silent scream.

Ronnie was feeling an agony he thought he'd left behind him with flesh and bone. But here it was again: pain, pain, pain.

He fluttered away from his mutilator, letting out what cry he could, while Maguire stumbled away up the lawn, his eyes huge. The man was close to madness, surely his mind was as good as broken. But that wasn't enough. He had to kill the bastard; that was his promise to himself and he intended to keep it.

The pain didn't disappear, but he tried to ignore it, putting all his energy into pursuing Maguire up the garden towards the house. But he was so weak now: the wind almost had mastery of him; gusting through his form and catching the frayed entrails of his body. He looked like a war-torn flag, fouled so it was scarcely recognizable, and just about ready to call it a day.

Except, except . . . Maguire.

Maguire reached the house, and slammed the door. The sheet pressed itself against the window, flapping ludicrously, its linen hands raking the glass, its almost-lost face demanding vengeance.

"Let me in," it said, "I *will* come in."

Maguire stumbled backwards across the room into the hall.

"Raquel . . ."

Where was the woman?

"Raquel . . . ?"

"Raquel . . ."

She wasn't in the kitchen. From the den, the sound of Tracy's singing. He peered in. The little girl was alone. She was sitting in the middle of the floor, headphones clamped over her ears, singing along to some favorite song.

"Mummy?" he mimed at her.

"Upstairs," she replied, without taking off the headphones.

Upstairs. As he climbed the stairs he heard the dogs barking down the garden. What was it doing? What was the fucker doing?

"Raquel . . . ?" His voice was so quiet he could barely hear it himself. It was as though he'd prematurely become a ghost in his own house.

There was no noise on the landing.

He stumbled into the brown-tiled bathroom and snapped on the light. It was flattering, and he had always liked to look at himself in it. The mellow radiance dulled the edge of age. But now it refused to lie. His face was that of an old and haunted man.

He flung open the airing cupboard and fumbled amongst the warm towels. There! a gun, nestling in scented comfort, hidden away for emergencies only. The contact made him salivate. He snatched the gun and checked it. All in working order. This weapon had brought Glass down once, and it could do it again. And again. And again.

He opened the bedroom door.

"Raquel—"

She was sitting on the edge of the bed, with Norton inserted between her legs. Both still dressed, one of Raquel's sumptuous breasts teased from her bra and pressed into Norton's accommodating mouth. She looked round, dumb as ever, not knowing what she'd done.

Without thinking, he fired.

The bullet found her open-mouthed, gormless as ever, and blew a sizeable hole in her neck. Norton pulled himself out, no necrophiliac he, and ran towards the window. Quite what he intended wasn't clear. Flight was impossible.

The next bullet caught Norton in the middle of the back,

and passed through his body, puncturing the window.

Only then, with her lover dead, did Raquel topple back across the bed, her breast spattered, her legs splayed wide. Maguire watched her fall. The domestic obscenity didn't disgust him; it was quite tolerable. Tit and blood and mouth and lost love and all; it was quite, quite tolerable. Maybe he was becoming insensitive.

He dropped the gun.

The dogs had stopped barking.

He slipped out of the room on to the landing, closing the door quietly, so as not to disturb the child.

Mustn't disturb the child. As he walked to the top of the stairs he saw his daughter's winsome face staring up at him from the bottom.

"Daddy."

He stared at her with a puzzled expression.

"There was someone at the door. I saw them passing the window."

He started to walk unsteadily down the stairs, one at a time. Slowly does it, he thought.

"I opened the door, but there was nobody there."

Wall. It must be Wall. He would know what to do for the best.

"Was it a tall man."

"I didn't see him properly, Daddy. Just his face. He was even whiter than you."

The door! Oh Jesus, the door! If she'd left it open. Too late.

The stranger came into the hall and his face crinkled into a kind of smile, which Maguire thought was about the worst thing he'd ever seen.

It wasn't Wall.

Wall was flesh and blood: the visitor was a ragdoll. Wall was a grim man; this one smiled. Wall was life and law and order. This thing wasn't.

It was Glass of course.

Maguire shook his head. The child, not seeing the thing wavering on the air behind her, misunderstood.

"What did I do wrong?" she asked.

Ronnie sailed past her up the stairs, more a shadow now

than anything remotely manlike, shreds of cloth trailing behind him. Maguire had no time to resist, nor will left to do so. He opened his mouth to say something in defense of his life, and Ronnie thrust his remaining arm, wound into a rope of linen, down Maguire's throat. Maguire choked on it, but Ronnie snaked on, past his protesting epiglottis, forging a rough way down his esophagus into Maguire's stomach. Maguire felt it there, a fullness that was like overeating, except that it squirmed in the middle of his body, raking his stomach wall and catching hold of the lining. It was all so quick, Maguire had no time to die of suffocation. In the event, he might have wished to go that way, horrid as it would have been. Instead, he felt Ronnie's hand convulse in his belly, digging deeper for a decent grip on his colon, on his duodenum. And when the hand had all it could hold, the fuckhead pulled out his arm.

The exit was swift, but for Maguire the moment would seemingly have no end. He doubled up as the disembowelling began, feeling his viscera surge up his throat, turning him inside out. His lights went out through his throat in a welter of fluids, coffee, blood, acid.

Ronnie pulled on the guts and hauled Maguire, his emptied torso collapsing on itself, towards the top of the stairs. Led by a length of his own entrails Maguire reached the top stair and pitched forward. Ronnie relinquished his hold and Maguire fell, head swathed in gut, to the bottom of the stairs, where his daughter still stood.

She seemed, by her expression, not the least alarmed; but then Ronnie knew children could deceive so easily.

The job completed, he began to totter down the stairs, uncoiling his arm, and shaking his head as he tried to recover a smidgen of human appearance. The effort worked. By the time he reached the child at the bottom of the stairs he was able to offer her something very like a human touch. She didn't respond, and all he could do was leave and hope that in time she'd come to forget.

Once he'd gone. Tracy went upstairs to find her mother. Racquel was unresponsive to her questions, as was the man on the carpet by the window. But there was something about him that fascinated her. A fat, red snake pressing out from his trousers. It made her laugh, it was such a silly little thing.

The girl was still laughing when Wall of the Yard appeared, late as usual. Though viewing the death dances the house had jumped to he was, on the whole, glad he'd been a late arrival at that particular party.

In the confessional of St. Mary Magdalene's the shroud of Ronnie Glass was now corrupted beyond recognition. He had very little feeling left in him, just the desire, so strong he knew he couldn't resist for very much longer, to let go of this wounded body. It had served him well; he had no complaints to make of it. But now he was out of breath. He could animate the inanimate no longer.

He wanted to confess though, wanted to confess so very badly. To tell the Father, to tell the Son, to tell the Holy Ghost what sins he'd performed, dreamt, longed for. There was only one thing for it: if Father Rooney wouldn't come to him then he'd go to Father Rooney.

He opened the door of the Confessional. The church was almost empty. It was evening now, he guessed, and who had the time for the lighting of candles when there was food to be cooked, love to be bought, life to be had? Only a Greek florist, praying in the aisle for his sons to be acquitted, saw the shroud stagger from the Confessional towards the door of the Vestry. It looked like some damn-fool adolescent with a filthy sheet slung over his head. The florist hated that kind of Godless behavior—look where it had got his children—he wanted to beat the kid around a bit, and teach him not to play silly beggars in the House of the Lord.

"Hey, you!" he said, too loudly.

The shroud turned to look at the florist, its eyes like two holes pressed in warm dough. The face of the ghost was so woebegone it froze the words on the florist's lips.

Ronnie tried the handle of the Vestry door. The rattling got him nowhere. The door was locked.

From inside, a breathless voice said:

"Who is it?" It was Father Rooney speaking.

Ronnie tried to reply, but no words would come. All he

could do was rattle, like any worthy ghost.

"Who is it?" asked the good Father again, a little impa-
tiently.

Confess me, Ronnie wanted to say, confess me, for I have
sinned.

The door stayed shut. Inside, Father Rooney was busy. He
was taking photographs for his private collection; his subject a
favorite lady of his by the name of Natalie. A daughter of vice
somebody had told him, but he couldn't believe that. She was
too obliging, too cherubic, and she wound a rosary around her
pert bosom as though she was barely out of a convent.

The jiggling of the handle had stopped now. Good, thought
Father Rooney. They'd come back, whoever they were. Noth-
ing was that urgent. Father Rooney grinned at the woman.
Natalie's lips pouted back.

In the church Ronnie hauled himself to the altar, and genu-
flected.

Three rows back the florist rose from his prayers, incensed
by this desecration. The boy was obviously drunk, the way he
was reeling, the man wasn't about to be frightened by a
tuppenny-colored deathmask. Cursing the desecrator in ripe
Greek, he snatched at the ghost as it knelt in front of the altar.

There was nothing under the sheet: nothing at all.

The florist felt the living cloth twitch in his hand, and
dropped it with a tiny cry. Then he backed off down the aisle,
crossing himself back and forth, back and forth, like a demented widow. A few yards from the door of the church he
turned tail and ran.

The shroud lay where the florist had dropped it. Ronnie,
lingering in the creases, looked up from the crumpled heap at
the splendor of the altar. It was radiant, even in the gloom of
the candlelit interior, and moved by its beauty, he was content
to put the illusion behind him. Unconfessed, but unfearful of
judgment, his spirit crept away.

After an hour or so Father Rooney unbolted the Vestry,
escorted the chaste Natalie out of the church, and locked the
front door. He peered into the Confessional on his way back,
to check for hiding children. Empty, the entire church was
empty. St. Mary Magdalene was a forgotten woman.

As he meandered, whistling, back to the Vestry he caught sight of Ronnie Glass' shroud. It lay sprawled on the altar steps, a forlorn pile of shabby cloth. Ideal, he thought, picking it up. There were some indiscreet stains on the Vestry floor. Just the job to wipe them up.

He sniffed the cloth, he loved to sniff. It smelt of a thousand things. Ether, sweat, dogs, entrails, blood, disinfectant, empty rooms, broken hearts, flowers and loss. Fascinating. This was the thrill of the Parish of Soho, he thought. Something new every day. Mysteries on the doorstep, on the altarstep. Crimes so numerous they would need an ocean of Holy Water to wash them out. Vice for sale on every corner, if you knew where to look.

He tucked the shroud under his arm.

"I bet you've got a tale to tell," he said, snuffing out the votive candles with fingers too hot to feel the flame.

SCAPE-GOATS

It wasn't a real island the tide had carried us on to, it was a lifeless mound of stones. Calling a hunch backed shit pile like this an island is flattery. Islands are oases in the sea: green and abundant. This is a forsaken place: no seals in the water around it, no birds in the air above it. I can think of no use for a place like this, except that you could say of it: I saw the heart of nothing, and survived.

"It's not on any of the charts," said Ray, poring over the map of the Inner Hebrides, his nail at the spot where he'd calculated that we should be. It was, as he'd said, an empty space on the map, just pale blue sea without the merest speck to sign the existence of this rock. It wasn't just the seals and the birds that ignored it then, the chart makers had too. There were one or two arrows in the vicinity of Ray's finger, marking the currents that should have been taking us north: tiny red darts on a paper ocean. The rest, like the world outside, was deserted.

Jonathan was jubilant of course, once he discovered that the place wasn't even to be found on the map; he seemed to feel instantly exonerated. The blame for our being here wasn't his any longer, it was the map makers': he wasn't going to be held responsible for our being beached if the mound wasn't even marked on the charts. The apologetic expression he'd worn since our unscheduled arrival was replaced with a look of self-satisfaction.

"You can't avoid a place that doesn't exist, can you?" he crowed. "I mean, can you?"

"You could have used the eyes God gave you," Ray flung back at him; but Jonathan wasn't about to be cowed by reasonable criticism.

"It was so sudden, Raymond," he said. "I mean, in this mist I didn't have a chance. It was on top of us before I knew it."

It had been sudden, no two ways about that. I'd been in the galley preparing breakfast, which had become my responsibility since neither Angela nor Jonathan showed any enthusiasm for the task, when the hull of the "Emmanuelle" grated on shingle, then ploughed her way, juddering, up on to the stony beach. There was a moment's silence: then the shouting began. I climbed up out of the galley to find Jonathan standing on deck, grinning sheepishly and waving his arms around to semaphore his innocence.

"Before you ask," he said, "I don't know how it happened. One minute we were just coasting along—"

"Oh Jesus Christ all-fucking Mighty," Ray was clambering out of the cabin, hauling a pair of jeans on as he did so, and looking much the worse for a night in a bunk with Angela. I'd had the questionable honor of listening to her orgasms all night; she was certainly demanding. Jonathan began his defense speech again from the beginning: "Before you ask—", but Ray silenced him with a few choice insults. I retreated into the confines of the galley while the argument raged on deck. It gave me no small satisfaction to hear Jonathan slanged; I even hoped Ray would lose his cool enough to bloody that perfect hook nose.

The galley was a slop bucket. The breakfast I'd been preparing was all over the floor and I left it there, the yolks of the eggs, the gammon and the french toasts all congealing in pools of split fat. It was Jonathan's fault; let him clear it up. I poured myself a glass of grapefruit juice, waited until the recriminations died down, and went back up.

It was barely two hours after dawn, and the mist that had shrouded this island from Jonathan's view still covered the sun. If today was anything like the week that we'd had so far, by noon the deck would be too hot to step on barefoot, but now, with the mist still thick, I felt cold wearing just the bottom of my bikini. It didn't matter much, sailing amongst the islands, what you wore. There was no one to see you. I'd got the best all over tan I'd ever had. But this morning the chill drove me back below to find a sweater. There was no wind: the cold was coming up out of the sea. It's still night down there, I thought, just a few yards off the beach; limitless night.

I pulled on a sweater, and went back on deck. The maps were out, and Ray was bending over them. His bare back was peeling from an excess of sun, and I could see the bald patch he tried to hide in his dirty yellow curls. Jonathan was staring at the beach and stroking his nose.

"Christ, what a place," I said.

He glanced at me, trying a smile. He had this illusion, poor Jonathan, that his face could charm a tortoise out of its shell, and to be fair to him there were a few women who melted if he so much as looked at them. I wasn't one of them, and it irritated him. I'd always thought his Jewish good looks too bland to be beautiful. My indifference was a red rag to him.

A voice, sleepy and pouting, drifted up from below deck. Our Lady of the Bunk was awake at last: time to make her late entrance, coyly wrapping a towel around her nakedness as she emerged. Her face was puffed up with too much red wine, and her hair needed a comb through it. Still she turned on the radiance, eyes wide, Shirley Temple with cleavage.

"What's happening, Ray? Where are we?"

Ray didn't look up from his computations, which earned him a frown.

"We've got a bloody awful navigator, that's all," he said.

"I don't even know what happened," Jonathan protested, clearly hoping for a show of sympathy from Angela. None was forthcoming.

"But where are we?" she asked again.

"Good morning, Angela," I said; I too was ignored.

"Is it an island?" she said.

"Of course it's an island: I just don't know which one yet," Ray replied.

"Perhaps it's Barra," she suggested.

Ray pulled a face. "We're nowhere near Barra," he said. "If you'll just let me retrace our steps—"

Retrace our steps, in the sea? Just Ray's Jesus fixation, I thought, looking back at the beach. It was impossible to guess how big the place was, the mist erased the landscape after a hundred yards. Perhaps somewhere in that grey wall there was human habitation.

Ray, having located the blank spot on the map where we were supposedly stranded, climbed down on to the beach and took a critical look at the bow. More to be out of Angela's way than anything else I climbed down to join him. The round stones of the beach were cold and slippery on the bare soles of my feet. Ray smoothed his palm down the side of the "Emmanuelle," almost a caress, then crouched to look at the damage to the bow.

"I don't think we're holed," he said, "but I can't be sure."

"We'll float off come high tide," said Jonathan, posing on the bow, hands on hips, "no sweat," he winked at me, "no sweat at all."

"Will we shit float off!," Ray snapped. "Take a look for yourself."

"Then we'll get some help to haul us off." Jonathan's confidence was unscathed.

"And you can damn well fetch someone, you asshole."

"Sure, why not? Give it an hour or so for the fog to shift and I'll take a walk, find some help."

He sauntered away.

"I'll put on some coffee," Angela volunteered.

Knowing her, that'd take an hour to brew. There was time for a stroll.

I started along the beach.

"Don't go too far, love," Ray called.

"No."

Love, he said. Easy word; he meant nothing by it.

The sun was warmer now, and as I walked I stripped off the sweater. My bare breasts were already brown as two nuts, and, I thought, about as big. Still, you can't have everything. At least I'd got two neurons in my head to rub together, which was more than could be said for Angela; she had tits like melons and a brain that'd shame a mule.

The sun still wasn't getting through the mist properly. It was filtering down on the island fitfully, and its light flattened everything out, draining the place of color or weight, reducing the sea and the rocks and the rubbish on the beach to one bleached-out grey, the color of over boiled meat.

After only a hundred yards something about the place began to depress me, so I turned back. On my right tiny, lisping waves crept up to the shore and collapsed with a weary slopping sound on the stones. No majestic rollers here: just the rhythmical slop, slop, slop of an exhausted tide.

I hated the place already.

Back at the boat, Ray was trying the radio, but for some reason all he could get was a blanket of white noise on every frequency. He cursed it awhile, then gave up. After half an hour, breakfast was served, though we had to make do with sardines, tinned mushrooms and the remains of the French toast. Angela served this feast with her usual aplomb, looking as though she was performing a second miracle with loaves and fishes. It was all but impossible to enjoy the food anyway; the air seemed to drain all the taste away.

"Funny isn't it—" began Jonathan.

"Hilarious," said Ray.

"—there's no fog horns. Mist, but no horns. Not even the sound of a motor; weird."

He was right. Total silence wrapped us up, a damp and smothering hush. Except for the apologetic slop of the waves and the sound of our voices, we might as well have been deaf.

I sat at the stern and looked into the empty sea. It was still grey, but the sun was beginning to strike other colors in it now: a somber green, and, deeper, a hint of blue-purple. Below the boat I could see strands of kelp and Maiden's Hair, toys to the tide, swaying. It looked inviting: and anything was better than the sour atmosphere on the "Emmanuelle".

"I'm going for a swim," I said.

"I wouldn't, love," Ray replied.

"Why not?"

"The current that threw us up here must be pretty strong, you don't want to get caught in it."

"But the tide's still coming in: I'd only be swept back to the beach."

"You don't know what cross currents there are out there.

Whirlpools even: they're quite common. Suck you down in a flash.''

I looked out to sea again. It looked harmless enough, but then I'd read that these were treacherous waters, and thought better of it.

Angela had started a little sulking session because nobody had finished her immaculately prepared breakfast. Ray was playing up to it. He loved babying her, letting her play damn stupid games. It made me sick.

I went below to do the washing up, tossing the slops out of the porthole into the sea. They didn't sink immediately. They floated in an oily patch, half-eaten mushrooms and slivers of sardines bobbing around on the surface, as though someone had thrown up on the sea. Food for crabs, if any self-respecting crab condescended to live here.

Jonathan joined me in the galley, obviously still feeling a little foolish, despite the bravado. He stood in the doorway, trying to catch my eye, while I pumped up some cold water into the bowl and half heartedly rinsed the greasy plastic plates. All he wanted was to be told I didn't think this was his fault, and yes, of course he was a kosher Adonis. I said nothing.

"Do you mind if I lend a hand?" he said.

"There's not really room for two," I told him, trying not to sound too dismissive. He flinched nevertheless: this whole episode had punctured his self-esteem more badly than I'd realized, despite his strutting around.

"Look," I said gently, "why don't you go back on deck: take in the sun before it gets too hot?"

"I feel like a shit," he said.

"It was an accident."

"An utter shit."

"Like you said, we'll float off with the tide."

He moved out of the doorway and down into the galley; his proximity made me feel almost claustrophobic. His body was too large for the space: too tanned, too assertive.

"I said there wasn't any room, Jonathan."

He put his hand on the back of my neck, and instead of shrugging it off I let it stay there, gently massaging the muscles. I wanted to tell him to leave me alone, but the lassitude of

the place seemed to have got into my system. His other hand
was palm down on my belly, moving up to my breast. I was indifferent to these ministrations: if he wanted this he could
have it.

Above deck Angela was gasping in the middle of a giggling
fit, almost choking on her hysteria. I could see her in my
mind's eye, throwing back her head, shaking her hair loose.
Jonathan had unbuttoned his shorts, and had let them drop.
The gift of his foreskin to God had been neatly made; his erection was so hygienic in its enthusiasm it seemed incapable of
the least harm. I let his mouth stick to mine, let his tongue ex-
plore my gums, insistent as a dentist's finger. He slid my bikini
down far enough to get access, fumbled to position himself,
then pressed in.

Behind him, the stair creaked, and I looked over his
shoulder in time to glimpse Ray, bending at the hatch and staring down at Jonathan's buttocks and at the tangle of our
arms. Did he see, I wondered, that I felt nothing; did he
understand that I did this dispassionately, and could only have
felt a twinge of desire if I substituted his head, his back, his
cock for Jonathan's? Soundlessly, he withdrew from the stair-
way; a moment passed, in which Jonathan said he loved me,
then I heard Angela's laughter begin again as Ray described
what he'd just witnessed. Let the bitch think whatever she
pleased: I didn't care.

Jonathan was still working at me with deliberate but
uninspired strokes, a frown on his face like that of a school-
boy trying to solve some impossible equation. Discharge came
without warning, signalled only by a tightening of his hold
on my shoulders, and a deepening of his frown. His thrusts
slowed and stopped; his eyes found mine for a flustered moment. I wanted to kiss him, but he'd lost all interest. He
withdrew still hard, wincing. "I'm always sensitive when I've
come," he murmured, hauling his shorts up. "Was it good for
you?"

I nodded. It was laughable; the whole thing was laughable.
Stuck in the middle of nowhere with this little boy of twenty-
six, and Angela, and a man who didn't care if I lived or died.
But then perhaps neither did I. I thought, for no reason, of the

slops on the sea, bobbing around, waiting for the next wave to catch them.

Jonathan had already retreated up the stairs. I boiled up some coffee, standing staring out of the porthole and feeling his come dry to a corrugated pearliness on the inside of my thigh.

Ray and Angela had gone by the time I'd brewed the coffee, off for a walk on the island apparently, looking for help.

Jonathan was sitting in my place at the stern, gazing out at the mist. More to break the silence than anything I said:

"I think it's lifted a bit."

"Has it?"

I put a mug of black coffee beside him.

"Thanks."

"Where are the others?"

"Exploring."

He looked round at me, confusion in his eyes. "I still feel like a shit."

I noticed the bottle of gin on the deck beside him.

"Bit early for drinking, isn't it?"

"Want some?"

"It's not even eleven."

"Who cares?"

He pointed out to sea. "Follow my finger," he said.

I leaned over his shoulder and did as he asked.

"No, you're not looking at the right place. Follow my finger—see it?"

"Nothing."

"At the edge of the mist. It appears and disappears. There! Again!"

I did see something in the water, twenty or thirty yards from the "Emmanuelle's" stern. Brown-colored, wrinkled, turning over.

"It's a seal," I said.

"I don't think so."

"The sun's warming up the sea. They're probably coming in to bask in the shallows."

"It doesn't look like a seal. It rolls in a funny way—"

"Maybe a piece of flotsam—"

"Could be."

He swigged deeply from the bottle.

"Leave some for tonight."

"Yes, mother."

We sat in silence for a few minutes. Just the waves on the beach. Slop. Slop. Slop.

Once in a while the seal, or whatever it was, broke surface, rolled, and disappeared again.

Another hour, I thought, and the tide will begin to turn. Float us off this little afterthought of creation.

"Hey!" Angela's voice, from a distance. "Hey, you guys!"

You guys she called us.

Jonathan stood up, hand up to his face against the glare of sunlit rock. It was much brighter now: and getting hotter all the time.

"She's waving to us," he said, disinterested.

"Let her wave."

"You guys!" she screeched, her arms waving. Jonathan cupped his hands around his mouth and bawled a reply:

"What do you want?"

"Come and see," she replied.

"She wants us to come and see."

"I heard."

"Come on," he said, "nothing to lose."

I didn't want to move, but he hauled me up by the arm. It wasn't worth arguing. His breath was inflammable.

It was difficult making our way up the beach. The stones were not wet with sea water, but covered in a slick film of grey-green algae, like sweat on a skull.

Jonathan was having even more difficulty getting across the beach than I was. Twice he lost his balance and fell heavily on his backside, cursing. The seat of his shorts was soon a filthy olive color, and there was a tear where his buttocks showed.

I was no ballerina, but I managed to make it, step by slow step, trying to avoid the large rocks so that if I slipped I wouldn't have far to fall.

Every few yards we'd have to negotiate a line of stinking seaweed. I was able to jump them with reasonable elegance but Jonathan, pissed and uncertain of his balance, ploughed through them, his naked feet completely buried in the stuff. It wasn't just kelp: there was the usual detritus washed up on any beach: the broken bottles, the rusting Coke cans, the scum-stained cork, globs of tar, fragments of crabs, pale yellow durex. And crawling over these stinking piles of dross were inch-long, fat-eyed blue flies. Hundreds of them, clambering over the shit, and over each other, buzzing to be alive, and alive to be buzzing.

It was the first life we'd seen.

I was doing my best not to fall flat on my face as I stepped across one of these lines of seaweed, when a little avalanche of pebbles began off to my left. Three, four, five stones were skipping over each other towards the sea, and setting another dozen stones moving as they jumped.

There was no visible cause for the effect.

Jonathan didn't even bother to look up; he was having too much trouble staying vertical.

The avalanche stopped: run out of energy. Then another: this time between us and the sea. Skipping stones: bigger this time than the last, and gaining more height as they leapt.

The sequence was longer than before: it knocked stone into stone until a few pebbles actually reached the sea at the end of the dance.

Plop.

Dead noise.

Plop. Plop.

Ray appeared from behind one of the big boulders at the height of the beach, beaming like a loon.

"There's life on Mars," he yelled and ducked back the way he'd come.

A few more perilous moments and we reached him, the sweat sticking our hair to our foreheads like caps.

Jonathan looked a little sick.

"What's the big deal?" he demanded.

"Look what we've found," said Ray, and led the way beyond the boulders.

The first shock.

Once we got to the height of the beach we were looking down on to the other side of the island. There was more of the same drab beach, and then sea. No inhabitants, no boats, no sign of human existence. The whole place couldn't have been more than half a mile across: barely the back of a whale.

But there was some life here; that was the second shock.

In the sheltering ring of the large, bald, boulders, which crowned the island was a fenced-in compound. The posts were rotting in the salt air, but a tangle of rusted barbed-wire had been wound around and between them to form a primitive pen. Inside the pen there was a patch of coarse grass, and on this pitiful lawn stood three sheep. And Angela.

She was standing in the penal colony, stroking one of the inmates and cooing in its blank face.

"Sheep," she said, triumphantly.

Jonathan was there before me with his snapped remark: "So what?"

"Well it's strange, isn't it?" said Ray. "Three sheep in the middle of a little place like this?"

"They don't look well to me," said Angela.

She was right. The animals were the worse for their exposure to the elements; their eyes were gummy with matter, and their fleeces hung off their hides in knotted clumps, exposing panting flanks. One of them had collapsed against the barbed-wire, and seemed unable to right itself again, either too depleted or too sick.

"It's cruel," said Angela.

I had to agree: it seemed positively sadistic, locking up these creatures without more than a few blades of grass to chew on, and a battered tin bath of stagnant water, to quench their thirst.

"Odd isn't is?" said Ray.

"I've cut my foot." Jonathan was squatting on the top of one of the flatter boulders, peering at the underside of his right foot.

"There's glass on the beach," I said, exchanging a vacant stare with one of the sheep.

"They're so deadpan," said Ray. "Nature's straight men."

Curiously, they didn't look so unhappy with their condition, their stares were philosophical. Their eyes said: I'm just a sheep, I don't expect you to like me, care for me, preserve me, except for your stomach's sake. There were no angry baas, no stamping of a frustrated hoof.

Just three grey sheep, waiting to die.

Ray had lost interest in the business. He was wandering back down the beach, kicking a can ahead of him. It rattled and skipped, reminding me of the stones.

"We should let them free," said Angela.

I ignored her; what was freedom in a place like this? She persisted, "Don't you think we should?"

"No."

"They'll die."

"Somebody put them here for a reason."

"But they'll *die.*"

"They'll die on the beach if we let them out. There's no food for them."

"We'll feed them."

"French toast and gin," suggested Jonathan, picking a sliver of glass from his sole.

"We can't just leave them."

"It's not our business," I said. It was all getting boring. Three sheep. Who cared if they lived or—

I'd thought that about myself an hour earlier. We had something in common, the sheep and I.

My head was aching.

"They'll die," whined Angela, for the third time.

"You're a stupid bitch," Jonathan told her. The remark was made without malice: he said it calmly, as a statement of plain fact.

I couldn't help grinning.

"What?" She looked as though she'd been bitten.

"Stupid bitch," he said again. "B-I-T-C-H."

Angela flushed with anger and embarrassment, and turned on him. "You got us stuck here," she said, lip curling.

The inevitable accusation. Tears in her eyes. Stung by his words.

"I did it deliberately," he said, spitting on his fingers and rubbing saliva into the cut. "I wanted to see if we could leave you here."

"You're drunk."

"And you're stupid. But I'll be sober in the morning."

The old lines still made their mark.

Outstripped, Angela started down the beach after Ray, trying to hold back her tears until she was out of sight. I almost felt some sympathy for her. She was, when it came down to verbal fisticuffs, easy meat.

"You're a bastard when you want to be," I told Jonathan; he just looked at me, glassy-eyed.

"Better be friends. Then I won't be a bastard to you."

"You don't scare me."

"I know."

The mutton was staring at me again. I stared back.

"Fucking sheep," he said.

"They can't help it."

"If they had any decency, they'd slit their ugly fucking throats."

"I'm going back to the boat."

"Ugly fuckers."

"Coming?"

He took hold of my hand: fast, tight, and held it in his hand like he'd never let go. Eyes on me suddenly.

"Don't go."

"It's too hot up here."

"Stay. The stone's nice and warm. Lie down. They won't interrupt us this time."

"You knew?" I said.

"You mean Ray? Of course I knew. I thought we put on quite a little performance."

He drew me close, hand over hand up my arm, like he was hauling in a rope. The smell of him brought back the galley, his frown, his muttered profession ("Love you"), the quiet retreat.

Déja vu.

Still, what was there to do on a day like this but go round in the same dreary circle, like the sheep in the pen? Round and round. Breathe, sex, eat, shit.

The gin had gone to his groin. He tried his best but he hadn't got a hope. It was like trying to thread spaghetti.

Exasperated, he rolled off me.

"Fuck. Fuck. Fuck."

Senseless word, once it was repeated, it had lost all its meaning, like everything else. Signifying nothing.

"It doesn't matter," I said.

"Fuck off."

"It really doesn't."

He didn't look at me, just stared down at his cock. If he'd had a knife in his hand at that moment, I think he'd have cut it off and laid it on the warm rock, a shrine to sterility.

I left him studying himself, and walked back to the "Emmanuelle". Something odd struck me as I went, something I hadn't noticed before. The blue flies, instead of jumping ahead of me as I approached, just let themselves be trodden on. Positively lethargic; or suicidal. They sat on the hot stones and popped under my soles, their gaudy little lives going out like so many lights.

The mist was disappearing at last, and as the air warmed up, the island unveiled its next disgusting trick: the smell. The fragrance was as wholesome as a roomful of rotting peaches, thick and sickly. It came in through the pores as well as the nostrils, like a syrup. And under the sweetness, something else, rather less pleasant than peaches, fresh or rotten. A smell like an open drain clogged with old meat: like the gutters of a slaughter house, caked with suet and black blood. It was the seaweed I assumed, although I'd never smelt anything to match the stench on any other beach.

I was halfway back to the "Emmanuelle", holding my nose as I stepped over the bands of rotting weed, when I heard the noise of a little murder behind me. Jonathan's whoops of satanic glee almost drowned the pathetic voice of the sheep as it was killed, but I knew instinctively what the drunken bastard had done.

I turned back, my heel pivotting on the slime. It was almost certainly too late to save one of the beasts, but maybe I could prevent him massacring the other two. I couldn't see the pen; it was hidden behind the boulders, but I could hear Jonathan's triumphant yells, and the thud, thud of his strokes. I knew what I'd see before it came into sight.

The grey-green lawn had turned red. Jonathan was in the pen with the sheep. The two survivors were charging back and forth in a rhythmical trot of panic, baaing in terror, while Jonathan stood over the third sheep, erect now. The victim had partially collapsed, its sticklike front legs buckled beneath it, its back legs rigid with approaching death. Its bulk shud-

dered with nervous spasms, and its eyes showed more white
than brown. The top of its skull had been almost entirely
dashed to pieces, and the grey hash of its brain exposed,
punctured by shards of its own bone, and pulped by the large
round stone that Jonathan was still wielding. Even as I
watched he brought the weapon down once more onto the
sheep's brain pan. Globs of tissue flew off in every direction,
speckling me with hot matter and blood. Jonathan looked like
some nightmare lunatic (which for that moment, I suppose, he
was). His naked body, so recently white, was stained as a
butcher's apron after a hard day's hammering at the abattoir.
His face was more sheep's gore than Jonathan—

The animal itself was dead. Its pathetic complaints had
ceased completely. It keeled over, rather comically, like a car-
toon character, one of its ears snagging the wire. Jonathan
watched it fall: his face a grin under the blood. Oh that grin: it
served so many purposes. Wasn't that the same smile he
charmed women with? The same grin that spoke lechery and
love? Now, at last, it was put to its true purpose: the gawping
smile of the satisfied savage, standing over his prey with a
stone in one hand and his manhood in the other.

Then, slowly, the smile decayed, as his senses returned.

"Jesus," he said, and from his abdomen a wave of revul-
sion climbed up his body. I could see it quite clearly; the way
his gut rolled as a throb of nausea threw his head forward,
pitching half-digested gin and toast over the grass.

I didn't move. I didn't want to comfort him, calm him, con-
sole him—he was simply beyond my help.

I turned away.

"Frankie," he said through a throat of bile.

I couldn't bring myself to look at him. There was nothing to
be done for the sheep, it was dead and gone; all I wanted to do
was run away from the little ring of stones, and put the sight
out of my head.

"Frankie."

I began to walk, as fast as I was able over such tricky ter-
rain, back down towards the beach and the relative sanity of
the "Emmanuelle".

The smell was stronger now: coming up out of the ground
towards my face in filthy waves.

Horrible island. Vile, stinking, insane island.

All I thought was hate as I stumbled across the weed and the filth. The "Emmanuelle" wasn't far off—

Then, a little pattering of pebbles like before. I stopped, balancing uneasily on the sleek dome of a stone, and looked to my left, where even now one of the pebbles was rolling to a halt. As it stopped another, larger pebble, fully six inches across, seemed to move spontaneously from its resting place, and roll down the beach, striking its neighbors and beginning another exodus towards the sea. I frowned: the frown made my head buzz.

Was there some sort of animal—a crab maybe—under the beach, moving the stones? Or was it the heat that in some way twitched them into life?

Again: a bigger stone—

I walked on, while behind the rattle and patter continued, one little sequence coming close upon another, to make an almost seamless percussion.

I began, without real focus or explanation, to be afraid.

Angela and Ray were sunning themselves on the deck of the "Emmanuelle".

"Another couple of hours before we can start to get the bitch off her backside," he said, squinting as he looked up at me.

I thought he meant Angela at first, then realized he was talking about floating the boat out to sea again.

"May as well get some sun." he smiled wanly at me.

"Yeah."

Angela was either asleep or ignoring me. Whichever, it suited me fine.

I slumped down on the sun deck at Ray's feet and let the sun soak into me. The specks of blood had dried on my skin, like tiny scabs. I picked them off idly, and listened to the noise of the stones, and the slop of the sea.

Behind me, pages were being turned. I glanced round. Ray, never able to lie still for very long, was flicking through a library book on the Hebrides he'd brought from home.

I looked back at the sun. My mother always said it burned a hole in the back of your eye, to look straight into the sun, but it was hot and alive up there; I wanted to look into its face. There was a chill in me—I don't know where it had come from—a chill in my gut and in between my legs—that wouldn't go away. Maybe I would have to burn it away by looking at the sun.

Some way along the beach I glimpsed Jonathan, tiptoeing down towards the sea. From that distance the mixture of blood and white skin made him look like some pie bald freak. He'd stripped off his shorts and he was crouching at the sea's edge to wash off the sheep.

Then, Ray's voice, very quietly: "Oh God," he said, in such an understated way that I knew the news couldn't be brilliant.

"What is it?"

"I've found out where we are."

"Good."

"No, not good."

"Why? What's wrong?" I sat upright, turning to him.

"It's here, in the book. There's a paragraph on this place."

Angela opened one eye. "Well?" she said.

"It's not just an island. It's a burial mound."

The chill in between my legs fed upon itself, and grew gross. The sun wasn't hot enough to warm me that deep, where I should be hottest.

I looked away from Ray along the beach again. Jonathan was still washing, splashing water up on to his chest. The shadows of the stones suddenly seemed very black and heavy, their edges pressed down on the upturned faces of—

Seeing me looking his way Jonathan waved.

Can it be there are corpses under those stones? Buried face up to the sun, like holiday makers laid out on a Blackpool beach?

The world is monochrome. Sun and shadow. The white tops of stones and their black underbellies. Life on top, death underneath.

"Burial?" said Angela. "What sort of burial?"

"War dead," Ray answered.

Angela: "What, you mean Vikings or something?"

"World War I, World War II. Soldiers from torpedoed troopships, sailors washed up. Brought down here by the Gulf Stream; apparently the current funnels them through the straits and washes them up on the beaches of the islands around here.''

"Washes them up?" said Angela.

"That's what it says."

"Not any longer though."

"I'm sure the occasional fisherman gets buried here still," Ray replied.

Jonathan had stood up, staring out to sea, the blood off his body. His hand shaded his eyes as he looked out over the blue-grey water, and I followed his gaze as I had followed his finger. A hundred yards out that seal, or whale, or whatever it was, had returned, lolling in the water. Sometimes, as it turned, it threw up a fin, like a swimmer's arm, beckoning.

"How many people were buried?" asked Angela, non-chalantly. She seemed completely unperturbed by the fact that we were sitting on a grave.

"Hundreds probably."

"Hundreds?"

"It just says 'many dead', in the book."

"And do they put them in coffins?"

"How should I know?"

What else could it be, this Godforsaken mound—but a cemetery? I looked at the island with new eyes, as though I'd just recognized it for what it was. Now I had a reason to despise its humpy back, its sordid beach, the smell of peaches.

"I wonder if they buried them all over," mused Angela, "or just at the top of the hill, where we found the sheep? Probably just at the top; out of the way of the water."

Yes, they'd probably had too much of water: their poor green faces picked by fish, their uniforms rotted, their dog tags encrusted with algae. What deaths; and worse, what journeys after death, in squads of fellow corpses, along the Gulf Stream to this bleak landfall. I saw them, in my mind's eye, the bodies of the soldiers, subject to every whim of the tide, borne backwards and forwards in a slush of rollers until a casual limb snagged on a rock, and the sea lost possession of them. With each receding wave uncovered; sodden and jellied brine, spat out by the sea to stink a while and be stripped by gulls.

I had a sudden, morbid desire to walk on the beach again,

armed with this knowledge, kicking over the pebbles in the hope of turning up a bone or two.

As the thought formed, my body made the decision for me. I was standing: I was climbing off the "Emmanuelle".

"Where are you off to?" said Angela.

"Jonathan," I murmured, and set foot on the mound.

The stench was clearer now: that was the accrued odor of the dead. Maybe drowned men got buried here still, as Ray had suggested, slotted under the pile of stones. The unwary yachtsman, the careless swimmer, their faces wiped off with water. At the feet the beach flies were less sluggish than they'd been: instead of waiting to be killed they jumped and buzzed ahead of my steps, with a new enthusiasm for life.

Jonathan was not to be seen. His shorts were still on the stones at the water's edge, but he'd disappeared. I looked out to sea: nothing: no bobbing head: no lolling, beckoning something.

I called his name.

My voice seemed to excite the files, they rose in seething clouds. Jonathan didn't reply.

I began to walk along the margin of the sea, my feet sometimes caught by an idle wave, as often as not left untouched. I realized I hadn't told Angela and Ray about the dead sheep. Maybe that was a secret between us four. Jonathan, myself, and the two survivors in the pen.

Then I saw him: a few yards ahead—his chest white, wide and clean, every speck of blood washed off. A secret it is then," I thought.

"Where have you been?" I called to him.

"Walking it off,"he called back.

"What off?"

"Too much gin," he grinned.

I returned the smile, spontaneously; he'd said he loved me in the galley; that counted for something.

Behind him, a rattle of skipping stones. He was no more than ten yards from me now, shamelessly naked as he walked; his gait was sober.

The rattle of stones suddenly seemed rhythmical. It was no longer a random series of notes as one pebble struck another—it was a beat, a sequence of repeated sounds, a tick-tap pulse.

No accident: intention.

Not chance: purpose.

Not stone: thought. Behind stone, with stone, carrying stone—

Jonathan, now close, was bright. His skin was almost luminous with sun on it, thrown into relief by the darkness behind him.

Wait—

—What darkness?

The stone mounted the air like a bird, defying gravity. A blank black stone, disengaged from the earth. It was the size of a baby: a whistling baby, and it grew behind Jonathan's head as it shimmered down the air towards him.

The beach had been flexing its muscles, tossing small pebbles down to the sea, all the time strengthening its will to raise this boulder off the ground and fling it at Jonathan.

It swelled behind him, murderous in its intention, but my throat had no sound to make worthy of my fright.

Was he deaf? His grin broke open again; he thought the horror on my face was a jibe at his nakedness, I realized. He doesn't understand—

The stone sheered off the top of his head, from the middle of his nose upwards, leaving his mouth still wide, his tongue rooted in blood, and flinging the rest of his beauty towards me in a cloud of wet red dust. The upper part of his head was split on to the face of the stone, its expression intact as it swooped towards me. I half fell, and it screamed past me, veering off towards the sea. Once over the water the assassin seemed to lose its will somehow, and faltered in the air before plunging into the waves.

At my feet, blood. A trail that led to where Jonathan's body lay, the open edge of his head towards me, its machinery plain for the sky to see.

I was still not screaming, though for sanity's sake I had to unleash the terror suffocating me. Somebody must hear me, hold me, take me away and explain to me, before the skipping pebbles found their rhythm again. Or worse, before the minds below the beach, unsatisfied with murder by proxy, rolled away their grave stones and rose to kiss me themselves.

But the scream would not come.

All I could hear was the patter of stones to my right and left. They intend to kill us all for invading their sacred ground. Stoned to death, like heretics.

Then, a voice.

"For Christ's sake—"

A man's voice; but not Ray's.

He seemed to have appeared from out of thin air: a short, broad man, standing at the sea's edge. In one hand a bucket and under his arm a bundle of coarsely cut hay. Food for the sheep, I thought, through a jumble of half-formed words. Food for sheep.

He stared at me, then down at Jonathan's body, his old eyes wild.

"What's gone on?" he said. The Gaelic accent was thick. "In the name of Christ what's gone on?"

I shook my head. It seemed loose on my neck, almost as though I might shake it off. Maybe I pointed to the sheep pen, maybe not. Whatever the reason he seemed to know what I was thinking, and began to climb the beach towards the crown of the island, dropping bucket and bundle as he went.

Half blind with confusion, I followed, but before I could reach the boulders he was out of their shadow again, his face suddenly shining with panic.

"Who did that?"

"Jonathan," I replied. I cast a hand towards the corpse, not daring to look back at him. The man cursed in Gaelic, and stumbled out of the shelter of the boulders.

"What have you done?" he yelled at me. "My Christ, what have you done? Killing their gifts."

"Just sheep," I said. In my head the instant of Jonathan's decapitation was playing over and over again, a loop of slaughter.

"They demand it, don't you see, or they rise—"

"Who rise?" I said, knowing. Seeing the stones shift.

"All of them. Put away without grief or mourning. But they've got the sea in them, in their heads—"

I knew what he was talking about: it was quite plain to me,

suddenly. The dead were here: as we knew. Under the stones. But they had the rhythm of the sea in them, and they wouldn't lie down. So to placate them, these sheep were tethered in a pen, to be offered up to their wills.

Did the dead eat mutton? No; it wasn't food they wanted. It was the gesture of recognition—as simple as that.

"Drowned," he was saying, "all drowned."

Then, the familiar patter began again, the drumming of stones, which grew, without warning, into an ear-splitting thunder, as though the entire beach was shifting.

And under the cacophony three other sounds: splashing, screaming and wholesale destruction.

I turned to see a wave of stones rising into the air on the other side of the island—

Again the terrible screams, wrung from a body that was being buffeted and broken.

They were after the "Emmanuelle". After Ray. I started to run in the direction of the boat, the beach rippling beneath my feet. Behind me, I could hear the boots of the sheep feeder on the stones. As we ran the noise of the assault became louder. Stones danced in the air like fat birds, blocking the sun, before plunging down to strike at some unseen target. Maybe the boat. Maybe flesh itself—

Angela's tormented screams had ceased.

I rounded the beachhead a few steps ahead of the sheep-feeder, and the "Emmanuelle" came into sight. It, and its human contents, were beyond all hope of salvation. The vessel was being bombarded by endless ranks of stones, all sizes and shapes; its hull was smashed, its windows, mast and deck shattered. Angela lay sprawled on the remains of the sun deck, quite obviously dead. The fury of the hail hadn't stopped however. The stones beat a tattoo on the remaining structure of the hull, and thrashed at the lifeless bulk of Angela's body, making it bob up and down as though a current were being passed through it.

Ray was nowhere to be seen.

I screamed then: and for a moment it seemed there was a lull in the thunder, a brief respite in the attack. Then it began again: wave after wave of pebbles and rocks rising off the beach and flinging themselves at their senseless targets. They would not be content, it seemed, until the "Emmanuelle" was reduced to flotsam and jetsam, and Angela's body was in small enough pieces to accommodate a shrimp's palate.

The sheepfeeder took hold of my arm in a grip so fierce it stopped the blood flowing to my hand.

"Come on," he said. I heard his voice but did nothing. I was waiting for Ray's face to appear—or to hear his voice calling my name. But there was nothing: just the barrage of the stones. He was dead in the ruins of the boat somewhere—smashed to smithereens.

The sheepfeeder was dragging me now, and I was following him back over the beach.

"The boat" he was saying, "we can get away in my boat—."

The idea of escape seemed ludicrous. The island had us on its back, we were its objects utterly.

But I followed, slipping and sliding over the sweaty rocks, ploughing through the tangle of seaweed, back the way we'd come.

On the other side of the island was his poor hope of life. A rowing boat, dragged up on the shingle: an inconsequential walnut shell of a boat.

Would we go to sea in that, like the three men in a sieve?

He dragged me, unresisting, towards our deliverance. With every step I became more certain that the beach would suddenly rise up and stone us to death. Maybe make a wall of itself, a tower even, when we were within a single step of safety. It could play any game it liked, any game at all. But then, maybe the dead didn't like games. Games are about gambles, and the dead had already lost. Maybe the dead act only with the arid certainty of mathematicians.

He half threw me into the boat, and began to push it out into the thick tide. No walls of stones rose to prevent our escape. No towers appeared, no slaughtering hail. Even the attack on the "Emmanuelle" had ceased.

Had they sated themselves on three victims? Or was it that the presence of the sheep feeder, an innocent, a servant of these willful dead, would protect me from their tantrums?

The rowing boat was off the shingle. We bobbed a little on the backs of a few limp waves until we were deep enough for the oars, and then we were pulling away from the shore and my savior was sitting opposite me, rowing for all he was worth, a dew of fresh sweat on his forehead, multiplying with every pull.

The beach receded; we were being set free. The sheep feeder seemed to relax a little. He gazed down at the swill of dirty water in the bottom of the boat and drew in half a dozen deep breaths; then he looked up at me, his wasted face drained of expression.

"One day, it had to happen—" he said, his voice low and heavy. "Somebody would spoil the way we lived. Break the rhythm."

It was almost soporific, the hauling of the oars, forward and back. I wanted to sleep, to wrap myself up in the tarpaulin I was sitting on, and forget. Behind us, the beach was a distant line. I couldn't see the "Emmanuelle."

"Where are we going?" I said.

"Back to Tiree," he replied. "We'll see what's to be done there. Find some way to make amends; to help them sleep soundly again."

"Do they eat the sheep?"

"What good is food to the dead? No. No, they have no need of mutton. They take the beasts as a gesture of remembrance."

Remembrance.

I nodded.

"It's our way of mourning them—"

He stopped rowing, too heartsick to finish his explanation, and too exhausted to do anything but let the tide carry us home. A blank moment passed.

Then the scratching.

A mouse noise, no more, a scrabbling at the underside of the boat like a man's nails tickling the planks to be let in. Not one man: many. The sound of their entreaties multiplied, the soft dragging of rotted cuticles across the wood.

In the boat, we didn't move, we didn't speak, we didn't believe. Even as we heard the worst—we didn't believe the worst.

A splash off to starboard; I turned and he was coming towards me, rigid in the water, borne up by unseen puppeteers

like a figure head. It was Ray; his body covered in killing
bruises and cuts: stoned to death then brought, like a gleeful
mascot, like proof of power, to spook us. It was almost as
though he were walking on water, his feet just hidden by the
swell, his arms hanging loosely by his side as he was hauled
towards the boat. I looked at his face: lacerated and broken.
One eye almost closed, the other smashed from its orbit.

Two yards from the boat, the puppeteers let him sink back
into the sea, where he disappeared in a swirl of pink water.

"Your companion?" said the sheep feeder.

I nodded. He must have fallen into the sea from the stern of
the "Emmanuelle". Now he was like them, a drowned man.
They'd already claimed him as their play thing. So they did
like games after all, they hauled him from the beach like
children come to fetch a playmate, eager that he should join
the horse play.

The scratching had stopped. Ray's body had disappeared
altogether. Not a murmur off the pristine sea, just the slop of
the waves against the boards of the boat.

I pulled at the oars—

"Row!" I screamed at the sheep feeder. "Row, or they'll
kill us."

He seemed resigned to whatever they had in mind to punish
us with. He shook his head and spat onto the water. Beneath
his floating phlegm something moved in the deep, pale forms
rolled and somersaulted, too far down to be clearly seen. Even
as I watched they came floating up towards us, their sea-
corrupted faces better defined with every fathom they rose,
their arms outstretched to embrace us.

A shoal of corpses. The dead in dozens, crab-cleaned and
fish-picked, their remaining flesh scarcely sitting on their
bones.

The boat rocked gently as their hands reached up to touch
it.

The look of resignation on the sheep feeder's face didn't
falter for a moment as the boat was shaken backwards and
forwards; at first gently, then so violently we were beaten
about like dolls. They meant to capsize us, and there was no
help for it. A moment later, the boat tipped over.

The water was icy; far colder than I'd anticipated, and it

took breath away. I'd always been a fairly strong swimmer. My strokes were confident as I began to swim from the boat, cleaving through the white water. The sheep feeder was less lucky. Like many men who live with the sea, he apparently couldn't swim. Without issuing a cry or a prayer, he sank like a stone.

What did I hope? That four was enough: that I could be left to thumb a current to safety? Whatever hopes of escape I had, they were short-lived.

I felt a soft, oh so very soft, brushing of my ankles and my feet, almost a caress. Something broke surface briefly close to my head. I glimpsed a grey back, as of a large fish. The touch on my ankle had become a grasp. A pulpy hand, mushed by so long in the water, had hold of me, and inexorably began to claim me for the sea. I gulped what I knew to be my last breath of air, and as I did so Ray's head bobbed no more than a yard from me. I saw his wounds in clinical detail—the water cleansed cuts were ugly flaps of white tissue, with a gleam of bone at their core. The loose eye had been washed away by now, his hair, flattened to his skull, no longer disguised the bald patch at his crown.

The water closed over my head. My eyes were open, and I saw my hard earned breath flashing past my face in a display of silver bubbles. Ray was beside me, consoling, attentive. His arms floated over his head as though he were surrendering. The pressure of the water distorted his face, puffing his cheeks out, and spilling threads of severed nerves from his empty eye socket like the tentacles of a tiny squid.

I let it happen. I opened my mouth and felt it fill with cold water. Salt burned my sinuses, the cold stabbed behind my eyes. I felt the brine burning down my throat, a rush of eager water where water shouldn't go—flushing air from my tubes and cavities, 'til my system was overwhelmed.

Below me, two corpses, their hair swaying loosely in the current, hugged my legs. Their heads lolled and danced on rotted ropes of neck muscle, and though I pawed at their hands, and their flesh came off the bone in grey, lace-edged pieces, their loving grip didn't falter. They wanted me, oh how dearly they wanted me.

Ray was holding me too, wrapping me up, pressing his face

to mine. There was no purpose in the gesture I suppose. He didn't know or feel, or love or care. And I, losing my life with every second, succumbing to the sea absolutely, couldn't take pleasure in the intimacy that I'd longed for.

Too late for love; the sunlight was already a memory. Was it that the world was going out—darkening towards the edges as I died—or that we were now so deep the sun couldn't penetrate so far? Panic and terror had left me—my heart seemed not to beat at all—my breath didn't come and go in anguished bursts as it had. A kind of peace was on me.

Now the grip of my companions relaxed, and the gentle tide had its way with me. A rape of the body: a ravaging of skin and muscle, gut, eye, sinus, tongue, brain.

Time had no place here. The days may have passed into weeks, I couldn't know. The keels of boats glided over and maybe we looked up from our rock hovels on occasion and watched them pass. A ringed finger was trailed in the water, a splashless puddle clove the sky, a fishing line trailed a worm. Signs of life.

Maybe the same hour as I died, or maybe a year later, the current sniffs me out of my rock and has some mercy. I am twitched from amongst the sea anemones and given to the tide. Ray is with me. His time too has come. The sea change has occurred; there is no turning back for us.

Relentlessly the tide bears us—sometimes floating, bloated decks for gulls, sometimes half sunk and nibbled by fish—bears us towards the island. We know the surge of the shingle, and hear, without ears, the rattle of the stones.

The sea has long since washed the plate clean of its leavings. Angela, the ''Emmanuelle'', and Jonathan, are gone. Only we drowned belong here, face up, under the stones, soothed by the rhythm of tiny waves and the absurd incomprehension of sheep.

HUMAN REMAINS

Some trades are best practiced by daylight, some by night. Gavin was a professional in the latter category. In midwinter, in midsummer, leaning against a wall, or poised in a doorway, a firefly cigarette hovering at his lips, he sold what sweated in his jeans to all comers.

Sometimes to visiting widows with more money than love, who'd hire him for a weekend of illicit meetings, sour, insistent kisses and perhaps, if they could forget their dead partners, a dry hump on a lavender-scented bed. Sometimes to lost husbands, hungry for their own sex and desperate for an hour of coupling with a boy who wouldn't ask their name.

Gavin didn't much care which it was. Indifference was a trademark of his, even a part of his attraction. And it made leaving him, when the deed was done and the money exchanged, so much simpler. To say, "Ciao," or "Be seeing you," or nothing at all to a face that scarcely cared if you lived or died: that was an easy thing.

And for Gavin, the profession was not unpalatable, as professions went. One night out of four it even offered him a grain of physical pleasure. At worst it was a sexual abattoir, all steaming skins and lifeless eyes. But he'd got used to that over the years.

It was all profit. It kept him in good shoes.

By day he slept mostly, hollowing out a warm furrow in the

bed, and mummifying himself in his sheets, head wrapped up
in a tangle of arms to keep out the light. About three or so,
he'd get up, shave and shower, then spend half an hour in
front of the mirror, inspecting himself. He was meticulously
self-critical, never allowing his weight to fluctuate more than a
pound or two to either side of his self-elected ideal, careful to
feed his skin if it was dry, or swab it if it was oily, hunting for
any pimple that might flaw his cheek. Strict watch was kept
for the smallest sign of veneral disease—the only type of
lovesickness he ever suffered. The occasional dose of crabs
was easily dispatched, but gonorrhea, which he'd caught
twice, would keep him out of service for three weeks, and that
was bad for business; so he policed his body obsessively, hurrying to the clinic at the merest sign of a rash.

It seldom happened. Uninvited crabs aside there was little to
do in that half hour of self-appraisal but admire the collision
of genes that had made him. He was wonderful. People told
him that all the time. Wonderful. The face, oh the face, they
would say, holding him tight as if they could steal a piece of
his glamour.

Of course there were other beauties available, through the
agencies, even on the streets if you knew where to search. But
most of the hustlers Gavin knew had faces that seemed, beside
his, unmade. Faces that looked like the first workings of a
sculptor rather than the finished article: unrefined, experi-
mental. Whereas he was made, entire. All that could be done
had been; it was just a question of preserving the perfection.

Inspection over, Gavin would dress, maybe regard himself
for another five minutes, then take the packaged wares out to
sell.

He worked the street less and less these days. It was
chancey; there was always the law to avoid, and the occasional psycho with an urge to clean up Sodom. If he was feeling really lazy he could pick up a client through the Escort
Agency, but they always creamed off a fat portion of the fee.

He had regulars of course, clients who booked his favors
month after month. A widow from Fort Lauderdale always
hired him for a few days on her annual trip to Europe; another
woman whose face he'd seen once in a glossy magazine called
him now and then, wanting only to dine with him and confide

her marital problems. There was a man Gavin called Rover, after his car, who would buy him once every few weeks for a night of kisses and confessions.

But on nights without a booked client he was out on his own finding a spec and hustling. It was a craft he had off perfectly. Nobody else working the street had caught the vocabulary of invitation better; the subtle blend of encouragement and detachment, of putto and wanton. The particular shift of weight from left foot to right that presented the groin at the best angle: so. Never too blatant: never whorish. Just casually promising.

He prided himself that there was seldom more than a few minutes between tricks, and never as much as an hour. If he made his play with his usual accuracy, eyeing the right disgruntled wife, the right regretful husband, he'd have them feed him (clothe him sometimes), bed him and bid him a satisfied goodnight all before the last tube had run on the Metropolitan Line to Hammersmith. The years of half-hour assignations, three blowjobs and a fuck in one evening, were over. For one thing he simply didn't have the hunger for it any longer, for another he was preparing for his career to change course in the coming years: from street hustler to gigolo, from gigolo to kept boy, from kept boy to husband. One of these days, he knew it, he'd marry one of the widows; maybe the matron from Florida. She'd told him how she could picture him spread out beside her pool in Fort Lauderdale, and it was a fantasy he kept warm for her. Perhaps he hadn't got there yet, but he'd turn the trick of it sooner or later. The problem was that these rich blooms needed a lot of tending, and the pity of it was that so many of them perished before they came to fruit.

Still, this year. Oh yes, this year for certain, it had to be this year. Something good was coming with the autumn, he knew it for sure.

Meanwhile he watched the lines deepen around his wonderful mouth (it was, without doubt, wonderful) and calculated the odds against him in the race between time and opportunity.

It was nine-fifteen at night. September 29th, and it was chilly, even in the foyer of the Imperial Hotel. No Indian summer to bless the streets this year: autumn had London in its jaws and was shaking the city bare.

The chill had got to his tooth, his wretched, crumbling tooth. If he'd gone to the dentist's, instead of turning over in his bed and sleeping another hour, he wouldn't be feeling this discomfort. Well, too late now, he'd go tomorrow. Plenty of time tomorrow. No need for an appointment. He'd just smile at the receptionist, she'd melt and tell him she could find a slot for him somewhere, he'd smile again, she'd blush and he'd see the dentist then and there instead of waiting two weeks like the poor nerds who didn't have wonderful faces.

For tonight he'd just have to put up with it. All he needed was one lousy punter—a husband who'd pay through the nose for taking it in the mouth—then he could retire to an all-night club in Soho and content himself with reflections. As long as he didn't find himself with a confession freak on his hands, he could spit his stuff and be done by half ten.

But tonight wasn't his night. There was a new face on the reception desk of the Imperial, a thin, shot-at face with a mismatched rug perched (glued) on his pate, and he'd been squinting at Gavin for almost half an hour.

The usual receptionist, Madox, was a closet-case Gavin had seen prowling the bars once or twice, an easy touch if you could handle that kind. Madox was putty in Gavin's hand; he'd even bought his company for an hour a couple of months back. He'd got a cheap rate too—that was good politics. But this new man was straight, and vicious, and he was on to Gavin's game.

Idly, Gavin sauntered across to the cigarette machine, his walk catching the beat of the muzack as he trod the maroon carpet. Lousy fucking night.

The receptionist was waiting for him as he turned from the machine, packet of Winston in hand.

"Excuse me . . . Sir." It was a practiced pronunciation that was clearly not natural. Gavin looked sweetly back at him.

"Yes?"

"Are you actually a resident at this hotel . . . Sir?"

"Actually—"

"If not, the management would be obliged if you'd vacate the premises immediately."

"I'm waiting for somebody."

"Oh?"

The receptionist didn't believe a word of it.

"Well just give me the name—"

"No need."

"Give me the name—," the man insisted, "and I'll gladly check to see if your . . . contact . . . is in the hotel."

The bastard was going to try and push it, which narrowed the options. Either Gavin could choose to play it cool, and leave the foyer, or play the outraged customer and stare the other man down. He chose, more to be bloodyminded than because it was good tactics, to do the latter.

"You don't have any right—" he began to bluster, but the receptionist wasn't moved.

"Look, sonny—" he said, "I know what you're up to, so don't try and get snotty with me or I'll fetch the police." He'd lost control of his elocution: it was getting further south of the river with every syllable. "We've got a nice clientele here, and they don't want no truck with the likes of you, see?"

"Fucker," said Gavin very quietly.

"Well that's one up from a cocksucker, isn't it?"

Touché.

"Now, sonny—you want to mince out of here under your own steam or be carried out in cuffs by the boys in blue?"

Gavin played his last card.

"Where's Mr. Madox? I want to see Mr. Madox: he knows me."

"I'm sure he does," the receptionist snorted, "I'm bloody sure he does. He was dismissed for improper conduct—" The artificial accent was re-establishing itself "—so I wouldn't try dropping his name here if I were you. O.K.? On your way."

Upper hand well and truly secured, the receptionist stood back like a matador and gestured for the bull to go by.

"The management thanks you for your patronage. Please don't call again."

Game, set and match to the man with the rug. What the hell; there were other hotels, other foyers, other receptionists.

He didn't have to take all this shit.

As Gavin pushed the door open he threw a smiling "Be see-ing you" over his shoulder. Perhaps that would make the tick sweat a little one of these nights when he was walking home and he heard a young man's step on the street behind him. It was a petty satisfaction, but it was something.

The door swung closed, sealing the warmth in and Gavin out. It was colder, substantially colder, than it had been when he'd stepped into the foyer. A thin drizzle had begun, which threatened to worsen as he hurried down Park Lane towards South Kensington. There were a couple of hotels on the High Street he could hole up in for a while; if nothing came of that he'd admit defeat.

The traffic surged around Hyde Park Corner, speeding to Knightsbridge or Victoria, purposeful, shining. He pictured himself standing on the concrete island between the two con-trary streams of cars, his fingertips thrust into his jeans (they were too tight for him to get more than the first joint into the pockets), solitary, forlorn.

A wave of unhappiness came up from some buried place in him. He was twenty-four and five months. He had hustled, on and off and on again, since he was seventeen, promising himself that he'd find a marriageable widow (the gigolo's pen-sion) or a legitimate occupation before he was twenty-five.

But time passed and nothing came of his ambitions. He just lost momentum and gained another line beneath the eye.

And the traffic still came in shining streams, lights signal-ling this imperative or that, cars full of people with ladders to climb and snakes to wrestle, their passage isolating him from the bank, from safety, with its hunger for destination.

He was not what he'd dreamed he'd be, or promised his secret self.

And youth was yesterday.

Where was he to go now? The flat would feel like a prison tonight, even if he smoked a little dope to talke the edge off the room. He wanted, no, he *needed* to be with somebody tonight. Just to see his beauty through somebody else's eyes. Be told how perfect his proportions were, be wined and dined and flattered stupid, even if it was by Quasimodo's richer, uglier brother. Tonight he needed a fix of affection.

•   •   •

The pickup was so damned easy it almost made him forget the
episode in the foyer of the Imperial. A guy of fifty-five or so,
well-heeled: Gucci shoes, a very classy overcoat. In a word:
quality.

Gavin was standing in the doorway of a tiny arthouse
cinema, looking over the times of the Truffaut movie they
were showing, when he became aware of the punter staring at
him. He glanced at the guy to be certain there was a pickup in
the offing. The direct look seemed to unnerve the punter; he
moved on; then he seemed to change his mind, muttered
something to himself, and retraced his steps, showing patently
false interest in the movie schedule. Obviously not too familiar
with this game, Gavin thought; a novice.

Casually Gavin took out a Winston and lit it, the flare of the
match in his cupped hands glossing his cheekbones golden.
He'd done it a thousand times, as often as not in the mirror
for his own pleasure. He had the glance up from the tiny fire
off pat: it always did the trick. This time when he met the
nervous eyes of the punter, the other didn't back away.

He drew on the cigarette, flicking out the match and letting
it drop. He hadn't made a pickup like this in several months,
but he was well satisfied that he still had the knack. The
faultless recognition of a potential client, the implicit offer in
eyes and lips, that could be construed as innocent friendliness
if he'd made an error.

This was no error, however, this was the genuine article.
The men's eyes were glued to Gavin, so enamored of him he
seemed to be hurting with it. His mouth was open, as though
the words of introduction had failed him. Not much of a face,
but far from ugly. Tanned too often, and too quickly: maybe
he'd lived abroad. He was assuming the man was English: his
prevarication suggested it.

Against habit, Gavin made the opening move.

"You like French movies?"

The punter seemed to deflate with relief that the silence between them had been broken.

"Yes," he said.

"You going in?"

The man pulled a face.

"I . . . I . . . don't think I will."

"Bit cold . . ."

"Yes. It is."

"Bit cold for standing around, I mean."

"Oh—yes."

The punter took the bait.

"Maybe . . . you'd like a drink?"

Gavin smiled.

"Sure, why not?"

"My flat's not far."

"Sure."

"I was getting a bit cheesed off, you know, at home."

"I know the feeling."

Now the other man smiled. "You are . . . ?"

"Gavin."

The man offered his leather-gloved hand. Very formal, businesslike. The grip as they shook was strong, no trace of his earlier hesitation remaining.

"I'm Kenneth," he said, "Ken Reynolds."

"Ken."

"Shall we get out of the cold?"

"Suits me."

"I'm only a short walk from here."

A wave of musty, centrally-heated air hit them as Reynolds opened the door of this apartment. Climbing the three flights of stairs had snatched Gavin's breath, but Reynolds wasn't slowed at all. Health freak maybe. Occupation? Something in the city. The handshake, the leather gloves. Maybe Civil Service.

"Come in, come in."

There was money here. Underfoot the pile of the carpet was lush, hushing their steps as they entered. The hallway was almost bare: a calendar hung on the wall, a small table with telephone, a heap of directories, a coatstand.

"It's warmer in here."

Reynolds was shrugging off his coat and hanging it up. His gloves remained on as he led Gavin a few yards down the hallway and into a large room.

"Let's have your jacket," he said.

"Oh . . . sure."

Gavin took off his jacket, and Reynolds slipped out into the hall with it. When he came in again he was working off his gloves; a slick of sweat made it a difficult job. The guy was still nervous: even on his home ground. Usually they started to calm down once they were safe behind locked doors. Not this one: he was a catalogue of fidgets.

"Can I get you a drink?"

"Yeah; that would be good."

"What's your poison?"

"Vodka."

"Surely. Anything with it?"

"Just a drop of water."

"Purist, eh?"

Gavin didn't quite understand the remark.

"Yeah," he said.

"Man after my own heart. Will you give me a moment—I'll just fetch some ice."

"No problem."

Reynolds dropped the gloves on a chair by the door, and left Gavin to the room. It, like the hallway, was almost stiflingly warm, but there was nothing homely or welcoming about it. Whatever his profession, Reynolds was a collector. The room was dominated by displays of antiquities, mounted on the walls, and lined up on shelves. There was very little furniture, and what there seemed odd: battered tubular frame chairs had no place in an apartment this expensive. Maybe the man was a university don, or a museum governor, something academic. This was no stockbroker's living room.

Gavin knew nothing about art, and even less about history, so the displays meant very little to him, but he went to have a closer look, just to show willing. The guy was bound to ask him what he thought of the stuff. The shelves were deadly dull. Bits and pieces of pottery and sculpture: nothing in its entirety, just fragments. On some of the shards there remained a glimpse of design, though age had almost washed the colors out. Some of the sculpture was recognizably human: part of a torso, or foot (all five toes in place), a face that was all but eaten away, no longer male or female. Gavin stifled a yawn. The heat, the exhibits and the thought of sex made him lethargic.

He turned his dulled attention to the wall-hung pieces. They were more impressive then the stuff on the shelves but they were still far from complete. He couldn't see why anyone would want to look at such broken things; what was the fascination? The stone reliefs mounted on the wall were pitted and eroded, so that the skins of the figures looked leprous, and the Latin inscriptions were almost wiped out. There was nothing beautiful about them: too spoiled for beauty. They made him feel dirty somehow, as though their condition was contagious.

Only one of the exhibits struck him as interesting: a tombstone, or what looked to him to be a tombstone, which was larger than the other reliefs and in slightly better condition. A man on a horse, carrying a sword, loomed over his headless enemy. Under the picture, a few words in Latin. The front legs of the horse had been broken off, and the pillars that bounded the design were badly defaced by age, otherwise the image made sense. There was even a trace of personality in the crudely made face: a long nose, a wide mouth; an individual.

Gavin reached to touch the inscriptions, but withdrew his fingers as he heard Reynolds enter.

"No, please touch it," said his host. "It's there to take pleasure in. Touch away."

Now that he'd been invited to touch the thing, the desire had melted away. He felt embarrassed; caught in the act.

"Go on," Reynolds insisted.

Gavin touched the carving. Cold stone, gritty under his fingertips.

"It's Roman," said Reynolds.

"Tombstone?"

"Yes. Found near Newcastle."

"Who was he?"

"His name was Flavinus. He was a regimental standard bearer."

What Gavin had assumed to be a sword was, on closer inspection, a standard. It ended in an almost erased motif: maybe a bee, a flower, a wheel.

"You an archaeologist, then?"

"That's part of my business. I research sites, occasionally oversee digs; but most of the time I restore artifacts."

"Like these?"

"Roman Britain's my personal obsession."

He put down the glasses he was carrying and crossed to the pottery-laden shelves.

"This is stuff I've collected over the years. I've never quite got over the thrill of handling objects that haven't seen the light of day for centuries. It's like plugging into history. You know what I mean?"

"Yeah."

Reynolds picked a fragment of pottery off the shelf.

"Of course all the best finds are claimed by the major collections. But if one's canny, one manages to keep a few pieces back. They were an incredible influence, the Romans. Civil engineers, roadlayers, bridge builders."

Reynolds gave a sudden laugh at his burst of enthusiasm.

"Oh hell," he said, "Reynolds is lecturing again. Sorry. I get carried away."

Replacing the pottery shard in its niche on the shelf, he returned to the glasses, and started pouring drinks. With his back to Gavin, he managed to say:? "Are you expensive?"

Gavin hesitated. The man's nervousness was catching and the sudden tilt of the conversation from the Romans to the price of a blowjob took some adjustment.

"It depends," he flannelled.

"Ah . . ." said the other, still busying himself with the glasses, "you mean what is the precise nature of my—er—requirement?"

"Yeah."

"Of course."

He turned and handed Gavin a healthy-sized glass of vodka. No ice.

"I won't be demanding of you," he said.

"I don't come cheap."

"I'm sure you don't," Reynolds tried a smile, but it wouldn't stick to his face, "and I'm prepared to pay you well. Will you be able to stay the night?"

"Do you want me to?"

Reynolds frowned into his glass.

"I suppose I do."

"Then yes."

The host's mood seemed to change, suddenly: indecision was replaced by a spurt of conviction.

"Cheers," he said, clinking his whisky-filled glass against Gavin's. "To love and life and anything else that's worth paying for."

The double-edged mark didn't escape Gavin: the guy was obviously tied up in knots about what he was doing.

"I'll drink to that," said Gavin and took a gulp of the vodka.

The drinks came fast after that, and just about his third vodka Gavin began to feel mellower than he'd felt in a hell of a long time, content to listen to Reynolds' talk of excavations and the glories of Rome with only one ear. His mind was drifting, an easy feeling. Obviously he was going to be here for the night, or at least until the early hours of the morning, so why not drink the punter's vodka and enjoy the experience for what it offered? Later, probably much later to judge by the way the guy was rambling, there'd be some drink-slurred sex in a darkened room, and that would be that. He'd had customers like this before. They were lonely, perhaps between lovers, and usually simple to please. It wasn't sex this guy was buying, it was company, another body to share his space awhile; easy money.

And then, the noise.

At first Gavin thought the beating sound was in his head, until Reynolds stood up, a twitch at his mouth. The air of well-being had disappeared.

"What's that?" asked Gavin, also getting up, dizzy with drink.

"It's all right—" Reynolds, palms were pressing him down into his chair. "Stay here—"

The sound intensified. A drummer in an oven, beating as he burned.

"Please, please stay here a moment. It's just somebody upstairs."

Reynolds was lying, the racket wasn't coming from upstairs. It was from somewhere else in the flat, a rhythmical thumping, that speeded up and slowed and speeded again.

"Help yourself to a drink," said Reynolds at the door, face flushed. "Damn neighbors . . ."

The summons, for that was surely what it was, was already subsiding.

"A moment only," Reynolds promised, and closed the door behind him.

Gavin had experienced bad scenes before: tricks whose lovers appeared at inappropriate moments; guys who wanted to beat him up for a price—one who got bitten by guilt in a hotel room and smashed the place to smithereens. These things happened. But Reynolds was different: nothing about him said weird. At the back of his mind, at the very back, Gavin was quietly reminding himself that the other guys hadn't seemed bad at the beginning. Ah hell; he put the doubts away. If he started to get the jitters every time he went with a new face he'd soon stop working altogether. Somewhere along the line he had to trust to luck and his instinct, and his instinct told him that this punter was not given to throwing fits.

Taking a quick swipe from his glass, he refilled it, and waited.

The noise had stopped altogether, and it became increasingly easier to rearrange the facts: maybe it had been an upstairs neighbor after all. Certainly there was no sound of Reynolds moving around in the flat.

His attention wandered around the room looking for something to occupy it awhile, and came back to the tombstone on the wall.

Flavinus the Standard Bearer.

There was something satisfying about the idea of having your likeness, however crude, carved in stone and put up on the spot where your bones lay, even if some historian was going to separate bones and stone in the fullness of time. Gavin's father had insisted on burial rather than cremation: How else, he'd always said, was he going to be remembered? Who'd ever go to an urn, in a wall, and cry? The irony was that nobody ever went to his grave either: Gavin had been perhaps twice in the years since his father's death. A plain stone bearing a name, a date, and a platitude. He couldn't even remember the year his father died.

People remembered Flavinus though; people who'd never known him, or a life like his, knew him now. Gavin stood up and touched the standard bearer's name, the crudely chased "FLAVINUS" that was the second word of the inscription.

Suddenly, the noise again, more frenzied than ever. Gavin turned away from the tombstone and looked at the door, half expecting Reynolds to be standing there with a word of explanation. Nobody appeared.

"Damn it."

The noise continued, a tattoo. Somebody, somewhere, was very angry. And this time there could be no self-deception: the drummer was here, on this floor, a few yards away. Curiosity nibbled Gavin, a coaxing lover. He drained his glass and went out into the hall. The noise stopped as he closed the door behind him.

"Ken?" he ventured. The word seemed to die at his lips.

The hallway was in darkness, except for a wash of light from the far end. Perhaps an open door. Gavin found a switch to his right, but it didn't work.

"Ken?" he said again.

This time the enquiry met with a response. A moan, and the sound of a body rolling, or being rolled, over. Had Reynolds had an accident? Jesus, he could be lying incapacitated within spitting distance from where Gavin stood: he must help. Why were his feet so reluctant to move? He had the tingling in his balls that always came with nervous anticipation; it reminded him of childhood hide-and-seek: the thrill of the chase. It was almost pleasurable.

And pleasure apart, could he really leave now, without knowing what had become of the punter? He had to go down the corridor.

The first door was ajar; he pushed it open and the room beyond was a book-lined bedroom/study. Street lights through the curtainless window fell on a jumbled desk. No Reynolds, no thrasher. More confident now he'd made the first move Gavin explored further down the hallway. The next door—the kitchen—was also open. There was no light from inside. Gavin's hands had begun to sweat: he thought of Reynolds trying to pull his gloves off, though they stuck to his palm.

What had he been afraid of? It was more than the pickup: there was somebody else in the apartment: somebody with a violent temper.

Gavin's stomach turned as his eyes found the smeared hand print on the door; it was blood.

He pushed the door, but it wouldn't open any further. There was something behind it. He slid through the available space, and into the kitchen. An unemptied waste bin, or a neglected vegetable rack, fouled the air. Gavin smoothed the wall with his palm to find the light switch, and the fluorescent tube spasmed into life.

Reynolds' Gucci shoes poked out from behind the door. Gavin pushed it to, and Reynolds rolled out of his hiding place. He'd obviously crawled behind the door to take refuge; there was something of the beaten animal in his tucked-up body. When Gavin touched him he shuddered.

"It's all right . . . it's me." Gavin prised a bloody hand from Reynold's face. There was a deep gouge running from his temple to his chin, and another, parallel with it but not as deep, across the middle of his forehead and his nose, as though he'd been raked by a two-pronged fork.

Reynolds opened his eyes. It took him a second only to focus on Gavin, before he said:

"Go away."

"You're hurt."

"Jesus' sake, go away. Quickly. I've changed my mind . . . You understand?"

"I'll fetch the police."

The man practically spat: "Get the fucking hell out of here, will you? Fucking bumboy!"

Gavin stood up, trying to make sense out of all this. The guy was in pain, it made him aggressive. Ignore the insults and fetch something to cover the wound. That was it. Cover the wound, and then leave him to his own devices. If he didn't want the police that was his business. Probably he didn't want to explain the presence of a pretty boy in his hothouse.

"Just let me get you a bandage—"

Gavin went back into the hallway.

Behind the kitchen door Reynolds said: "Don't," but the

bumboy didn't hear him. It wouldn't have made much difference if he had. Gavin liked disobedience. Don't was an invitation.

Reynolds put his back to the kitchen door, and tried to edge
his way upright, using the doorhandle as purchase. But his
head was spinning: a carousel of horrors, round and round,
each horse uglier than the last. His legs doubled up under him,
and he fell down like the senile fool he was. Damn. Damn.
Damn.

Gavin heard Reynolds fall, but he was too busy arming
himself to hurry back into the kitchen. If the intruder who'd
attacked Reynolds was still in the flat, he wanted to be ready
to defend himself. He rummaged through the reports on the
desk in the study and alighted on a paper knife which was lying beside a pile of unopened correspondence. Thanking God
for it, he snatched it up. It was light, and the blade was thin
and brittle, but properly placed it could surely kill.

Happier now, he went back into the hall and took a moment
to work out his tactics. The first thing was to locate the
bathroom, hopefully there he'd find a bandage for Reynolds.
Even a clean towel would help. Maybe then he could get some
sense out of the guy, even coax him into an explanation.

Beyond the kitchen the hallway made a sharp left. Gavin
turned the corner, and dead ahead the door was ajar. A light
burned inside: water shone on tiles. The bathroom.

Clamping his left hand over the right hand that held the
knife, Gavin approached the door. The muscles of his arms
had become rigid with fear: would that improve his strike if it
was required? he wondered. He felt inept, graceless, slightly
stupid.

There was blood on the doorjamb, a palm print that was
clearly Reynolds'. This was where it had happened—Reynolds
had thrown out a hand to support himself as he reeled back
from his assailant. If the attacker was still in the flat, he must
be here. There was nowhere else for him to hide.

Later, if there was a later, he'd probably analyze this situation and call himself a fool for kicking the door open, for encouraging this confrontation. But even as he contemplated the
idiocy of the action he was performing it, and the door was

swinging open across tiles strewn with water-blood puddles, and any moment there'd be a figure there, hook-handed, screaming defiance.

No. Not at all. The assailant wasn't here; and if he wasn't here, he wasn't in the flat.

Gavin exhaled, long and slow. The knife sagged in his hand, denied its pricking. Now, despite the sweat, the terror, he was disappointed. Life had let him down, again—snuck his destiny out of the back door and left him with a mop in his hand not a medal. All he could do was play nurse to the old man and go on his way.

The bathroom was decorated in shades of lime; the blood and tiles clashed. The translucent shower curtain, sporting stylized fish and seaweed, was partially drawn. It looked like the scene of a movie murder: not quite real. Blood too bright: light too flat.

Gavin dropped the knife in the sink, and opened the mirrored cabinet. It was well stocked with mouth washes, vitamin supplements, and abandoned toothpaste tubes, but the only medication was a tin of Elastoplast. As he closed the cabinet door he met his own features in the mirror, a drained face. He turned on the cold tap full, and lowered his head to the sink; a splash of water would clear away the vodka and put some color in his cheeks.

As he cupped the water to his face, something made a noise behind him. He stood up, his heart knocking against his ribs, and turned off the tap. Water dripped off his chin and his eyelashes, and gurgled down the waste pipe.

The knife was still in the sink, a hand's-length away. The sound was coming from the bath, from *in* the bath, the inoffensive slosh of water.

Alarm had triggered flows of adrenalin, and his senses distilled the air with new precision. The sharp scent of lemon soap, the brilliance of the turquoise angel fish flitting through lavender kelp on the shower curtain, the cold droplets on his face, the warmth behind his eyes: all sudden experiences, details his mind had passed over 'til now, too lazy to see and smell and feel to the limits of its reach.

You're living in the real world, his head said (it was a revelation), and if you're not very careful you're going to die there.

Why hadn't he looked in the bath? Asshole. Why not the bath?

"Who's there?" he asked, hoping against hope that Reynolds had an otter that was taking a quiet swim. Ridiculous hope. There was blood here, for Christ's sake.

He turned from the mirror as the lapping subsided—do it! do it!—and slid back the shower curtain on its plastic hooks. In his haste to unveil the mystery he'd left the knife in the sink. Too late now: the turquoise angels concertinaed, and he was looking down into the water.

It was deep, coming up to within an inch or two of the top of the bath, and murky. A brown scum spiralled on the surface, and the smell off it was faintly animal, like the wet fur of a dog. Nothing broke the surface of the water.

Gavin peered in, tryuing to work out the form at the bottom, his reflection floating amid the scum. He bent closer, unable to puzzle out the relation of shapes in the silt, until he recognized the crudely-formed fingers of a hand and he realized he was looking at a human form curled up into itself like a fetus, lying absolutely still in the filthy water.

He passed his hand over the surface to clear away the muck, his reflection shattered, and the occupant of the bath came clear. It was a statue, carved in the shape of a sleeping figure, only its head, instead of being tucked up tight, was cranked round to stare up out of the blur of sediment towards the surface. Its eyes were painted open, two crude blobs on a roughly carved face; its mouth was a slash, its ears ridiculous handles on its bald head. It was naked: its anatomy no better realized than its features: the work of an apprentice sculptor. In places the paint had been corrupted, perhaps by the soaking, and was lifting off the torso in grey, globular strands. Underneath, a core of dark wood was uncovered.

There was nothing to be frightened of here. An *objet d'art* in a bath, immersed in water to remove a crass paintjob. The lapping he'd heard behind him had been some bubbles rising from the thing, caused by a chemical reaction. There: the fright was explained. Nothing to panic over. Keep beating my heart, as the barman at the Ambassador used to say when a new beauty appeared on the scene.

Gavin smiled at the irony; this was no Adonis.

"Forget you ever saw it."

Reynolds was at the door. The bleeding had stopped, staunched by an unsavory rag of a handkerchief pressed to the side of his face. The light of the tiles made his skin bilious: his pallor would have shamed a corpse.

"Are you all right? You don't look it."

"I'll be fine . . . just go, please."

"What happened?"

"I slipped. Water on the floor. I slipped, that's all."

"But the noise . . ."

Gavin was looking back into the bath. Something about the statue fascinated him. Maybe its nakedness, and that second strip it was slowly performing underwater: the ultimate strip: off with the skin.

"Neighbors, that's all."

"What is this?" Gavin asked, still looking at the unfetching dollface in the water.

"It's nothing to do with you."

"Why's it all curled up like that? Is he dying?"

Gavin looked back to Reynolds to see the response to that question, the sourest of smiles, fading.

"You'll want money."

"No."

"Damn you! You're in business aren't you? There's notes beside the bed; take whatever you feel you deserve for your wasted time—" He was appraising Gavin. "—and your silence."

Again the statue: Gavin couldn't keep his eyes off it, in all its crudity. His own face, puzzled, floated on the skin of the water, shaming the hand of the artist with its proportions.

"Don't wonder," said Reynolds.

"Can't help it."

"This is nothing to do with you."

"You stole it . . . is that right? This is worth a mint and you stole it."

Reynolds pondered the question and seemed, at last, too tired to start lying.

"Yes. I stole it."

"And tonight somebody came back for it—"

Reynolds shrugged.

"—Is that it? Somebody came back for it?"

"That's right. I stole it . . ." Reynolds was saying the lines by rote, ". . . and somebody came back for it."

"That's all I wanted to know."

"Don't come back here, Gavin whoever you are. And don't try anything clever, because I won't be here."

"You mean extortion?" said Gavin, "I'm no thief."

Reynolds' look of appraisal rotted into contempt.

"Thief or not, be thankful. If it's in you." Reynolds stepped away from the door to let Gavin pass. Gavin didn't move.

"Thankful for what?" he demanded. There was an itch of anger in him; he felt, absurdly, rejected, as though he was being foisted off with a half-truth because he wasn't worthy enough to share this secret.

Reynolds had no more strength left for explanation. He was slumped against the doorframe, exhausted.

"Go," he said.

Gavin nodded and left the guy at the door. As he passed from bathroom into hallway a glob of paint must have been loosened from the statue. He heard it break surface, heard the lapping at the edge of the bath, could see, in his head, the way the ripples made the body shimmer.

"Goodnight," said Reynolds, calling after him.

Gavin didn't reply, nor did he pick up any money on his way out. Let him have his tombstones and his secrets.

On his way to the front door he stepped into the main room to pick up his jacket. The face of Flavinus the Standard Bearer looked down at him from the wall. The man must have been a hero, Gavin thought. Only a hero would have been commemorated in such a fashion. He'd get no remembrance like that; no stone face to mark his passage.

He closed the front door behind him, aware once more that his tooth was aching, and as he did so the noise began again, the beating of a fist against a wall.

Or worse, the sudden fury of a woken heart.

•   •   •

The toothache was really biting the following day, and he went to the dentist midmorning, expecting to coax the girl on the desk into giving him an instant appointment. But his charm was at a low ebb, his eyes weren't sparkling quite as luxuriantly as usual. She told him he'd have to wait until the following Friday, unless it was an emergency. He told her it was: she told him it wasn't. It was going to be a bad day: an aching tooth, a lesbian dentist receptionist, ice on the puddles, nattering women on every street corner, ugly children, ugly sky.

That was the day the pursuit began.

Gavin had been chased by admirers before, but never quite like this. Never so subtle, so surreptitious. He'd had people follow him round for days, from bar to bar, from street to street, so doglike it almost drove him mad. Seeing the same longing face night after night, screwing up the courage to buy him a drink, perhaps offering him a watch, cocaine, a week in Tunisia, whatever. He'd rapidly come to loathe that sticky adoration that went bad as quickly as milk, and stank to high Heaven once it had. One of his most ardent admirers, a knighted actor he'd been told, never actually came near him, just followed him around, looking and looking. At first the attention had been flattering, but the pleasure soon became irritation, and eventually he'd cornered the guy in a bar and threatened him with a broken head. He'd been so wound up that night, so sick of being devoured by looks, he'd have done some serious harm if the pitiful bastard hadn't taken the hint. He never saw the guy again; half thought he'd probably gone home and hanged himself.

But this pursuit was nowhere near as obvious, it was scarcely more than a feeling. There was no hard evidence that he had somebody on his tail. Just a prickly sense, every time he glanced round, that someone was slotting themselves into the shadows, or that on a night street a walker was keeping pace with him, matching every click of his heel, every hesitation in his step. It was like paranoia, except that he wasn't paranoid. If he was paranoid, he reasoned, somebody would tell him.

Besides, there were incidents. One morning the cat woman who lived on the landing below him idly enquired who his visitor was: the funny one who came in late at night and waited on the stairs hour after hour, watching his room. He'd had no such visitor: and knew no one who fitted the description.

Another day, on a busy street, he'd ducked out of the throng into the doorway of an empty shop and was in the act of lighting a cigarette when somebody's reflection, distorted through the grime on the window, caught his eye. The match burned his finger, he looked down as he dropped it, and when he looked up again the crowd had closed round the watcher like an eager sea.

It was a bad, bad feeling: and there was more where that came from.

Gavin had never spoken with Preetorius, though they'd exchanged an occasional nod on the street, and each asked after the other in the company of mutual acquaintances as though they were dear friends. Preetorius was a black, somewhere between forty-five and assassination, a glorified pimp who claimed to be descended from Napoleon. He'd been running a circle of women, and three or four boys, for the best part of a decade, and doing well from the business. When he first began work, Gavin had been strongly advised to ask for Preetorius' patronage, but he'd always been too much of a maverick to want that kind of help. As a result he'd never been looked upon kindly by Preetorius or his clan. Nevertheless, once he became a fixture on the scene, no one challenged his right to be his own man. The word was that Preetorius even admitted a grudging admiration for Gavin's greed.

Admiration or no, it was a chilly day in Hell when Preetorius actually broke the silence and spoke to him.

"White boy."

It was towards eleven, and Gavin was on his way from a bar off St. Martin's Lane to a club in Covent Garden. The street still buzzed: there were potential punters amongst the theatre and movie-goers, but he hadn't got the appetite for it tonight. He had a hundred in his pocket, which he'd made the day before and hadn't bothered to bank. Plenty to keep him going.

His first thought when he saw Preetorius and his pie-bald goons blocking his path was: they want my money.

"White boy."

Then he recognized the flat, shining face. Preetorius was no street thief; never had been, never would be.

"White boy, I'd like a word with you."

Preetorius took a nut from his pocket, shelled it in his palm, and popped the kernel into his ample mouth.

"You don't mind do you?"

"What do you want?"

"Like I said, just a word. Not too much to ask, is it?"

"O.K. What?"

"Not here."

Gavin looked at Preetorius' cohorts. They weren't gorillas, that wasn't the black's style at all, but nor were they ninety-eight pound weaklings. This scene didn't look, on the whole, too healthy.

"Thanks, but no thanks." Gavin said, and began to walk, with as even a pace as he could muster, away from the trio. They followed. He prayed they wouldn't, but they followed. Preetorius talked at his back.

"Listen. I hear bad things about you," he said.

"Oh yes?"

"I'm afraid so. I'm told you attacked one of my boys."

Gavin took six paces before he answered. "Not me. You've got the wrong man."

"He recognized you, trash. You did him some serious mischief."

"I told you: not me."

"You're a lunatic, you know that? You should be put behind fucking bars."

Preetorius was raising his voice. People were crossing the street to avoid the escalating argument.

Without thinking, Gavin turned off St. Martin's Lane into Long Acre, and rapidly realized he'd made a tactical error. The crowds thinned substantially here, and it was along trek through the streets of Convent Garden before he reached another center of activity. He should have turned right instead of left, and he'd have stepped onto Charing Cross Road. There would have been some safety there. Damn it, he couldn't turn round, not and walk straight into them. All he could do was walk (not run; never run with a mad dog on your heels) and hope he could keep the conversation on an even keel.

Preetorius: "You've cost me a lot of money."

"I don't see—"

"You put some of my prime boy meat out of commission. It's going to be a long time 'til I get that kid back on the market. He's shit scared, see?"

"Look . . . I didn't do anything to anybody."

"Why do you fucking lie to me, trash? What have I ever done to you, you treat me like this?"

Preetorius picked up his pace a little and came up level with Gavin, leaving his associates a few steps behind.

"Look . . ." he whispered to Gavin, "kids like that can be tempting, right? That's cool. I can get into that. You put a little boy pussy on my plate I'm not going to turn my nose up at it. But you hurt him: and when you hurt one of my kids, I bleed too."

"If I'd done this like you say, you think I'd be walking the street?"

"Maybe you're not a well man, you know? We're not talking about a couple of bruises here, man. I'm talking about you taking a shower in a kid's blood, that's what I'm saying. Hanging him up and cutting him everywhere, then leaving him on my fuckin' stair wearing a pair of fuckin' socks. You getting my message now, white boy? You read my message?"

Genuine rage had flared as Preetorius described the alleged crimes, and Gavin wasn't sure how to handle it. He kept his silence, and walked on.

"That kid idolized you, you know? Thought you were essential reading for an aspirant bumboy. How'd you like that?"

"Not much."

"You should be fuckin' flattered, man, 'cause that's about as much as you'll ever amount to."

"Thanks."

"You've had a good career. Pity it's over."

Gavin felt iced lead in his belly: he'd hoped Preetorius was going to be content with a warning. Apparently not. They were here to damage him: Jesus, they were going to hurt him, and for something he hadn't done, didn't even know anything about.

"We're going to take you off the street, white boy. Permanently."

"I did nothing."

"The kid knew you, even with a stocking over your head he knew you. The voice was the same, the clothes were the same. Face it, you were recognized. Now take the consequences."

"Fuck you."

Gavin broke into a run. As an eighteen year old he'd sprinted for his country: he needed that speed again now. Behind him Preetorius laughed (such sport!) and two sets of feet pounded the pavement in pursuit. They were close, closer—and Gavin was badly out of condition. His thighs were aching after a few dozen yards, and his jeans were too tight to run in easily. The chase was lost before it began.

"The man didn't tell you to leave," the white goon scolded, his bitten fingers digging into Gavin's biceps.

"Nice try." Preetorius smiled, sauntering towards the dogs and the panting hare. He nodded, almost imperceptibly, to the other goon.

"Christian?" he asked.

At the invitation Christian delivered a fist to Gavin's kidneys. The blow doubled him up, spitting curses.

Christian said: "Over there." Preetorius said: "Make it snappy," and suddenly they were dragging him out of the light into an alley. His shirt and his jacket tore, his expensive shoes were dragged through dirt, before he was pulled upright, groaning. The alley was dark and Preetorius' eyes hung in the air in front of him, dislocated.

"Here we are again," he said. "Happy as can be."

"I . . . didn't touch him," Gavin gasped.

The unnamed cohort, Not Christian, put a ham hand in the middle of Gavin's chest, and pushed him back against the end wall of the alley. His heel slid in muck, and though he tried to stay upright his legs had turned to water. His ego too: this was no time to be courageous. He'd beg, he'd fall down on his knees and lick their soles if need be, anything to stop them doing a job on him. Anything to stop them spoiling his face.

That was Preetorius' favorite pastime, or so the street talk went: the spoiling of beauty. He had a rare way with him, could maim beyond hope of redemption in three strokes of his razor, and have the victim pocket his lips as a keepsake.

Gavin stumbled forward, palms slapping the wet ground. Something rotten-soft slid out of its skin beneath his hand.

Not Christian exchanged a grin with Preetorius.

"Doesn't he look delightful?" he said.

Preetorius was crunching a nut. "Seems to me—" he said, "—the man's finally found his place in life."

"I didn't touch him," Gavin begged. There was nothing to do but deny and deny: and even then it was a lost cause.

"You're guilty as hell," said Not Christian.

"Please."

"I'd really like to get this over with as soon as possible," said Preetorius, glancing at his watch, "I've got appointments to keep, people to pleasure."

Gavin looked up at his tormentors. The sodium-lit street was a twenty-five-yard dash away, if he could break through the cordon of their bodies.

"Allow me to rearrange your face for you. A little crime of fashion."

Preetorius had a knife in his hand. Not Christian had taken a rope from his pocket, with a ball on it. The ball goes in the mouth, the rope goes round the head—you couldn't scream if you life depended on it. This was it.

Go!

Gavin broke from his grovelling position like a sprinter from his block, but the slops greased his heels, and threw him off balance. Instead of making a clean dash for safety he stumbled sideways and fell against Christian, who in turn fell back.

There was a breathless scrambling before Preetorius stepped in, dirtying his hands on the white trash, and hauling him to his feet.

"No way out, fucker," he said, pressing the point of the blade against Gavin's chin. The jut of the bone was clearest there, and he began the cut without further debate—tracing the jawline, too hot for the act to care if the trash was gagged or not. Gavin howled as blood washed down his neck, but his cries were cut short as somebody's fat fingers grappled with his tongue, and held it fast.

His pulse began to thud in his temples, and windows, one behind the other, opened and opened in front of him, and he was falling through them into unconsciousness.

Better to die. Better to die. They'd destroy his face: better to die.

Then he was screaming again, except that he wasn't aware of making the sound in his throat. Through the slush in his ears he tried to focus on the voice, and realized it was Preetorius' scream he was hearing, not his own.

His tongue was released; and he was spontaneously sick. He staggered back, puking, from a mess of struggling figures in front of him. A person, or persons, unknown had stepped in, and prevented the completion of his spoiling. There was a body sprawled on the floor, face up. Not Christian, eyes open, life shut. God: someone had killed for him. *For him.*

Gingerly, he put his hand up to his face to feel the damage. The flesh was deeply lacerated along his jawbone, from the middle of his chin to within an inch of his ear. It was bad, but Preetorius ever organized, had left the best delights to the last, and had been interrupted before he'd slit Gavin's nostrils or taken off his lips. A scar along his jawbone wouldn't be pretty, but it wasn't disastrous.

Somebody was staggering out of the mêlée towards him—Preetorius, tears on his face, eyes like golf balls.

Beyond him Christian, his arms useless, was staggering towards the street.

Preetorius wasn't following: why?

His mouth opened; an elastic filament of saliva, strung with pearls, depended from his lower lip.

"Help me," he appealed, as though his life was in Gavin's power. One large hand was raised to squeeze a drop of mercy out of the air, but instead came the swoop of another arm, reaching over his shoulder and thrusting a weapon, a crude blade, into the black's mouth. He gargled it a moment, his throat trying to accommodate its edge, its width, before his attacker dragged the blade up and back, holding Preetorius' neck to steady him against the force of the stroke. The startled faced divided, and heat bloomed from Preetorius' interior, warming Gavin in a cloud.

The weapon hit the alley floor, a dull clank. Gavin glanced

at it. A short, wide-bladed sword. He looked back at the dead man.

Preetorius stood upright in front of him, supported now only by his executioner's arm. His gushing head fell forward, and the executioner took the bow as a sign, neatly dropping Preetorius' body at Gavin's feet. No longer eclipsed by the corpse, Gavin met his savior face to face.

It took him only a moment to place those crude features: the startled, lifeless eyes, the gash of a mouth, the jug handle ears. It was Reynolds' statue. It grinned, its teeth too small for its head. Milk teeth, still to be shed before the adult form. There was, however, some improvement in its appearance, he could see that even in the gloom. The brow seemed to have swelled; the face was altogether better proportioned. It remained a painted doll, but it was a doll with aspirations.

The statue gave a stiff bow, its joints unmistakably creaking, and the absurdity, the sheer absurdity of this situation welled up in Gavin. It bowed, damn it, it smiled, it murdered: and yet it couldn't possibly be alive, could it? Later, he would disbelieve, he promised himself. Later he'd find a thousand reasons not to accept the reality in front of him: blame his blood-starved brain, his confusion, his panic. One way or another he'd argue himself out of this fantastic vision, and it would be as though it had never happened.

If he could just live with it a few minutes longer.

The vision reached across and touched Gavin's jaw, lightly, running its crudely carved fingers along the lips of the wound Preetorius had made. A ring on its smallest finger caught the light: a ring identical to his own.

"We're going to have a scar," it said.

Gavin knew its voice.

"Dear me: pity," it said. It was speaking with *his* voice. "Still, it could be worse."

His voice. God, his, his, his.

Gavin shook his head.

"Yes," it said, understanding that he'd understood.

"Not me."

"Yes."

"Why?"

It transferred its touch from Gavin's jawbone to its own,

marking out the place where the wound should be, and even as it made the gesture its surface opened, and it grew a scar on the spot. No blood welled up: it had no blood.

Yet wasn't that his own, even brow it was emulating, and the piercing eyes, weren't they becoming his, and the wonderful mouth?

"The boy?" said Gavin, fitting the pieces together.

"Oh the boy . . ." It threw its unfinished glance to Heaven. "What a treasure he was. And how he snarled."

"You washed in his blood?"

"I need it." It knelt to the body of Preetorius and put its finger in the split head. "This blood's old, but it'll do. The boy was better."

It daubed Preetorius' blood on its cheek, like war paint. Gavin couldn't hide his disgust.

"Is he such a loss?" the effigy demanded.

The answer was no, of course. It was no loss at all that Preetorius was dead, no loss that some drugged, cocksucking kid had given up some blood and sleep because this painted miracle needed to feed its growth. There were worse things than this every day, somewhere; huge horrors. And yet—

"You can't condone me," it prompted, "its not in your nature is it? Soon it won't be in mine either. I'll reject my life as a tormentor of children, because I'll see through *your* eyes, share *your* humanity . . ."

It stood up, its movements still lacking flexibility.

"Meanwhile, I must behave as I think fit."

On its cheek, where Preetorius' blood had been smeared, the skin was already waxier, less like painted wood.

"I am a thing without a proper name," it pronounced. "I am a wound in the flank of the world. But I am also that perfect stranger you always prayed for as a child, to come and take you, call you beauty, lift you naked out of the street and through Heaven's window. Aren't I? Aren't I?"

How did it know the dreams of his childhood? How could it have guessed that particular emblem, of being hoisted out of a street full of plague into a house that was Heaven?

"Because I am yourself," it said, in reply to the unspoken question, "made perfectable."

Gavin gestured towards the corpses.

"You can't be me. I'd never have done this."

It seemed ungracious to condemn it for its intervention, but the point stood.

"Wouldn't you?" said the other. "I think you would."

Gavin heard Preetorius' voice in his ear. "A crime of fashion." Felt again the knife at his chin, the nausea, the helplessness. Of course he'd have done it, a dozen times over he'd have done it, and called it justice.

It didn't need to hear his accession, it was plain.

"I'll come and see you again," said the painted face. "Meanwhile—if I were you—" it laughed, "—I'd be going."

Gavin locked eyes with it a beat, probing it for doubts, then started towards the road.

"Not that way. This!"

It was pointing towards a door in the wall, almost hidden behind festering bags of refuse. That was how it had come so quickly, so quietly.

"Avoid the main streets, and keep yourself out of sight. I'll find you again, when I'm ready."

Gavin needed no further encouragement to leave. Whatever the explanations of the night's events, the deeds were done. Now wasn't the time for questions.

He slipped through the doorway without looking behind him: but he could hear enough to turn his stomach. The thud of fluid on the ground, the pleasurable moan of the miscreant: the sounds were enough for him to be able to picture its toilet.

Nothing of the night before made any more sense the morning after. There was no sudden insight into the nature of the waking dream he'd dreamt. There was just a series of stark facts.

In the mirror, the fact of the cut on his jaw, gummed up and aching more badly than his rotted tooth.

In the newspapers, the reports of two bodies found in the Covent Garden area, known criminals viciously murdered in what the police described as a "gangland slaughter".

In his head, the inescapable knowledge that he would be found out sooner or later. Somebody would surely have seen him with Preetorius, and spill the beans to the police. Maybe even Christian, if he was so inclined, and they'd be there, on his step, with cuffs and warrants. Then what could he tell them, in reply to their accusations? That the man who did it was not a man at all, but an effigy of some kind, that was by degrees becoming a replica of himself? The question was not whether he'd be incarcerated, but which hole they'd lock him in, prison or asylum?

Juggling despair with disbelief, he went to the casualty department to have his face seen to, where he waited patiently for three and a half hours with dozens of similar walking wounded.

The doctor was unsympathetic. There was no use in stitches now, he said, he said, the damage was done: the wound could and would be cleaned and covered, but a bad scar was now unavoidable. Why didn't you come last night, when it happened? the nurse asked. He shrugged: what the hell did they care? Artificial compassion didn't help him an iota.

As he turned the corner with his street, he saw the cars outside the house, the blue light, the cluster of neighbors grinning their gossip. Too late to claim anything of his previous life. By now they had possession of his clothes, his combs, his perfumes, his letters—and they'd be searching through them like apes after lice. He'd seen how thorough-going these bastards could be when it suited them, how completely they could seize and parcel up a man's identity. Eat it up, suck it up: they could erase you as surely as a shot, but leave you a living blank.

There was nothing to be done. His life was theirs now to sneer at and salivate over: even have a nervous moment, one or two of them, when they saw his photographs and wondered if perhaps they'd paid for this boy themselves, some horny night.

Let them have it all. They were welcome. From now on he would be lawless, because laws protect possessions and he had none. They'd wiped him clean, or as good as: he had no place to live, nor anything to call his own. He didn't even have fear: that was the strangest thing.

He turned his back on the street and the house he'd lived in for four years, and he felt something akin to relief, happy that his life had been stolen from him in its squalid entirety. He was the lighter for it.

Two hours later, and miles away, he took time to check his

pockets. He was carrying a banker's card, almost a hundred pounds in cash, a small collection of photographs, some of his parents and sister, mostly of himself; a watch, a ring, and a gold chain round his neck. Using the card might be dangerous—they'd surely have warned his bank by now. The best thing might be to pawn the ring and the chain, then hitch North. He had friends in Aberdeen who'd hide him awhile.

But first—Reynolds.

It took Gavin an hour to find the house where Ken Reynolds lived. It was the best part of twenty-four hours since he'd eaten and his belly complained as he stood outside Livingstone Mansions. He told it to keep its peace, and slipped into the building. The interior looked less impressive by daylight. The tread of the stair carpet was worn, and the paint on the balustrade filthied with use.

Taking his time he climbed the three flights to Reynolds' apartment, and knocked.

Nobody answered, nor was there any sound of movement from inside. Reynolds had told him of course: don't come back—I won't be here. Had he somehow guessed the consequences of sicking that thing into the world?

Gavin rapped on the door again, and this time he was certain he heard somebody breathing on the other side of the door.

"Reynolds . . ." he said, pressing to the door, "I can hear you."

Nobody replied, but there was somebody in there, he was sure of it. Gavin slapped his palm on the door.

"Come on, open up. Open up, you bastard."

A short silence, then a muffled voice. "Go away."

"I want to speak to you."

"Go away, I told you, go away. I've nothing to say to you."

"You owe me an explanation, for God's sake. If you don't open this fucking door I'll fetch someone who will."

An empty threat, but Reynolds responded: "No! Wait. Wait."

There was the sound of a key in the lock, and the door was opened a few paltry inches. The flat was in darkness beyond the scabby face that peered out at Gavin. It was Reynolds sure enough, but unshaven and wretched. He smelt unwashed, even through the crack in the door, and he was wearing only a stained shirt and a pair of pants, hitched up with a knotted belt.

"I can't help you. Go away."

"If you'll let me explain—" Gavin pressed the door, and Reynolds was either too weak or too befuddled to stop him opening it. He stumbled back into the darkened hallway.

"What the fuck's going on in here?"

The place stank of rotten food. The air was evil with it. Reynolds let Gavin slam the door behind him before producing a knife from the pocket of his stained trousers.

"You don't fool me," Reynolds gleamed, "I know what you've done. Very fine. Very clever."

"You mean the murders? It wasn't me."

Reynolds poked the knife towards Gavin.

"How many blood baths did it take?" he asked, tears in his eyes. "Six? Ten?"

"I didn't kill anybody."

". . . monster."

The knife in Reynolds' hand was the paper knife Gavin himself had wielded. He approached Gavin with it. There was no doubt: he had every intention of using it. Gavin flinched, and Reynolds seemed to take hope from his fear.

"Had you forgotten what it was like, being flesh and blood?"

The man had lost his marbles.

"Look . . . I just came here to talk."

"You came here to kill me. I could reveal you . . . so you came to kill me."

"Do you know who I am?" Gavin said.

Reynolds sneered: "You're not the queer boy. You look like him, but you're not."

"For pity's sake . . . I'm Gavin . . . Gavin—"

The words to explain, to prevent the knife pressing any closer, wouldn't come.

"Gavin, you remember?" was all he could say.

Reynolds faltered a moment, staring at Gavin's face.

"You're sweating," he said. the dangerous stare fading in his eyes.

Gavin's mouth had gone so dry he could only nod.

"I can see," said Reynolds, "you're sweating."

He dropped the point of the knife.

"It could never sweat," he said, "Never had, never would have, the knack of it. You're the boy . . . not it. The boy."

His face slackened, its flesh a sack which was almost emptied.

"I need help," said Gavin, his voice hoarse. "You've got to tell me what's going on."

"You want an explanation?" Reynolds replied, "you can have whatever you can find."

He led the way into the main room. The curtains were drawn, but even in the gloom Gavin could see that every antiquity it had contained had been smashed beyond repair. The pottery shards had been reduced to smaller shards, and those shards to dust. The stone reliefs were destroyed, the tombstone of Flavinus the Standard Bearer was rubble.

"Who did this?"

"I did," said Reynolds.

"Why?"

Reynolds sluggishly picked his way through the destruction to the window, and peered through a slit in the velvet curtains.

"It'll come back, you see," he said, ignoring the question.

Gavin insisted: "Why destroy it all?"

"It's a sickness," Reynolds replied. "Needing to live in the past."

He turned from the window.

"I stole most of these pieces," he said, "over a period of many years. I was put in a position of trust, and I misused it."

He kicked over a sizeable chunk of rubble: dust rose.

"Flavinus lived and died. That's all there is to tell. Knowing his name means nothing, or next to nothing. It doesn't make Flavinus real again: he's dead and happy."

"The statue in the bath?"

Reynolds stopped breathing for a moment, his inner eye meeting the painted face.

"You thought I was it, didn't you? When I came to the door."

"Yes. I thought it had finished its business."

"It imitates."

Reynolds nodded. "As far as I understand its nature," he said, "yes, it imitates."

"Where did you find it?"

"Near Carlisle. I was in charge of the excavation there. We found it lying in the bathhouse, a statue curled up into a ball beside the remains of an adult male. It was a riddle. A dead man and a statue, lying together in a bathhouse. Don't ask me what drew me to the thing, I don't know. Perhaps it works its will through the mind as well as the physique. I stole it, brought it back here."

"And you fed it?"

Reynolds stiffened.

"Don't ask."

"I *am* asking. You fed it?"

"Yes."

"You intended to bleed me, didn't you? That's why you brought me here: to kill me, and let it wash itself—"

Gavin remembered the noise of the creature's fists on the sides of the bath, that angry demand for food, like a child beating on its cot. He'd been so close to being taken by it, lamb like.

"Why didn't it attack me the way it did you? Why didn't it just jump out of the bath and feed on me?"

Reynolds wiped his mouth with the palm of his hand.

"It saw your face, of course."

Of course: it saw my face, and wanted it for itself, and it couldn't steal the face of a dead man, so it let me be. The rationale for its behavior was fascinating, now it was revealed: Gavin felt a taste of Reynolds' passion, unveiling mysteries.

"The man in the bathhouse. The one you uncovered—"

"Yes . . .?"

"He stopped it doing the same thing to him, is that right?"

"That's probably why his body was never moved, just sealed up. No one understood that he'd died fighting a creature that was stealing his life."

The picture was near as damn it complete; just anger remaining to be answered.

This man had come close to murdering him to feed the effigy. Gavin's fury broke surface. He took hold of Reynolds by shirt and skin, and shook him. Was it his bones or teeth that rattled?

"It's almost got my face." He stared into Reynolds' blood-shot eyes. "What happens when it finally has the trick off pat?"

"I don't know."

"You tell me the worst—Tell me!"

"It's all guesswork," Reynolds replied.

"Guess then!"

"When it's perfected its physical imitation, I think it'll steal the one thing it can't imitate: your soul."

Reynolds was past fearing Gavin. His voice had sweetened, as though he was talking to a condemned man. He even smiled.

"Fucker!"

Gavin hauled Reynolds' face yet closer to his. White spittle dotted the old man's cheek.

"You don't care! You don't give a shit, do you?"

He hit Reynolds across the face, once, twice, then again and again, until he was breathless.

The old man took the beating in absolute silence, turning his face up from one blow to receive another, brushing the blood out of his swelling eyes only to have them fill again.

Finally, the punches faltered.

Reynolds, on his knees, picked pieces of tooth off his tongue.

"I deserved that," he murmured.

"How do I stop it?" said Gavin.

Reynolds shook his head.

"Impossible," he whispered, plucking at Gavin's hand. "Please," he said, and taking the fist, opened it and kissed the lines.

Gavin left Reynolds in the ruins of Rome, and went into the street. The interview with Reynolds had told him little he hadn't guessed. The only thing he could do now was find this beast that had his beauty, and best it. If he failed, he failed attempting to secure his only certain attribute: a face that was wonderful. Talk of souls and humanity was for him so much wasted air. He wanted his face.

There was rare purpose in his step as he crossed Kensington. After years of being the victim of circumstance he saw circumstance embodied at last. He would shake sense from it, or die trying.

In his flat Reynolds drew aside the curtain to watch a picture of evening fall on a picture of a city.

No night he would live through, no city he'd walk in again. Out of sighs, he let the curtain drop, and picked up the short stabbing sword. The point he put to his chest.

"Come on," he told himself and the sword, and pressed the hilt. But the pain as the blade entered his body a mere half inch was enough to make his head reel: he knew he'd faint before the job was half done. So he crossed to the wall, steadied the hilt against it, and let his own body weight impale him. That did the trick. He wasn't sure if the sword had skewered him through entirely, but by the amount of blood he'd surely killed himself. Though he tried to arrange to turn, and so drive the blade all the way home as he fell on it, he fluffed the gesture, and instead fell on his side. The impact made him aware of the sword in his body, a stiff, uncharitable presence transfixing him utterly.

It took him well over ten minutes to die, but in that time, pain apart, he was content. Whatever the flaws of his fifty-seven years, and they were many, he felt he was perishing in a way his beloved Flavinus would not have been ashamed of.

Towards the end it began to rain, and the noise on the roof made him believe God was burying the house, sealing him up forever. And as the moment came, so did a splendid delusion: a hand, carrying a light, and escorted by voices, seemed to break through the wall, ghosts of the future come to excavate his history. He smiled to greet them, and was about to ask what year this was when he realized he was dead.

The creature was far better at avoiding Gavin than he'd been at avoiding it. Three days passed without its pursuer snatching sight of hide or hair of it.

But the fact of its presence, close, but never too close, was indisputable. In a bar someone would say: "Saw you last night on the Edgware Road" when he'd not been near the place, or "How'd you make out with that Arab then?" or "Don't you speak to your friends any longer?"

And God, he soon got to like the feeling. The distress gave way to a pleasure he'd not known since the age of two: ease.

So what if someone else was working his patch, dodging the law and the street wise alike; so what if his friends (what friends? Leeches) were being cut by this supercilious copy; so what if his life had been taken from him and was being worn to its length and its breadth in lieu of him? He could sleep, and know that he, or something so like him it made no difference, was awake in the night and being adored. He began to see the creature not as a monster terrorizing him, but as his tool, his public persona almost. It was substance: he shadow.

He woke, dreaming.

It was four-fifteen in the afternoon, and the whine of traffic was loud from the street below. A twilight room; the air breathed and rebreathed and breathed again so it smelt of his lungs. It was over a week since he'd left Reynolds to the ruins, and in that time he'd only ventured out from his new digs (one tiny bedroom, kitchen, bathroom) three times. Sleep was more important now than food or exercise. He had enough dope to keep him happy when sleep wouldn't come, which was seldom, and he'd grown to like the staleness of the air, the flux of light through the curtainless window, the sense of a world elsewhere which he had no part of or place in.

Today he'd told himself he ought to go out and get some fresh air, but he hadn't been able to raise the enthusiasm. Maybe later, much later, when the bars were emptying and he wouldn't be noticed, then he'd slip out of his cocoon and see what could be seen. For now, there were dreams—

Water.

He'd dreamt water; sitting beside a pool in Fort Lauderdale, a pool full of fish. And the splash of their leaps and dives was continuing, an overflow from sleep. Or was it the other way round? Yes; he had been hearing running water in his sleep and his dreaming mind had made an illustration to accompany the sound. Now awake, the sound continued.

It was coming from the adjacent bathroom, no longer running, but lapping. Somebody had obviously broken in while he was asleep, and was now taking a bath. He ran down the short list of possible intruders: the few who knew he was here. There was Paul: a nascent hustler who'd bedded down on the floor two nights before; there was Chink, the dope dealer; and a girl from downstairs he thought was called Michelle. Who was he kidding? None of these people would have broken the lock on the door to get in. He knew very well who it must be. He was just playing a game with himself, enjoying the process of elimination, before he narrowed the options to one.

Keen for reunion, he slid out from his skin of sheet and duvet. His body turned to a column of gooseflesh as the cold air encased him, his sleep erection hid its head. As he crossed the room to where his dressing gown hung on the back of the door he caught sight of himself in the mirror, a freeze frame from an atrocity film, a wisp of a man, shrunk by cold, and lit by a rainwater light. His reflection almost flickered, he was so insubstantial.

Wrapping the dressing gown, his only freshly purchased garment, around him, he went to the bathroom door. There was no noise of water now. He pushed the door open.

The warped linoleum was icy beneath his feet; and all he wanted to do was to see his friend, then crawl back into bed. But he owed the tatters of his curiosity more than that: he had questions.

The light through the frosted glass had deteriorated rapidly in the three minutes since he'd woken: the onset of night and a rain storm congealing the gloom. In front of him the bath was almost filled to overflowing, the water was oil-slick calm, and dark. As before, nothing broke surface. It was lying deep, hidden.

How long was it since he'd approached a lime-green bath in a lime-green bathroom, and peered into the water? It could have been yesterday: his life between then and now had become one long night. He looked down. It was there, tucked up, as before, and asleep, still wearing all its clothes as though it had had no time to undress before it hid itself. Where it had been bald it now sprouted a luxuriant head of hair, and its features were quite complete. No trace of a painted face remained: it had a plastic beauty that was his own absolutely, down to the last mole. Its perfectly finished hands were crossed on its chest.

The night deepened. There was nothing to do but watch it sleep, and he became bored with that. It had traced him here, it wasn't likely to run away again, he could go back to bed. Outside the rain had slowed the commuters' homeward journey to a crawl, there were accidents, some fatal; engines overheated, hearts too. He listened to the chase; sleep came and went. It was the middle of the evening when thirst woke him again: he was dreaming water, and there was the sound as it had been before. The creature was hauling itself out of the bath, was putting its hand to the door, opening it.

There it stood. The only light in the bedroom was coming from the street below; it barely began to illuminate the visitor.

"Gavin? Are you awake?"

"Yes," he said.

"Will you help me?" it asked. There was no trace of threat in its voice, it asked as a man might ask his brother, for kinship's sake.

"What do you want?"

"Time to heal."

"Heal?"

"Put on the light."

Gavin switched on the lamp beside the bed and looked at the figure at the door. It no longer had its arms crossed on its chest, and Gavin saw that the position had been covering an appalling shotgun wound. The flesh of its chest had been blown open, exposing its colorless innards. There was, of course, no blood: that it would never have. Nor, from this distance, could Gavin see anything in its interior that faintly resembled human anatomy.

"God Almighty," he said.

"Preetorius had friends," said the other, and its fingers touched the edge of the wound. The gesture recalled a picture of the wall of his mother's house. Christ in Glory—the Sacred Heart floating inside the Saviour—while his fingers, pointing to the agony he'd suffered, said: "This was for you."

"Why aren't you dead?"

"Because I'm not yet alive," it said.

Not yet: remember that, Gavin thought. It has intimations of mortality.

"Are you in pain?"

"No," it said sadly, as though it craved the experience, "I feel nothing. All the signs of life are cosmetic. But I'm learning." It smiled. "I've got the knack of the yawn, and the fart." The idea was both absurd and touching; that it would aspire to farting, that a farcical failure in the digestive system was for it a precious sign of humanity.

"And the wound?"

"—is healing. Will heal completely in time."

Gavin said nothing.

"Do I disgust you?" it asked, without inflection.

"No."

It was staring at Gavin with perfect eyes, his perfect eyes.

"What did Reynolds tell you?" it asked.

Gavin shrugged.

"Very little."

"That I'm a monster? That I suck out the human spirit?"

"Not exactly."

"More or less."

"More or less," Gavin conceded.

It nodded. "He's right," it said. "In his way, he's right. I need blood: that makes me monstrous. In my youth, a month ago, I bathed in it. Its touch gave wood the appearance of flesh. But I don't need it now: the process is almost finished. All I need now—"

It faltered; not, Gavin thought, because it intended to lie, but because the words to describe its condition wouldn't come.

"What do you need?" Gavin pressed it.

It shook its head, looking down at the carpet. "I've lived several times, you know. Sometimes I've stolen lives and got away with it. Lived a natural span, then shrugged off that face and found another. Sometimes, like the last time, I've been challenged, and lost—"

"Are you some kind of machine?"

"No."

"What then?"

"I am what I am. I know of no others like me; though why should I be the only one? Perhaps there *are* others, many others: I simply don't know of them yet. So I live and die and live again, and learn nothing—" the word was bitterly pronounced, "—of myself. Understand? You know what you are because you see others like you. If you were alone on earth, what would you know? What the mirror told you, that's all. The rest would be myth and conjecture."

The summary was made without sentiment.

"May I lie down?" it asked.

It began to walk towards him, and Gavin could see more clearly the fluttering in its chest cavity, the restless, incoherent forms that were mushrooming there in place of the heart. Sighing, it sank face down on the bed, its clothes sodden, and closed its eyes.

"We'll heal," it said. "Just give us time."

Gavin went to the door of the flat and bolted it. Then he dragged a table over and wedged it under the handle. Nobody could get in and attack it in sleep: they would stay here together in safety, he and it, he and himself. The fortress secured, he brewed some coffee and sat in the chair across the room from the bed and watched the creature sleep.

The rain rushed against the window heavily one hour, lightly the next. Wind threw sodden leaves against the glass and they clung there like inquisitive moths; he watched them sometimes, when he tired of watching himself, but before long he'd want to look again, and he'd be back staring at the casual beauty of his outstretched arm, the light flicking the wrist bone, the lashes. He fell asleep in the chair about midnight, with an ambulance complaining in the street outside, and the rain coming again.

It wasn't comfortable in the chair, and he'd surface from sleep every few minutes, his eyes opening a fraction. The creature was up: it was standing by the window, now in front of the mirror, now in the kitchen. Water ran: he dreamt water. The creature undressed: he dreamt sex. It stood over him, its chest whole, and he was reassured by its presence: he dreamt, it was for a moment only, himself lifted out of a street through a window into Heaven. It dressed in his clothes: he murmured his assent to the theft in his sleep. It was whistling: and there was a threat of day through the window, but he was too dozy to stir just yet, and quite content to have the whistling young man in his clothes live for him.

At last it leaned over the chair and kissed him on the lips, a brother's kiss, and left. He heard the door close behind it.

After that there were days, he wasn't sure how many, when he stayed in the room, and did nothing but drink water. This thirst had become unquenchable. Drinking and sleeping, drinking and sleeping, twin moons.

The bed he slept on was damp at the beginning from where the creature had laid, and he had no wish to change the sheets. On the contrary he enjoyed the wet linen, which his body dried out too soon. When it did he took a bath himself in the water the thing had lain in and returned to the bed dripping wet, his skin crawling with cold, and the scent of mildew all around. Later, too indifferent to move, he allowed his bladder free rein while he lay on the bed, and that water in time became cold, until he dried it with his dwindling body heat.

But for some reason, despite the icy room, his nakedness, his hunger, he couldn't die.

He got up in the middle of the night of the sixth or seventh day, and sat on the edge of the bed to find the flaw in his resolve. When the solution didn't come he began to shamble around the room much as the creature had a week earlier, standing in front of the mirror to survey his pitifully changed body, watching the snow shimmer down and melt on the sill.

Eventually, by chance, he found a picture of his parents he remembered the creature staring at. Or had he dreamt that? He thought not: he had a distinct idea that it had picked up this picture and looked at it.

That was, of course, the bar to his suicide: that picture. There were respects to be paid. Until then how could he hope to die?

He walked to the Cemetery through the slush wearing only a

pair of slacks and a tee-shirt. The remarks of middle-aged
women and school children went unheard. Whose business but
his own was it if going barefoot was the death of him? The
rain came and went, sometimes thickening towards snow, but
never quite achieving its ambition.

There was a service going on at the church itself, a line of
brittle colored cars parked at the front. He slipped down the
side into the churchyard. It boasted a good view, much spoiled
today by the smoky veil of sleet, but he could see the trains
and the high-rise flats; the endless rows of roofs. He ambled
amongst the headstones, by no means certain of where to find
his father's grave. It had been sixteen years: and the day
hadn't been that memorable. Nobody had said anything il-
luminating about death in general, or his father's death
specifically, there wasn't even a social gaffe or two to mark
the day: no aunt broke wind at the buffet table, no cousin
took him aside to expose herself.

He wondered if the rest of the family ever came here:
whether indeed they were still in the country. His sister had
always threatened to move out: go to New Zealand, begin
again. His mother was probably getting through her fourth
husband by now, poor sod, though perhaps she was the pitiable one, with her endless chatter barely concealing the panic.

Here was the stone. And yes, there were fresh flowers in the
marble urn that rested amongst the green marble chips. The
old bugger had not lain here enjoying the view unnoticed. Obviously somebody, he guessed his sister, had come here seeking a little comfort from Father. Gavin ran his fingers over the
name, the date, the platitude. Nothing exceptional: which was
only right and proper, because there'd been nothing exceptional about him.

Staring at the stone, words **came** spilling out, as though
Father was sitting on the edge **of** the grave, dangling his feet,
raking his hair across his **gleaming** scalp, pretending, as he
always pretended, to care.

"What do you think, eh?"

Father wasn't impressed.

"Not much, am I?" **Gavin** confessed.

You said it, son.

"Well I was always careful, like you told me. There aren't any bastards out there, going to come looking for me."

Damn pleased.

"I wouldn't be much to find, would I?"

Father blew his nose, wiped it three times. Once from left to right, again left to right, finishing right to left. Never failed. Then he slipped away.

"Old shithouse."

A toy train let out a long blast on its horn as it passed and Gavin looked up. There he was—himself—standing absolutely still a few yards away. He was wearing the same clothes he'd put on a week ago when he'd left the flat. They looked creased and shabby from constant wear. But the flesh! Oh, the flesh was more radiant than his own had ever been. It almost shone in the drizzling light; and the tears on the doppelganger's cheeks only made the features more exquisite.

"What's wrong?" said Gavin.

"It always makes me cry, coming here." It stepped over the graves towards him, its feet crunching on gravel, soft on grass. So real.

"You've been here before?"

"Oh yes. Many times, over the years—"

Over the years? What did it mean, over the years? Had it mourned here for people it had killed?

As if in answer:

"—I come to visit Father. Twice, maybe three times a year."

"This isn't your father," said Gavin, almost amused by the delusion. "It's mine."

"I don't see any tears on your face," said the other.

"I feel . . ."

"Nothing," his face told him. "You feel nothing at all, if you're honest."

That was the truth.

"Whereas I . . ." the tears began to flow again, its nose ran, "I will miss him until I die."

It was surely playacting, but if so why was there such grief in its eyes: and why were its features crumpled into ugliness as it wept. Gavin had seldom given in to tears: they'd always made him feel weak and ridiculous. But this thing was proud of tears, it gloried in them. They were its triumph.

And even then, knowing it had overtaken him, Gavin could find nothing in him that approximated grief.

"Have it," he said. "Have the snots. You're welcome."

The creature was hardly listening.

"Why is it all so painful?" it asked, after a pause. "Why is it loss that makes me human?"

Gavin shrugged. What did he know or care about the fine art of being human? The creature wiped its nose with its sleeve, sniffed, and tried to smile through its unhappiness.

"I'm sorry," it said, "I'm making a damn fool of myself. Please forgive me."

It inhaled deeply, trying to compose itself.

"That's all right," said Gavin. The display embarrassed him, and he was glad to be leaving.

"Your flowers?" he asked as he turned from the grave.

It nodded.

"He hated flowers."

The thing flinched.

"Ah."

"Still, what does he know?"

He didn't even look at the effigy again; just turned and started up the path that ran beside the church. A few yards on, the thing called after him:

"Can you recommend a dentist?"

Gavin grinned, and kept walking.

It was almost the commuter hour. The arterial road that ran by the church was already thick with speeding traffic: perhaps it was Friday, early escapees hurrying home. Lights blazed brilliantly, horns blazed.

Gavin stepped into the middle of the flow without looking to right or left, ignoring the squeals of brakes, and the curses, and began to walk amongst the traffic as if he were idling in an open field.

The wing of a speeding car grazed his leg as it passed, another almost collided with him. Their eagerness to get somewhere, to arrive at a place they would presently be itching to depart from again, was comical. Let them rage at him, loathe him, let them glimpse his featureless face and go home haunted. If the circumstances were right, maybe one of them would panic, swerve, and run him down. Whatever. From now on he belonged to chance, whose Standard Bearer he would surely be.